ICEBERG

JENNIFER A. NIELSEN

ICEBERG

SCHOLASTIC PRESS · NEW YORK

Library of Congress Cataloging-in-Publication Data available

ISBN 978-1-338-79502-8

10 9 8 7 6 5 4 3 2 1   23 24 25 26 27

Printed in Italy   183

First edition, March 2023

Book design by Christopher Stengel

For Johan Svensson, a distant cousin and third-class passenger, who at age 14 snuck onto the boat deck and finally made it onto Lifeboat 13. Thanks for your courage.

CHAPTER ONE

Before the End Came

In the end, in those final minutes before the *Titanic* sank into its grave, some people would jump overboard, taking their chances in the icy water. They had little hope of surviving, but if they continued clinging to the rails, they'd have no chance at all.

Others, resigned to their fate, stepped back and listened to the small group of musicians, playing on even as the water crept higher onto the deck. Maybe that was better, to seek peace in the inevitable.

Others still made themselves heroes in the end, working until their last breath was swallowed up in an ocean of water, hoping to give those on deck another minute of life. They might have proven themselves to be the finest among us.

Yet the stories will be told of those who had no choice.

Stories of those who ran for the nearest stairwells, hoping to reach a higher deck, or praying for the chance to reach a lifeboat, but found themselves trapped behind watertight doors, without a chance to survive.

I know these stories are true. Because I was one of them.

CHAPTER
TWO

Everything Seemed Perfect

Wednesday, April 10, 1912

A British legend from nine hundred years ago describes the Viking king Canute, who had his throne carried to the shores of Southampton. There on the beach, he stood before the mighty ocean and commanded the incoming tide to stop so as not to wet his royal robes.

But the water was indifferent to the command and flowed onto the shores, soaking the great king's robes. Dripping with ocean water, the king turned to his followers to say, "Even with all my power, I am nothing compared to the heavens and earth. I worship the heavens, and I respect the might of this world."

My father used to tell me that story every time he returned from his fishing trips. But that was years ago. I was twelve years old now, and far older in my mind, as I'd never cared much for childish things. Except for Papa's story. I did used to love that, and every word came rushing back to me on the day I first saw the *Titanic*.

Because here I was now, on the very same shores of Southampton, England. Although I wasn't down on the beach, but on the port above it, staring up at a ship that aimed to defy King Canute's words.

The *Titanic* was everything the papers had described: as powerful as the Titans of mythology, and as elegant as if it were a floating castle. It did not respect the might of this world because it *was* the might of this world.

The *Titanic* was also the largest man-made moving object in the world. Taller than the great pyramids of Egypt, or any cathedral of Europe; as long as four city blocks. Each of its four smokestacks was wide enough that a locomotive could drive through it, and its anchors were said to weigh fifteen tons each. Indeed, the *Titanic* was so bold in appearance that the newspapers called it the world's first unsinkable ship.

The ship that claimed it would command the very tides of the ocean.

I'd done my research. On a four-day walk from my home in the southern tip of England to the ports of Southampton, I'd pulled newspapers from every rubbish bin I could find, scouring the pages for any information on the White Star Line's newest and grandest ship.

But reading about it did little to prepare me for the wonder of actually seeing it.

I wasn't the only one standing in awe. A vast crowd had gathered to watch the *Titanic* depart on its maiden voyage.

I couldn't begin to guess at how many people had come, but surely it was in the tens of thousands. Men lifted children to their shoulders, and women stood on their toes for a better look at the ship, or to crane their necks in hopes of seeing any of the wealthy and famous passengers.

Those passengers weren't boarding here at the dock level, naturally. If life had elevated them above us common folk, then the gangplank itself also had to be elevated. The wealthiest passengers had a separate entrance, bringing them directly into the upper decks of the ship.

Meanwhile, those of us in the poorer class moved among the cargo, waiting in endless lines for what appeared to be a doctor's inspection before we'd be allowed on board.

The variety of people in line amazed me. I'd never seen so many people who must have come from all parts of the world. Some traveled alone, and others with entire families.

I understood the gleam in their eyes, the excitement of being part of this adventure of traveling to a new country. America was supposed to be a land where even the poorest person had a chance to build a life for themselves, sometimes even to find wealth.

That wouldn't be my future. Papa had died two years ago during a storm at sea. Mum had done her best to support us, but each month we had fallen further behind. Then two weeks ago, we had received a letter from my mum's sister in America. She had heard of our difficulties and was inviting me to come to America and work alongside her in a garment factory. The work would be difficult and sometimes dangerous, she'd said, but I could board with her free of charge, then send nearly everything I earned home to my family.

While Mum had read me the letter, her forehead had lined with wrinkles, each line deeper than the one above it. And when she finished, she set it down, saying, "I'm so very sorry, Hazel. What do you think?"

I'd thought it sounded horrible. Until that letter came, I'd had big dreams for my life, plans and possibilities that filled my imagination. I was going to make something of my life.

The letter from my aunt ended those dreams. I wanted to tell my mum no, even to beg her to let me stay in England. But I couldn't do it, not when every rainstorm brought dripping water through our roof. Not when all of my four younger brothers needed new shoes and went barefoot most of the time. Mum had recently sold her wedding ring to pay a debt that was overdue. The truth was that there were no dreams to be had here at home.

So I'd made myself smile back at Mum and said, "I'll go."

She had wrapped me in her arms. "You are a better daughter than I deserve. The amount you earn may save our family, and perhaps in time, it will prove to be a good thing for you too."

Perhaps. But I rather doubted it.

That was how I ended up here, at the Southampton port, staring up at the ship destined to carry me to America, with every last farthing Mum could scrape together to pay for my passage.

Finally, it was my turn in line at the ticket booth. "Third-class ticket," I told the woman inside the booth. "Traveling alone, and I'm willing to share a room if they don't snore too loud."

She had frowned back at me and answered, "Three pounds."

Mum had given me a shoulder bag to hold the money, and enough food for my walk, so I'd spent nothing along the way. But I knew there were barely over two pounds inside the bag. Not enough.

I asked the woman, "How much if they do snore loud?"

"Prices in third class go up to eight pounds." She frowned at me, then looked at the person in line behind me. "Next, please."

And just like that, I was out of the line.

I turned to face the ship again. The easiest answer to the "what now" question looming ahead of me was to return home. After all, I had the perfect excuse.

But then I remembered Mum's last words to me before I left.

She had hugged me tight, then said, "If I didn't believe this is the only way to save our family, I wouldn't give you up for anything in the world."

I needed to get on board that ship. With or without a ticket.

I wouldn't get through on the third-class gangplank. The officers taking tickets were watching for stowaways, for on a few occasions I saw passengers slinking back down the gangplank, obviously turned away. That's what would happen to me. There had to be another way.

I was so intent on studying the ship that I jumped when I felt a tap on my shoulder. I turned to see a rather pretty girl in a light blue dress with a lace collar and with a very fine hat over her long blonde hair, curled at the ends. If she stood still enough, I'd almost have believed she was a museum painting.

In my first look at her, I already understood who she was. Mum said some people breathed wealth. They inhaled air but exhaled money, getting richer almost without trying. This girl breathed wealth.

"Pardon me," she said, "but I've become separated from my governess. Have you seen her? A tall, slender woman, dressed all in black."

"I haven't seen her." I tried to speak with the same polite tone as she had used, but my words sounded as ordinary as I was, standing in my coarse fabric dress without a single stitch of lace, and an old coat that had belonged to Papa, too long for me. I had no hat, and my brown hair would've been in tangles if I had not taken the trouble this morning to pull it into two braids.

The girl smiled kindly. "My name is Sylvia Thorngood."

I arched a brow. "Any relation to Edgar Thorngood?"

"He's my father."

I couldn't stop my jaw from dropping wide open. Everyone knew that name, even here in England. The family fortune was said to be worth over a million dollars.

"What's your name?" Sylvia asked.

"Hazel Rothbury."

"Rothbury." She spoke slowly, letting my name flow over her tongue as if a slow pronunciation would help her recall which of her father's wealthy friends I was related to.

The answer was simple: none of them.

Still, Sylvia widened her smile. "I am very happy to meet you. Are you boarding the ship as well?"

"Yes, I'm traveling to America." I'd already noted the difference in our accents. "You must be going home."

"I am. I've been in England with my governess, visiting my grandparents. Who will you be visiting in America?"

I opened my mouth but had no idea how to answer. It was humiliating to explain that my journey would end in a garment factory, changing bobbins or threading needles for ten hours a day. Sylvia was looking at me like a friend. I didn't want her to think of me as a servant.

So I only said, "I'll be staying with my aunt in New York." That was the most I wanted to say about that.

"There is so much to see and do in New York," she said. "You will have such a wonderful time!"

"Miss Thorngood, there you are!" The woman hurrying toward us was tall and rail thin with graying hair pulled back into a tight bun, and wearing layers of black. Either she was in mourning, or else miserable old spinsters had inspired her sad fashion choices.

"My apologies, Miss Gruber. I became lost, but now I've met a new friend." Sylvia gestured to me. "Miss Hazel Rothbury is headed to New York to stay with her aunt. Perhaps we could have them over for supper one evening."

I flushed with embarrassment and quietly said, "I don't think . . . my aunt would not know your family."

"The Thorngoods know everyone . . . in New York's high society." Miss Gruber eyed the shoulder bag at my side. "No luggage?"

"I had a long walk here. Couldn't pack much with me."

"And you have a ticket?"

I couldn't admit the truth, not with Miss Gruber already looking down on me, literally. So I nodded. "Of course I do."

Sylvia clapped her hands together. "I have a lovely idea. Let's not wait until we reach New York to know each other better. Perhaps one evening you might join us on the ship. There won't be many people on board our age, so let's decide to be friends now."

"That would be fun," I agreed, though I had no intention of ever meeting her for a meal. I'd feel lucky enough just to get onto this ship.

"Miss Rothbury will likely be too busy washing and ironing her dress to have time for a supper," Miss Gruber observed.

That might be true. On my walk to Southampton, I had slept in a barn each night, and often tramped through the cold rain along muddy roads.

If Miss Gruber understood why my dress was dirty, maybe she would not have been so sharp with me now. Or maybe she was so sharp *because* she understood that, because the very fact that I had been bold enough to speak to her ward was offense enough.

"Come now, Miss Thorngood," Miss Gruber said. "Have a pleasant voyage, Miss Rothbury."

The tone of her voice was unmistakable. She didn't care whether my voyage was pleasant or the greatest disaster in a century. She just didn't want me to interfere with *her* voyage.

I waved goodbye, then headed toward the stern of the ship, where passengers had deposited their trunks and large pieces of baggage to be transported into the *Titanic*'s cargo hold. Crewmen were busy loading each piece, but each time they left with a piece of luggage, I had two or three minutes to look around.

Most of the trunks I saw were locked from the outside or had exterior latches. Finally, I found a simpler one that merely closed. I opened it and saw it filled with a woman's clothes. It took some effort to fit inside and still have room to breathe, but I did it, and lowered the lid without being noticed.

This was a terrible idea. I knew that as well as I knew this was breaking the law, a disgrace to my family's good reputation, and likely was a fair amount dangerous.

But it was the only plan I had. Several minutes later, the trunk was picked up by a crewman, who then called, "Oi, this one's heavy. Lend a hand, mate?"

A second crewman came to pick up the trunk, and before I knew it, I was being carried on board the *Titanic*.

CHAPTER
THREE

It Was Time for Adventure

My trunk was lowered with a heavy clunk, then the crewman who had spoken before said, "If we get many more trunks as heavy as that one, it'll bring down the ship."

"Watch what you say," his crewmate replied sharply. "That's not the kind of joke to be makin' on board."

The apology offered faded along with their footsteps, but I waited a minute longer to be sure they were gone. I couldn't wait too long, though, or they might come back with more cargo. I pushed on the lid, but it opened only a fraction of an inch before it hit on something above me. I pushed the lid again, but it wouldn't open.

I was trapped!

Panic filled me as I weighed my options, though I actually had a single option and it was awful. My only way out of this trunk would be to wait for the crewmen to return. Then I'd have to call out and get their attention.

Which meant I'd be scolded and kicked off the ship, and the *Titanic* would leave port without me. I'd have to go home and tell Mum I'd failed, and then try to answer her question that would have no good answer: "What will our family do now?"

I needed another option, anything else but to give myself up now. Yet after several more failed attempts at escape, when I heard the crewmen return, I called out, "Help!"

I had shouted it plenty loud enough, but I'd also shouted at the very moment in which the ship blew its horn. Nobody heard me.

"Looks like the captain wants to be underway soon," one of the crewmen said. "We'd better hurry."

"Move that trunk," the second crewmen said. "This one will fit better in that spot."

"What do you have there? Are those ostrich feathers?"

"If you like it, there's another eleven crates still to be loaded. I'd reckon somewhere out there is a whole continent of ostriches wonderin' what happened to all their feathers."

I was ready to call out again, but felt my trunk being dragged out from wherever it had been set, then nearly dropped on the ground.

"Careful, mate," the crewman said. "Let's get the rest, then we'll organize everything after we set off."

This time when they left and I pushed on the lid, it opened. I drew in a great gulp of air as I climbed out, then tried to get my bearings. The cargo area was very large but filling up quickly with barrels and trunks and parcels and crates. Some were so large they must have been loaded on by machines earlier this morning. One in particular took up the entire corner of the cargo area. Curious about it, I walked closer and saw a stamp on the side that identified it as a Renault automobile. I wished I could have seen that for myself. I was sure it would be grand.

But I had no time to waste. I grabbed my small bag, closed the trunk up tight, and left. I hoped whoever picked up the trunk next would be different crewmen than before. Otherwise, they'd be sure to notice the difference in weight. They'd know someone had snuck on board.

But I couldn't worry about that now. Instead, I tiptoed out of the cargo room into a corridor of plain metal walls and floors. The engines rumbled loudly beneath my feet, telling me I was somewhere low in the ship. Straight ahead was a stairway leading upward. That was my escape . . . until I heard heavy footsteps coming down.

I couldn't be discovered here, so I looked around for a place to hide and found a small alcove behind the stairs. I quickly ducked into it, barely in time to see two pairs of tall, soot-blackened boots walking down.

"So the captain's decided, then—we're still leaving port?" one of the men asked.

A man with a lower voice and strong Scottish accent replied, "He decided, or his bosses decided for him. It's hardly the first time any of us have been at sea with the ship on fire."

My ears perked up. Had he just said that the *Titanic* was on fire?

"Maybe not," the first man replied. "But the coal bins on this ship are higher than we're used to. I reckon we'll be fighting that fire for most of the way to New York."

"Then you'd better get back to work," said his Scottish friend. "I need to stop at the lavatory, then I'll meet you in Boiler Room Six."

Boiler Room Six? Was that the location of the fire? It had to be.

The first man replied, "All I can say is that I wish I'd refused this job. You think the firemen who got off the ship here in Southampton might've known something we don't?"

"I figure most people know things I don't," came the reply before they were too far away for me to hear them anymore.

I sat there for a very long time, unsure of what to do.

The captain knew about the fire, yet gave the order to leave anyway. And the men who'd spoken seemed more concerned about the work of putting out the fire rather than the danger of the fire to the ship. So perhaps fires on ships were not that unusual.

Yet one man had said other firemen left the ship here in Southampton. Why would they have left, unless they knew the fire posed some danger to the *Titanic*?

I squeezed out from my hiding place and hurried up three flights of stairs until I finally made it to a deck identified for third-class passengers. The corridors were already full with passengers bustling about, but most people seemed eager to be outside, so I allowed myself to be carried along with them.

We emerged onto the rear deck of the ship, an enormous area already filled with passengers who were making their way around the wood benches in hopes of finding a place to stand at the rails. Those already at the rails were waving goodbye to friends and loved ones, brushing away tears of sadness, yet somehow still smiling with excitement for the journey ahead.

Since I had no one to wave goodbye to, I studied those around me instead. Most were dressed in clothes as simple as mine. Many were speaking in excited voices, in languages I did not recognize. Some had darker skin, or fairer skin than mine, but in that moment, we were all together, excited for the adventure we were about to share.

As I watched, I took a seat on one of the benches. How I wished I had a notebook and pen so that I could write down everything I was seeing. I glanced around me, hoping someone nearby had some paper I could borrow, but no such luck.

A boy near my age crossed in front of me, his arms full of luggage bags. He was dressed in a dark suit with light buttons and had coal-black hair beneath a sailor's hat. He stopped when he saw me and gave a polite nod.

"You're not interested in watching us leave?" he asked.

I shrugged. "There's no room for me at the rails."

He craned his head toward the crowd. "Ah yes, I see the problem. Come with me if you'd like. I'll show you a better view, but you've got to do as I say. It'll be worth your trouble, Miss."

I grinned and nodded. My adventure was beginning, and we had not yet even left port.

CHAPTER
FOUR

Time to Plan

The boy led me back down some stairs to the inside passage-ways, then as we walked, he turned back long enough to say, "My name is Charlie Blight. I'm a porter here."

"I thought you must be a porter," I said. "No one else could carry so many bags at once."

He chuckled. "I can always take a little bit more."

"My name is Hazel Rothbury."

"And you're traveling in third class?"

I hesitated. I was a traveler, and I was here in third class. As long as he didn't ask if I had a ticket, I supposed I could answer with some measure of honesty.

"Yes," I said. "Third class. That's where I'll be."

He went on, unaware of my hesitation. "You'll never get a proper view of the harbor from here. I've got to deliver these bags up top. Want to come along?"

A waist-high gate was ahead of us, with a sign clearly posted on the wall beside it: NOTICE: 3RD CLASS PASSENGERS ARE NOT ALLOWED FORWARD OF THIS.

I stopped there. "Charlie, I'm not allowed."

His grin came with a mischievous wink. "Unfortunately, on the first day, sometimes the third-class passengers get a little lost."

I smiled back at him. So that was his plan.

I followed him up several more flights of stairs until we finally exited on an upper deck. It was different here, very different from anywhere I'd seen in my life. This passageway was lined with dark-paneled wooden walls, fine art, and elegant chandeliers. Beyond that was an entrance to a stairway of oak railings above carved wood panels. If the stairs had been paved in gold, I would not have been surprised.

"That'll be the Grand Staircase," Charlie said. "Sometimes when I walk on it, I imagine that I am in the finest estate in all of Europe."

"I wouldn't know about that." I had never been inside any fine estate. I'd passed by them often enough, on the way to market with a basket of eggs to sell. Walking past an estate probably wasn't the same thing as standing in one.

"Me neither," Charlie said. "But on the Grand Staircase, I can imagine. And at least you don't have to imagine the view." He nodded toward an empty railing overlooking the harbor and much of Southampton. "That spot is for you. I'll deliver these bags and be back in fifteen minutes."

I smiled, but rather than look down at the harbor, I began

studying this promenade, trying to soak in every detail of what I was seeing.

As I studied the passengers themselves, I began to understand why Miss Gruber had scolded me about my hair. The women who strolled along this deck had perfect hair without a single wisp out of place, and they wore tailored suits or hand-beaded dresses with fur wraps and sparkling jewelry. Their hats were wide and elegant, and everyone seemed to have a lady's maid following close behind.

The men on this deck wore dark suits, and many carried walking sticks. They greeted each other warmly and quickly found the name of someone they both knew, often a name I'd seen in the newspapers, Americans such as Rockefeller or Carnegie, or here in Britain, our own King George.

My father had only ever owned one suit, and it was frayed at the seams and elbows. He had only one pair of shoes, so he'd wear the same ones to church as he did to board the fishing boats. Papa had been a proud man. It was hard on him not to have any Sunday best to wear.

While I stood at the railings, another couple passed by, eventually stopping less than a meter away. They looked similar to the others here, but I did notice a few differences. The woman, with a mound of brown hair tucked up beneath her large hat, certainly had the fur coat and jewelry like the other women on deck, but her boots were scuffed and the heels were worn and uneven. The man had a fine suit, but it didn't fit him quite right. I wondered if it might have been made for someone else.

Even so, they would travel in very different circles from mine, ones made of silver and gold. Mine were made of straw and tin.

The man gestured at the port below. "At last we are leaving all of this behind! A new life awaits us in America, a better life."

"*If* our plan works." His wife seemed nervous. I noticed her pulling at a bit of ribbon that had come loose on one sleeve. "We can't be sure that the money is even on board."

"Where else would it be? I've written down everything we must do before we reach New York. Follow the plan and we'll be fine."

She was still unconvinced. "If our name should be noticed on the passenger list . . ."

"Mollison is a common enough name," he said. "Besides, nobody who sees that list will think twice about us."

Now his wife began to smile. "True. And even if someone does, we can always claim to be the unfortunate relations of *those* Mollisons."

He scoffed. "Speaking of unfortunate relations—"

"Now don't you start. We wouldn't be on board right now without the kindness shown to us."

He pulled a paper from his coat, rose colored and folded in thirds. "What kindness? If we don't get that money, we'll be in serious trouble."

"We'll get the money." The wife—Mrs. Mollison—turned to him. "But my dear, promise that you won't ruin this trip by spending all your time playing cards."

20

"I must stay in practice." Mr. Mollison straightened his tie. "A lucky game might be the only way our plan works."

"Or you could lose and sink us back into debt. Besides, I'll end up doing the real work while you're off gambling," she replied.

"If you ever watched me play, my dear, you would know that proper gambling is very hard work." Mr. Mollison offered his wife an arm. "Come now, we should begin meeting with others, see if we can get ourselves an invitation to join some-one important for supper."

I rolled my eyes as I listened and was very happy when the Mollisons finally left. These were not people I ever wished to know. If they were traveling in first class, then I wanted to be anywhere else.

Shortly after they left, the *Titanic*'s horn sounded, signal-ing that we were about to get underway. The engines had been humming below us, but now they began to churn, and I felt a gentle sway as the ship slowly began moving.

The crowd at the port cheered even louder and waved. Yet we had barely left the side of the dock when another horn sounded far below us, giving an urgent warning. Somewhere nearby, I heard a series of whistles, the officers passing signals to each other. Something was definitely wrong.

A gentleman passing by leaned over the rails and said to another man with him, "That ship below is getting sucked into our wake!"

I leaned over as well and saw two smaller ships within the *Titanic*'s wake. One of them appeared to have snapped free from its mooring rope, which was now lying on the water. A second ship moved to intervene, preventing the first ship from being pulled closer to the *Titanic*.

The man beside me breathed a sigh of relief, and when I looked at him, he simply said, "We certainly don't want a repeat of what happened to the *Olympic* last fall. A near disaster, that one."

I tilted my head, with no idea what he was referencing. I had read about the *Olympic*. That was the *Titanic*'s sister ship, already at sea. But I'd never heard anything about a near disaster.

"Captain Edward Smith was in command of the *Olympic* that day, and he commands this ship now," the man continued. "Let's hope he doesn't put a hole in this ship too."

Captain Smith had put a hole in the *Olympic*?

"Pardon me, sir," I said. "Would you happen to have a bit of paper and a pen?"

He frowned at me, then reached into a pocket and pulled out a small, used envelope, and a pen from another pocket. I thanked him, then immediately wrote down the question at the top of my mind.

What disaster almost happened to the Olympic?

I folded my fingers around the pen, letting an idea seep inside my imagination, an idea so bold that I barely dared to think of it. Yet here it was, demanding my attention, so I finally gave it rein.

Maybe my dreams didn't have to end. Maybe this was my one remaining chance to turn this dream into a reality.

There was another way to earn the money that my family so desperately needed.

I could write.

Here I was, on the greatest ship ever built, and on its maiden voyage. Newspapers throughout Europe and America would be anxious to print the first story about life on board the *Titanic*.

I could provide it.

And it would begin with the truth. That the *Titanic* sailed from Southampton on April 10, 1912, led by a captain who may have nearly created a disaster with his former ship.

And who was now in command of a ship with a terrible secret.

Our ship was on fire.

TITANIC DEPARTS ON MAIDEN VOYAGE

THE UNSINKABLE LUXURY LINER

April 10, 1912 - Today, Southampton bid farewell to its new wonder of the world, the R.M.S. Titanic. This grand centerpiece of the White Star Line is the largest manmade object ever built, capable of carrying more than 3,300 passengers and crew.

Over 100,000 eager onlookers came to bid farewell to the passengers, as follows:

First Class............750
Second Class............500
Steerage..............1100
Crew............800

Rumors are circulating that first-class passengers may include actors, writers, and businessmen such as John Jacob Astor, Benjamin Guggenheim, Isidor Straus, and renowned fashion designer, Lady Duff Gordon.

Additionally, the Titanic will be captained by Edward John Smith, with 43 years of experience at sea. Also traveling are Thomas Andrews, the ship's designer, and White Star Chairman, J. Bruce Ismay.

White Star Line has said this ship is designed to be "unsinkable," and at first sight of this magnificent queen of the seas, there can be little doubt of that.

The Titanic is expected to arrive in New York after approximately one week at sea. Truly, this will be a voyage worth remembering for all time.

CHAPTER
FIVE

Gates Divided Us

Charlie returned soon after we had left port, though he had new bags in hand now.

"I can help you with those," I offered.

But he only smiled and hoisted them higher in his arms. "It's as I told you before. I can always take a bit more. Besides, these are to be delivered to the cargo hold on the Orlop Deck. No passengers allowed there. But I'll walk you back down to your room if you need to know the way."

"I know the way," I quickly replied. Since I literally had nowhere to go, it didn't matter much where I went now.

I had taken only a few steps forward when a ship's officer dressed in a black suit with gold buttons and gold trim on his sleeves approached us. A badge on his suit identified him as Officer Kent.

His voice was stern as he spoke to Charlie. "Mr. Blight, is this passenger with you?"

If the officer's tone worried Charlie, he didn't let it show. With an eye on me, he said, "She must be lost. I'm taking her back to third class right now."

Now Officer Kent turned to me, and I was certain I didn't hide my worry at all. "We're glad you're on board with us, miss, but you'll see the signs posted for the third-class areas. See that you keep to them."

"Yes, sir." I turned and followed Charlie, who only smiled as he led me toward the stairway. Once we were alone, I said, "That wasn't funny. I could have gotten into real trouble!"

"Not on the first day," he replied. "Now *tomorrow*, you'd best not find yourself anywhere on this deck. They have to keep the passengers in their proper areas."

"Because the wealthy pay more for the nicer spaces."

Charlie shook his head. "Oh no, miss. It's the lice."

"Lice!" That was an insult. "I have no lice."

"I'm glad to hear it since I've just walked you around half the ship. But some third-class passengers can't say the same. The doctors probably explained that before you came on board."

"Of course they explained that," I said. To everyone else. Not to me.

Charlie continued, "We have to separate the classes, to protect the first- and second-class passengers."

By then, we were passing through the same gate we had crossed to enter the first-class promenade. "Then that's what these gates are for?" I asked. "Protection from the poor?"

"It's no offense, Miss Rothbury. I've got no money myself. The gates are there for more than the lice. A few gates on this ship go floor to ceiling and can be locked if necessary. I've never heard the reason why, but I do wonder if they're not to protect the women and children in an emergency." He glanced over at me. "All of them. Not just those on the top decks."

"What do you mean?" I still had the pen and envelope from the gentleman—he had told me I could keep them—but Charlie was walking fast enough that there wasn't time for me to pull them out.

"You've heard of the French ship called *La Bourgogne*, I assume."

"No."

He glanced over at me, looking truly surprised. "Then you must not study maritime history."

My father had been a fisherman. I knew a few things about boats, but nothing about their history.

He said, "Fourteen years ago, *La Bourgogne* was considered one of the fastest ships in the world."

"Like the *Titanic*!"

Charlie frowned. "You'd best not compare that ship to ours, because you see, early one morning, *La Bourgogne* collided with a British ship."

I thought of the man who'd said Captain Smith put a hole in the *Olympic*, but for now, I stayed quiet. I wanted to hear more about this French ship.

Charlie continued, "Most passengers were asleep at the

time of the collision, and so the crew made a tremendous fuss, creating enough noise to panic the passengers and make them hurry from their beds. But as it turned out, most of the panic came from the crew. Many of them couldn't swim, and there weren't enough lifeboats for everyone on board."

"That doesn't make sense," I said. "Surely it would be irresponsible for a ship to launch without enough lifeboats for everyone on board."

Charlie merely arched a brow, then continued. "The crew began fighting for their own places on the lifeboats. As the passengers became more anxious, the crewmen fought back, including several large stokers. They threatened the passengers away from the lifeboats. So many people were fighting that no one was left to actually lower the lifeboats into the water. When they counted the survivors, most were crew members who had put their own lives first." He frowned over at me. "Perhaps the gates are there to remind the crew that in any disaster, women and children will get on the lifeboats first."

By now, I well understood why he would not want any comparisons between the *Titanic* and *La Bourgogne*. What a tragic end for that French ship!

Which led me once again to think about the fire, and whether it should be a concern here on the *Titanic*.

But it also raised another question in my mind. "Charlie, if there should be a problem on board the *Titanic*, would they lock the gates? Because if that kept crewmen from going to the upper decks, wouldn't it also keep a lot of passengers locked below as well?"

Charlie stopped walking and looked directly at me, his eyes solidly focused on mine. "If there ever is a problem, do not wait to find out. You get to your feet, and you move toward safety. I've shown you how to get to those upper decks. If necessary, see that you get there."

THE EVENING POST

6 O'CLOCK PM EDITION   NEW YORK, WED JULY 5, 1898   PRICE ONE CENT

SINKING OF FRENCH SHIP LA BOURGOGNE.

A CREW OF COWARDS!

562 LIVES LOST.

Women and Children Last!

Halifax, Nova Scotia — It is common knowledge that on any voyage over the cold North Atlantic waters, travelers may encounter patches of thick fog.

Such was the case with the French liner La Bourgogne, carrying 725 souls on board when it collided with another ship, the ill-fated Cromartyshire. As the ship began to sink, chaos broke out among passengers and crew for the few places available on lifeboats.

What followed was a display of cowardice beneath even the most dishonorable sailor.

May this tragedy never be repeated again.

CHAPTER
SIX

Secrets United Us

C harlie and I walked on a little farther. I knew he'd have to excuse himself soon to deliver the bags he carried. If I was going to ask him about the fire, this was my chance.

So when the passageway was clear, I turned to him. "I overheard some men talking earlier. They said the *Titanic* is on fire. Is that true?"

Charlie glanced around to see if anyone else had heard, then immediately stopped and lowered every bag in his arms. The cheerful expression he had worn changed too, from a pleasant smile into something as stern as Officer Kent had been. Looking around him, he said, "Hush, please, miss. You can't ask such questions so openly."

"Why not? Is it true?"

"Doesn't matter. We're at sea now. What do you think would happen if the passengers heard that? You'd cause a riot on board. We don't need a problem like that."

"Is a riot any worse than a ship on fire?"

"Please lower your voice." He looked around again, desperation in his eyes. "You said you heard some men talking about it?"

"Two crewmen. They were filthy, covered in ash."

"Ah, you saw some of our firemen. We call them the Black Gang, because of that soot. They've got the hardest job on board, in my opinion."

"So they're the ones to put out the fires?"

"Of course, when it's necessary."

When it's *necessary*? I rolled my eyes at the obvious. "Aren't they trying to put out this fire?"

"Certainly they are, but they also have to load coal into the boilers to build up the fires that keep the *Titanic* moving. It's difficult work, but without the firemen, this ship would be dead in the water."

"Dead in the water? That's a terrible thing to say on the open seas."

He chuckled. "I hadn't thought about that. My apologies."

This time I lowered my voice. "They said the . . . trouble is in Boiler Room Six. Can you explain the problem to me?"

His eyes darted. He obviously didn't want to answer but clearly knew exactly what I was talking about. When I continued to stare at him, he finally gave in. "To keep moving, the *Titanic* requires more than six thousand tons of coal every day. It's all got to be stored somewhere."

I tried to do the math for that. There were coal mines not far from my house, so I'd seen the bins that stored a single ton of coal. Each one was as large as a kitchen table. If the *Titanic* required six thousand tons of coal each day over a weeklong journey, I couldn't imagine the storage space that would be needed.

"The coal is stored in separate bins," he said. "Each one is enormous, three stories high. If a fire starts, the firemen have got to shovel it out from the bottom and drop it into one of the boilers. Of course, that'll mean new coal falls into the fire and that lights up too."

"How did the fire start?"

Charlie sighed. "That's the way coal is, miss. Once it's exposed to air, it's got to be kept wet or given space to breathe. Otherwise, you might see it heatin' up itself."

My eyes widened. "Coal can start its own fire?"

"They call it spontaneous combustion, and it happens on ships more often than anyone knows. Which means you've got no reason to worry. They've dealt with this kind of thing before, and the firemen know what to do now."

"How long has the fire been burning?"

Charlie looked around once again. "Hush, miss, please!" He lowered his voice and added, "By the time anyone detects a coal fire, it's likely been goin' on for some time. From what I hear, it might've been burnin' for two or three weeks already."

"Three weeks!" I stood up straighter, genuinely alarmed. "And the captain let us leave the port anyway?"

"Of course he did. He gets reports on it regularly, so he already knows more than either of us about the situation. And if he saw fit to leave port, then it's because we're in no danger."

I didn't understand that. How could a three-week-old fire not pose a danger to the ship?

And yet, I had never stepped foot on a ship of this size before. Captain Smith had. And Charlie was right. The ship's captain would never put his passengers in danger.

Unless . . .

This was the *Titanic*'s maiden voyage and all the newspapers were watching. Did the captain feel he had to leave port? Surely an announcement that the finest ship in the fleet was burning while full of passengers would be disastrous for the cruise line.

I pulled out the scrap of paper and pen. "Is there any reason that the ship had to leave Southampton when it did? Why couldn't we have waited until the . . . problem was out?"

Charlie fixed his eyes on the pen. "You're taking notes?"

"I have to. I'm going to write a story about the *Titanic*. I need to understand the fire before I can write about it."

"You can't write about this!" Charlie said. "You could ruin our reputation!"

"People have the right to know the truth."

"They don't have to know it from me." Charlie picked up the bags he had dropped to the floor earlier. "It's a beautiful day, and we'll soon have France in sight. I trust you can find your cabin on your own."

"Charlie, I'm sorry," I called after him, but he didn't say another word. He merely turned the corner and left me there alone.

MALE HELP WANTED

Wanted - Strong men with a sense of adventure, for work as firemen on R.M.S. Titanic. Experienced stokers, greasers, trimmers, also needed. Apply at Southampton Docks by Wed, Apr 10, ready to travel.

CHAPTER
SEVEN

Then I Found a Teacher

Charlie had left me on E Deck, which as far as I could tell was mostly third-class cabins and crewmen areas. I began searching there for a place where I might stay that night. It had to be comfortable enough to keep me alive for the next week, but not so comfortable that other passengers would discover it.

I took my time to explore the different areas of E Deck. There was one very long and wide corridor that must have run nearly the entire length of the ship. As I walked it, I heard a man passing by explain to his friend that this was called Scotland Road.

I wondered if the actual Scotland Road in Liverpool was as crowded and busy as this passageway. With so many people going in every direction, I'd never succeed in hiding here.

After more searching, I found a stairway to the next deck below, F Deck. I'd passed through this deck earlier, after escaping the cargo hold, but this time, a wonderful smell of freshly baked bread filled the air. Until this very moment, I would've said that my mum baked the best-smelling bread in the world, but that was no longer true. I followed the scent to the entrance for the third-class saloon. Mum had warned me to bring some food of my own, as ships only provided food to the upper-class passengers. But she was wrong about the *Titanic*. There seemed to be plenty of food for third-class passengers, and my mouth began watering for a single taste of it.

I hadn't listened to Mum's warning. I had worried the money she'd sent with me might not be enough, so I'd purchased no food before coming to the docks this morning. Everyone on board the *Titanic* would be well-fed, except for me.

The thought crashed into me, stirring up my hunger. But I couldn't linger on my empty stomach, no matter how loud it was complaining. I had no ticket. I'd have to find food some other way.

Hoping for a distraction, I decided to replace the comforting smell of warm bread with the adventurous scent of a salty ocean breeze. After some asking around, I found the poop deck, the third-class promenade at the rear of the ship. From here, I could see the first-class promenade, though we were separated by plenty of gates, ladders, and a well deck below.

By now, I had seen the views from the front of the ship, so I understood why they would be reserved for the first-class passengers. Who else would look ahead in their lives, anticipating their next business deal, their next work of art, their next move to add another hundred dollars to their pocketbooks?

The views from the side of the ship would belong to the

second class. They would see the ship moving forward, but their views would never change. I wondered if that was true of their lives as well, steadily achieving some success in the world, but never enough to get ahead.

I was at the back of the ship, and I thought it must be the finest view possible. Because here, the people sat and looked at where they had come from: poverty, hunger, every struggle to survive. And now they were leaving all of it behind.

Once again, I thought of how different my journey was from most of the passengers' here. They wanted to leave— they had chosen this adventure. I only wanted to return home and be with my family.

Before leaving, Mum had described New York to me. "People say it is one of the greatest cities in the world. Once you are there, I'm sure you'll love it so much, you'll barely think of our simple life at home again."

The very opposite was true. I doubted there would ever be a day in my life when I did not wish I was home again. But if I did become a journalist, perhaps I could bring in enough money with my writing that I could travel back home anytime I wanted.

I pulled out the envelope I'd borrowed, but it was so full of notes by now, I needed more paper. I scanned the deck until I saw a small paper in the corner that must have blown free in the breeze. I started toward it until the breeze carried it upward once again, depositing the paper just past a gate with a sign that warned third-class passengers away. I still would've tried to reach the paper, but a deckhand was nearby, keeping watch over the area.

As I began looking for another piece of paper, my eyes traveled up another level to the first-class promenade, the very place I had stood with Charlie when the ship launched. That's what the readers would be interested in. If I was going to sell my first news story, I needed to write about life on board for the wealthiest passengers, not the poorest ones.

Which meant my next decision would be either brilliant or utterly foolish. Or both.

I needed a way back onto the first-class promenade.

I glanced over at the deckhand. He didn't seem to be going anywhere, but I did remember the gate that Charlie had led me through earlier. Hadn't he said that on the first day, the officers would be more lenient about mistakes? I hoped so because I intended to make another one. A deliberate, planned mistake.

I'd taken only a few steps inside before I crossed paths with an older woman wearing a long cream dress, her graying hair in a high bun. She seemed steady on her feet, but was noticeably leaning on a cane with a brass handle in the shape of an eagle's head. She'd been watching me for some time but finally asked, "Would you be kind enough to help an old woman down the stairs?"

I was headed in the opposite direction, so it was a most inconvenient time to remember the one rule of manners that my mother was careful to have taught me: "No matter your hurry, there is always time for courtesy."

Mum would be ashamed of me now if I ignored that, so I smiled and offered the woman my arm, leading her off the poop deck.

"You're traveling alone?" the woman asked.

My first instinct was to lie, just to avoid any further questions. Except my conscience was already filled with as much guilt as it could manage, so I said, "I'm alone, but I'm quite capable of managing for myself this week."

"Are you? What's your name, child?"

"Hazel Rothbury."

"It's lovely to meet you, Hazel. My name is Mrs. Ruth Abelman."

There was a quiet dignity about Mrs. Abelman. She didn't strike me as the typical third-class passenger, but then again, I wasn't even in third class, so I was in no position to judge.

"Are you traveling alone too, Mrs. Abelman?"

"I'm very much alone, I'm afraid. Widowed several years ago and with my only daughter lost in a factory fire last year in New York." She smiled over at me, a sad smile that perfectly mirrored the way I felt whenever I spoke about my father. "I'm going to the United States to settle some personal matters, and after that, I don't know what I'll do. I am quickly approaching the age where I shall be useless to the world."

"That can't be true," I said, hoping to cheer her up. "My mum says the only useless creatures are mosquitoes. Everything and everyone else have a role to play in this world."

Mrs. Abelman laughed. "I did, once. Six weeks ago, I was a governess, always came with the highest recommendations. Then one day, some items in the household went missing. My employers accused me of the crime and I was dismissed."

"Why would they think it was you?"

Her smile faded. "Some fools will believe the worst rumors about a person simply because she is poor, or because she is wealthy, or because she doesn't care about money at all. Some will do the same simply because I am Jewish."

I'd never met anyone who was Jewish before, but I already liked Mrs. Abelman. I said, "Maybe one day everyone will know the truth," which made her smile.

At the bottom of the first set of stairs, Mrs. Abelman paused to look me over again. "I hope you won't be needing someone to look after you while you're on board this ship? Because I'm too old to fuss about that now."

"Oh no, ma'am." That was the last thing I wanted. "I used to help my mother keep house, and work with my brothers on our farm. I have taught myself from borrowed books by candlelight every night. If you judge me by my years, I know that I am young. But my mind is old enough to make this journey on my own."

Mrs. Abelman hummed as she looked me over once again, this time with a little more respect, I thought. "To speak like that, either you believe that you are intelligent and capable of solving problems as they come your way. Or else you are a bold young woman who knows what she wants and is unafraid to reach for it. Which one is true?"

I considered her question for several seconds, unsure of how to answer. Finally, with a shrug, I said, "Ma'am, I believe that both are true."

She continued to eye me. "If that is true, then if trouble comes this week, I trust you will find a way out of it."

I was far more likely to cause trouble than to avoid it. At least, that's what Mum had always said about me.

Mrs. Abelman kept walking, forcing me to continue on with her down the passageway. "When I was your age, I used to be full of questions. My father used to tell me so many questions would bring trouble into my life. Then he would add that there was only one way out of that trouble."

This sounded like something I needed to know. "What was that way out?"

She winked at me. "I had to find the answers." She pointed to my shoulder bag. "You must be a curious young lady too. I believe I saw you with a pen earlier."

"Yes, ma'am, but I don't have any paper. Would you have any I could borrow? Even a scrap will do. I hope to write a news story about this ship."

Mrs. Abelman smiled. "You wish to be a journalist? Are you a good writer? Curious?" She leaned toward me. "How will you know what to write about?"

"I think I'll just know." Mrs. Abelman arched one brow, but I added, "My mum says I get premonitions—that means I have a sense for when something is going to happen."

"I know what premonitions are."

"I had a feeling you'd say that," I said with a wink. "Anyway, I think I'll know when I've found the right story to write about."

"Then you'll need plenty of paper." Mrs. Abelman's smile widened. She reached into her own bag and withdrew a notebook with a brown leather cover and a latch to hold the notebook closed. "You may write in this, and I cannot wait to read your news story."

I shook my head. "I can't accept this. It's much too nice."

"Then you may borrow it. Return it when your story is finished, and I will use any paper that is left."

I brought the notebook to my chest, taking in the wonderful smell of leather and paper. "Thank you so much."

"You are very welcome. At first I had planned to travel on the *Californian*. I should have kept those tickets. I'm sure there would have been fewer stairs. However, I can continue on from here." She set her walking stick firmly down on the deck. "I shall not think twice about looking after you. If, however, you find yourself in need of some company, I don't care much for these adults with whom I am forced to socialize for the next week, but I do like children. I should enjoy spending some time with you."

"I'd like that too, Mrs. Abelman," I said, turning to leave.

She called after me, "Remember, Hazel, that it is your duty to write the truth. A good journalist will write the truth, not protect the secrets."

I nodded back at her, but she could not possibly have known how heavy that request was. Because I knew only one secret about the *Titanic* so far, and it was big enough that it could ruin White Star's reputation.

If the *Titanic* held any more secrets, I would have to write about them too. People needed to know the truth.

I planned to tell it.

CHAPTER
EIGHT

Then I Found a Friend

That first night, I slept in the well beneath one of the third-class stairways. Or rather, I huddled there, shivering with cold, my muscles aching against the hard metal floor. My eyes opened with the slightest sound, and on more than one occasion I had to press myself deeper into the shadows to avoid being seen by crewmen who were changing shifts or passengers who might've enjoyed a late-night outing before finally returning to their cabins.

I wanted to wish for a cabin of my own, for a place I knew would be safe, for a blanket to wrap myself in, and perhaps for a guarantee of a morsel of food come morning.

But I didn't make the wish. I'd learned long ago that wishes never did any good. I couldn't wish food onto my family's table, or light back into Mum's eyes. I certainly couldn't wish Papa alive again.

Eventually, I'd learned that doing was more important than wishing.

So I'd begun to work hard and to sacrifice what I wanted for what my family needed. I'd learned to be bold and to take risks when necessary. That's what had kept my family going for the past two years. It's how I would help them now.

I curled up tighter beneath the stairway and tried to ignore my hunger. After all, I'd known from the moment I stepped aboard the *Titanic* that this would be my lot for the next week. I simply had to endure the best I could. And hopefully, very soon, find something to eat.

The dining saloon wasn't far from where I sat. The wonderful smell of warm bread that had filled the corridors earlier in the day was back again, along with the scent of a hearty stew and the sweet aroma of oranges.

That food had to be prepared somewhere nearby. Perhaps later today, I'd try to find the kitchen. Maybe there'd be some scraps I could sneak away to eat.

I'd have to be careful, though. If I was caught, how would I explain why I was looking for scraps when food was available to everyone?

Everyone . . . with a ticket.

Once I thought it was safe to leave, I crawled out from beneath the stairs, though I stood too quickly and banged my head on the handle of a partially hidden door. I grimaced and was rubbing my head when I entered the corridor . . . and almost screamed out loud.

There stood Charlie, leaning against the wall, watching me without a hint of surprise. Watching me without any expression at all, actually. I truly didn't know if he was amused to have frightened me, or if he was irritated to have been kept waiting until I came out.

I stared at him for what seemed like a very long time, with no idea what to say. He stared back, saying nothing. I wasn't about to start this conversation and neither was he, apparently.

Finally, he gave in. "Well?"

That wasn't much for me to work with, so I decided to give him nothing in return. "There's no rule against exploring stairwells."

"But there is a rule against being a stowaway," he replied. "A lot of rules, actually. This is a crime."

My shoulders fell. "How did you know?"

He said, "Last night, I checked the passenger list. No one by the name of Hazel Rothbury has a ticket here on the *Titanic*. In fact, there are no Rothburys on board at all. I have to report this."

I stepped toward him, my voice trembling now with fear. "Please don't report me."

What would the punishment be for stowing away? I could imagine all sorts of possibilities. Would I spend time in the brig, or face a public humiliation, or be fined and sent to a workhouse? Each idea was worse than the one before.

"Those are the rules," he said. "I'm sorry, but I've got no other choice."

He turned to leave, but I darted forward and grabbed his arm. "I planned to pay for my ticket, I swear that. I just don't have the money right now."

"That's called theft. You should've saved up like everyone else did, bought the ticket properly, and then come on board."

With my other hand, I reached into my shoulder bag and pulled out the money inside. "This is all we had. My mum thought it would be enough, but it isn't. I can give you this much for a ticket, but it will leave me with nothing to find my aunt once we're in New York."

"Then you shouldn't have gotten on this ship."

"I had no choice. We're destitute, Charlie. My brothers are hungry; the bank is threatening to take our home. But if I can reach New York, I can get work in a garment factory and begin sending some money home."

Charlie turned toward me again and folded his arms, obviously still skeptical. "If you send that money to your family, where will you get the money for this ticket?"

I held up my notebook. "I'll sell my story to a newspaper! I swear to you, every cent I earn will go to repaying this ticket."

Then Charlie blinked again and his doubt returned. "Nobody buys newspaper stories from children, or from girls of any age."

"Maybe they will if I write it well enough. That's why I asked you those questions last night! If I get answers, then I can give them a story that no one else can. Please help me, Charlie. You told me that you come from poverty too, so you know that sometimes we have to do desperate things."

Charlie stared at me, slowly shaking his head. I tried not to be irritated by that, but I was. After all, I had finally been completely honest with him and now he was doubting me? If I had wanted to lie, I certainly could have invented a more believable story than that. This was the full truth, and I didn't know how to convince him any other way.

At last, he pushed past me to open the closet where I had banged my head. He grabbed something from it, closed the closet door, then said, "Wait here. I really wish you would have told me all of this sooner. It would have gone easier for you."

After he marched away, I looked up the stairs, debating whether to run, but where could I possibly go now? Besides, if I had made things worse by waiting a day to confess my crimes, I could only imagine how much worse still they would be if I tried to run now.

So I waited, but it felt like hours passed by with no sign of Charlie. Twice I had to hide again from other crew members or passengers in the area, and still there wasn't a trace of him. Hunger was gnawing at me, I was sleepy from the long night, and my patience was thin. So when I finally saw him heading toward me, I didn't care what punishment was coming my way. I only wanted to be angry with him for making me wait so long to be punished.

Without a smile or single change of expression, he said, "Come with me, Miss Rothbury."

"Could you call me Hazel, please?" If he used my name, that would mean we were friends.

But in the same stern voice, he only repeated, "Come with me."

So we were not friends. I forgot my anger now and simply began to worry. "Charlie, please."

I followed him down the passageway, because I had little choice, all the while wondering what awful thing was waiting for me ahead. My hands even began shaking and I wished for a coat with pockets so I could hide them. Not that Charlie would care, obviously.

He stopped halfway down the passageway, then unfolded his hand, and I saw a key in it. He pushed it into the lock of one of the cabin doors, then turned the handle to open the door.

"The closet you opened, was this key in it?" I asked.

He frowned. "You need to forget ever seeing that closet. It's not for passengers."

The door handle clicked and Charlie stepped aside, then gestured for me to enter.

"What are you doing?" I asked.

I stepped into the cabin with a bed for one and a blanket folded on top. Straight ahead of me was a table with two oranges, two rolls, a tall glass of milk, and a bowl of porridge.

Tears filled my eyes. Was this all for me?

Forgetting my anger and worry, I nearly dove at the food and began taking it in with the largest bites I could manage.

Charlie stood in the doorway, waiting until I remembered him again. I turned back to him and smiled, hoping for an explanation.

He set the key beside me on the table and said, "My room's on this same deck, so I knew not every cabin was filled. But you must promise to pay for your ticket after you sell that newspaper story."

"Yes, of course."

"And when you write your story, you must agree not to be one of those American muckrakers who's only trying to ruin my employers. You can be fair and honest, but write about what is good about this ship."

"I can do that." So far, other than the fire . . . and the possible story about what Captain Smith did to the *Olympic* last fall, I saw nothing about the *Titanic* other than its majesty. That was when I made my decision about what I wanted to write: why the *Titanic* was a new world wonder. I would tell the great story of this ship.

Charlie smiled back at me. "Then as far as anyone knows, you are now a legal passenger on board the *Titanic*. Nobody will question you for walking the corridors or eating in the saloon, or for roaming the ship wherever any other third-class passenger may go. You're going to reach America and save your family, and pay back this ticket, Miss Hazel. I know you will."

Hazel.

So we were friends after all.

If it wouldn't have been completely inappropriate, I would have wrapped my arms around Charlie's neck and given him an enormous hug of appreciation.

As it was, I merely said, "Thank you again. I really can't . . ." And when I couldn't think of any good way to finish that sentence, I had no other choice.

I wrapped my arms around Charlie's neck and gave him an enormous hug of appreciation.

CHAPTER
NINE

Every Second Counts

Thursday, April 11, 1912

The day I left home, Mum warned me that third-class passengers were treated more like cattle than good people. I realized now that wasn't true on the *Titanic*. In fact, the room Charlie had given me felt like a room in a palace.

After he left, I spent the next hour exploring my new cabin. It sat directly against the ship's metal hull, so the outer wall was curved, fitting with the angle of the ship. It had painted white walls with a pretty pink linoleum floor. The bed had a real mattress with soft linens, and most exciting, I had my very own washbasin. Even at home, I had to use the pump in our kitchen or go outside to wash my face.

The engines hummed from the lower decks, creating a strange vibration throughout my body, but when I climbed onto the bunk, the hum and the ship's gentle sway tempted me to close my eyes.

When I finally awoke, I was hungry again. I sat up, disoriented, then remembered that I could eat on board now. I jumped to the floor, quickly washed my face and tidied my dress and my hair, then put my bag over my shoulder.

At the door, I paused, whispering, "You'll pay them back, you'll pay them back." I'd promised Charlie that I would, and I could not disappoint him.

Minutes later, I stopped again at the entrance to the dining saloon. What if Charlie was wrong? What if they knew I didn't really belong in here?

"Sit anywhere you'd like, miss," a waiter said as he passed by.

I nodded, unclenched my fists, then walked inside, taking the seat nearest to the doors so that I could run if necessary. At this same table was a Greek family on my left and two women on my right who might have been sisters. In front of me was a pitcher of milk and some bread. One of the sisters took some bread for herself, so I did the same, then poured myself a glass of milk.

A waiter came toward me and I put my head down, hoping he'd turn in another direction. What if he asked for my ticket? He stood right behind me, not speaking a word. I got ready to run.

"I hope you're still hungry," he said, setting a bowl of soup with a slice of roast beef in front of me. I stared down at the food in complete disbelief. Could they have possibly mixed up our menu with that of the first class? This was a feast!

The two women beside me were piling butter on fresh-baked bread as their soup cooled in their bowls. "Surely they can't eat any finer than this on those upper decks," one woman said.

"It's better than I've had for most of my life," the other woman replied.

I agreed with the women. Every bite tasted better than the last, and that wasn't only because I'd nearly been starving until this morning.

The younger of the two women added, "They say the *Olympic* is nothing compared to the *Titanic*."

My ears perked up. I knew how rude it was to eavesdrop, but they were speaking loudly, so I had no choice but to listen. Surely any good journalist would say the same thing.

"What of the linens on the beds—" the older woman began.

Linens? My readers wouldn't care about the linens. There were far more important issues in the world. So I leaned toward them and said, "Pardon the interruption, but the *Olympic* is our sister ship, I believe."

The older woman frowned at me. Only one person in the world would think linens were more interesting than a near disaster with the *Olympic*, and she was at my table.

But the younger woman smiled kindly. "Right you are. The *Olympic* has a similar design to our ship here, but it's been at sea for months now."

"Did something happen to it when Captain Smith was in charge?" She squinted back at me, so I added, "An accident, perhaps?"

Both women's eyes widened, and I worried that I'd made a mistake by speaking so boldly. Of course it was a mistake. I'd just accused our ship's captain of . . . something bad. I thought I should know if the accusation was true.

"You are speaking of Captain Edward Smith, who now commands the *Titanic*?" the older woman asked. "Dear girl, he is the finest captain on any ship in the world. You don't know what you are talking about."

"Actually . . ." The younger woman waited until she had her sister's attention, then said, "I did read something in the newspapers."

I leaned forward, hoping she would say more. And to my great delight, she continued, "Last September, Captain Smith was in command of the *Olympic*. The ship left Southampton, same as we did yesterday, but a British warship was leaving the harbor too. Some people believed that Captain Smith and the warship's commander were in a race out of port. It might've all been a bit of fun—the new ocean liner competing against one of Britain's finest battleships—but it was hardly responsible behavior. There they were, testing who commanded the fastest ship."

"The battleship would win, of course," her sister said. "It's been proven at war."

"Indeed it has. But could it beat a ship with the size and might of the *Olympic*?" The younger woman smiled. "The waterway narrowed, forcing the two ships closer together. The more powerful *Olympic* pulled the warship into its wake, and the two boats collided, leaving an enormous gash in the hull of the *Olympic*, tall enough for a grown man to stand inside."

The older woman gasped. "Impossible! The *Olympic* would never have survived that."

"But it did. The *Olympic* safely returned to port for repairs." She glanced at me. "It returned safely . . . under the command of Captain Smith."

I was about to point out that it only needed to return because Captain Smith might have been foolish enough to race, but before I could, the older sister spoke. "I daresay if the *Olympic* can take on damage like that and stay afloat, then nothing will ever bring down the *Titanic*."

My spirits brightened at that thought. "Thank you both," I said as the women stood to leave. At least one mystery in my notebook was solved.

Or else a new mystery was introduced.

The first woman said, "There is one difference between the ships. The *Olympic* has a double hull. The *Titanic* does not. If the warship crashed into us as it did with the *Olympic*, we would not have fared so well."

I immediately reached for my notebook and wrote my next question to be solved.

What is a double hull?

Whatever it was, it had to be important, maybe even the difference between a near disaster and an actual disaster.

I looked up to ask the women about it, but they had already gone. But they couldn't leave, not when I had so many new questions to ask them! So I folded up my notebook and hurried out of the saloon, wondering which way they'd gone.

I found them again on the poop deck, staring out over the railing at the shores of Ireland, our final dock before leaving for America. I looked out over the railing too. As I did, my stomach began to feel strange, a touch of seasickness perhaps. But it came with a recurring thought to get off the ship here and find a new route to America.

I'd felt this same way the morning Papa left for work—the last morning he would ever leave our home. My stomach had been in knots during breakfast, knowing something was wrong.

But wasn't that the very reason to stay on the *Titanic*, to figure out if something here was wrong? If I left the *Titanic*, I would never write my story, I would never see it printed in a newspaper, and I would never become a journalist.

It was settled, then. I was staying here.

Eventually, the horn sounded from the boat deck, signaling that the *Titanic* was leaving Ireland to head for the open seas.

The two women had left, but only minutes later, a young couple took their place near the rails. The wife put a tissue to her eyes as they gazed out over the fading Irish coastline. She was so pretty, and so sad. I couldn't help but stare at her.

"Whatever is the matter, dear?" Her husband spoke with a distinct Irish accent.

"My mam said she had a bad feeling about this trip," she replied. "She begged me not to go. I s'pose I'm still thinking about her."

"Your mam is just feeling lonesome to see her lovely daughter go across the ocean." The husband put an arm around his wife. "But you'll see, New York isn't so far away. I heard that the ship made excellent time here, and she'll go even faster once we're in open water."

"I did hear that this is a very fast ship," his wife agreed.

That struck me as interesting, so once again I pulled my notebook from my bag and added two more questions to it:

What is the top speed for the Titanic?
If the ship has to stop for any reason, how long would it take?

I glanced up as the wife gasped and pointed upward toward the first-class promenade. "Who do you think that is?"

Her husband squinted. "My dear, I'm sure that I don't know."

"That's John Jacob Astor. I saw a picture of him in the newspaper last week. It must be him! Imagine that, a man as famous as he is on board this very ship!"

I turned to look as well, craning my head until I spotted him. Mr. Astor was one of the wealthiest men in the world. He had recently married a pretty young woman named Madeleine, who was now walking by his side.

"People say he is as fine a man as ever there was," the wife said, then quickly turned to her husband. "Other than you, of course!"

He smiled. "Maybe they only say that because he's so rich. Just you wait. I'll make my fortune in America too. One day, you'll dress just as beautifully as Mrs. Astor up there."

I glanced that way again for a second look, but this time

the Astors had passed out of my sight. Instead, I saw a more familiar figure waving at me.

I walked toward the rails to see her better. Sure enough, there was Sylvia Thorngood, standing on the first-class promenade, trying to get my attention. I smiled and waved back, surprised that she was still friendly to me, even now that it was obvious I was in third class.

Then my smile widened. Perhaps Sylvia didn't care about my class. Perhaps she was like Mr. Astor, as fine a person as ever there was.

But my smile almost instantly fell, along with my hand. Directly behind Sylvia was her governess, Miss Gruber. She was speaking to the very same woman I'd overheard at the deck rails yesterday when we departed, Mrs. Mollison. Something about her and her husband made my stomach bunch into knots. They were not good people.

I knew that because they had spoken of a plan to get money from someone on board. Were they talking about Sylvia Thorngood's money? Maybe so, because I couldn't think of any other reason why Mrs. Mollison would want to talk with that sour Miss Gruber.

Maybe it was nothing, but I thought I should warn Sylvia, at least. She had been kind to me, and if I were any sort of friend, I would find a way past the gates and the well deck, up to the first-class promenade, where I could tell her to stay away from the Mollisons.

But there was no point in trying. The crewmen roaming

the promenades would stop me and send me back to third class. The last thing I needed was anyone's attention.

There was nothing I could do for Sylvia, so with feelings of regret, I waved goodbye, then went back inside. I was no kind of friend at all.

CHAPTER
TEN

A Second Hull

By lunchtime, I was back in the saloon, seated before a bowl of vegetable soup I had yet to touch and a half-finished orange. I hadn't eaten any fruit for the past winter and the orange tasted even better than I remembered them. This time, I shared a table with two young families, each with babies in their arms. I didn't understand their language, but it became clear that they were exchanging parenting advice.

I pulled out my notebook and began to write. I didn't need help with parenting. I needed help with life.

"You do love that notebook." I looked up and saw Charlie standing across the table from me, hands in his pockets and a wide smile on his face. "Wouldn't be surprised if you had it filled before we reach New York."

"I'll do my best." I smiled back. "Thanks again, for what you did."

He blushed a little. "Now, if I were someone with any manners, I'd brush my hand through the air and say, 'Oh no, Miss Hazel, it wasn't any trouble at all.' Then you'd lean forward and say, 'But, Charlie, of course it was a lot of trouble. I can't imagine the risks you must have taken to get that room for me.' Then finally, I'd realize that it would do no good to deny it any longer and accept your thanks." While I laughed, he drew in a breath before continuing. "So I will save you the effort and merely say that it was a fair amount of trouble, and a risk that I know I should not have taken, but I did so because I think of you as a friend, and friends help each other. So I am happy to accept your thanks."

I laughed again, though he'd lost me about halfway through his speech. I did understand one thing clearly: We were friends now.

But although I was grateful and despite our new friendship, I also remembered that I still had questions for him. So I invited him to sit and when he did, I leaned across the table and lowered my voice. "Is there any more news, about the—"

Before I finished, his smile disappeared, just as it had the first time I'd tried to question him. He looked around and kept his voice low. "Do you mean, what's down below?"

I nodded eagerly. He knew exactly what I was talking about. "Surely you've heard something by now."

For several seconds he stared back at me, his mouth hanging open, as if I had just revealed that the earth was about to separate and swallow us whole.

Finally, he leaned in again, this time whispering, "I asked another friend of mine on board, he's a trimmer—that means he carries coal from the bunkers to the boiler rooms. He says they're working to get that fire out as soon as possible, for the sake of the ship."

"So we are in danger, then?"

"Oh no, the bunker should contain the fire. But I heard with the coal strikes back in England, we only have enough coal on board to barely reach New York. With this fire, we may run out before we get there."

"Is that why the ship is going fast?" I asked. "To get to New York before we run out?"

"I think it's the other way around," Charlie said. "Because of the fire, there's extra coal in the boilers, causing the ship to go fast. That's why we're at risk to run out."

I thought about that. "So you're saying the *Titanic* has to travel fast, or else we'll run out of coal before we reach New York?"

"Aye, miss. Imagine how embarrassin' that would be for White Star, if its flagship can't even reach port. Captain Smith will keep us going fast all the way into New York Harbor."

He started to leave but I lifted my notebook. "I have other questions. What does the crew think about being captained by the same man who nearly sank the *Olympic*?"

"The crew thinks it's wonderful, of course." His face fell into a frown. "Please don't ask me such questions. I need this job, and I'm grateful for it. I'll talk about any facts that you'd already find in the papers, but no gossip from the past. I won't turn on my employers by reporting problems to you."

"But if there are problems—"

"If there are problems, then the ship is designed to protect us from them. The people who built the *Titanic* have a lot of experience, more than either of us. They know what they're doing. No ship has ever been finer or stronger."

"So it's true, then. This is an unsinkable ship?"

Charlie shrugged. "Personally, I believe if an unsinkable ship ever was built, this is it." He pointed to my notebook. "Mind my words: If you ask too many questions, you'll only create unnecessary worry for yourself."

I hardly felt that a ship's fire was an *unnecessary* worry, but I did have other questions waiting to be asked.

"Could you tell me, then, what is a double hull?"

Charlie blinked back at me before his smile widened. "Now that is a question I can answer." With his good mood restored, Charlie left, returning a minute later with two empty soup bowls.

He lifted one of the bowls and held it up to look around its sides. "This is a good, strong bowl. Not a single crack. Liquid won't get in or out. Consider this bowl the hull of a ship."

Now he set that bowl into the second bowl. "This is a double hull, two layers to protect the ship. What happens if this outer hull gets a crack in it?"

"I suppose water would leak inside," I said.

Charlie reached for the pitcher and poured some water into the outer bowl. "If there is a leak in the outer hull, would the ship sink?"

I shook my head. "No, because the inner hull is protected."

"Exactly! With a double hull, even if the outer layer fails, water still won't get inside the ship itself."

"I would guess that has saved a number of lives."

Charlie's face lit up. "It has. This is what saved the *Olympic*."

I had one more question for Charlie, though I was nervous to ask it. "What about the *Titanic*'s hull?"

He shrugged. "Double layer on the bottom. It's not exactly the same as a double hull, but it is double thick. If we scrape a rock in shallow waters, we should be fine."

"Only on the bottom? What about the sides of the *Titanic*? Are those double hulls too?"

Charlie paused for a very long time, then said, "No, they are not. If we get scraped on the sides, we could be in real trouble."

CHAPTER
ELEVEN

A Second Try

Charlie's words hit me like a brick. I didn't know much about shipbuilding—I didn't know anything about it, in fact—except for one thing: A double hull sounded a great deal safer than a single hull.

Even Charlie seemed unsettled. He ran a hand through his hair and slowly shook his head.

"Charlie?"

"Huh?"

He looked over at me and must have seen the worry in my eyes, because he forced a smile to his face. Literally, he did. I saw him make the effort. Before it faded away, he said, "Of course, there are other safety measures in place, so with any problem, we'd still stay afloat a very long time. So don't you worry, Miss Hazel. When you do, a line forms across your forehead, and one day I reckon that line will stay there forever. I believe you worry too much."

"I don't think you worry enough." I leaned forward. "Did the captain order all of the crewmen to say whatever was necessary to help passengers feel safe?"

"Yes." Then he quickly added, "As I told you before, that's because you are safe. A safer ship has never been built than the *Titanic*."

"But what about—"

He must've sensed that another difficult question was coming because he stood to leave. "My apologies, but I need to get back to work."

I didn't want to get him in trouble for talking with me. Still, I was disappointed. I liked spending time with Charlie. "Thank you for the visit."

"My pleasure, Miss Hazel." Charlie cocked his head. "That's not the right word. This wasn't a pleasant conversation at all, and it might put a worry line on my own forehead for a while, but I'm glad we could talk."

I smiled and waved goodbye, but he was only a few steps away when he groaned and turned back to me.

He said, "We were so busy discussing all the terrible news that I nearly forgot the very happy reason I came to see you."

"Oh?"

"I was sent here to deliver a private message from a Miss Sylvia Thorngood up on B Deck. She asked if you would join her for dinner this evening at seven o'clock in the Café Parisien."

I stared down at my bowl of soup. "They'll have a dinner here."

"They'll have tea and some scones or bits of cheese. Nothing like what you'll find up top."

I shook my head. "You know very well that I can't go up there. I'm not allowed."

"No, you aren't, but if I were in your situation, I'd ignore that rule and find a way up there. Do you know what it means to get an invitation like this? If you were to refuse her, that would be considered quite rude."

I had no wish to offend Sylvia, but if I was caught, my good intentions would not be enough to save me.

"I'll stand out. Everyone will know I shouldn't be there."

"How is that?" Charlie looked genuinely confused. "Do you plan to announce your poverty at the door?"

"Of course not, but they'll see it, the same way that I see their wealth."

"I've served the wealthy for this entire first day at sea, and would you guess what I've noticed?"

"What's that?"

"Turns out, they get dressed, same as you and me, one leg at a time into their trousers."

My nose wrinkled. "The rich don't dress the same at all. They have servants to dress them."

"All right, well then, did you know the wealthy burp the same as us? They pass wind—"

I quickly looked around. "Charlie!"

"Well, it's true! My point is that you have nothing to be ashamed of. People are the same everywhere. Either they'll accept you as you are or they won't, but if they don't, that says more about them as snobs than you as comin' from poverty."

That wasn't at all what worried me, but I did appreciate him trying to help. "Thank you," I said.

Charlie seemed to know what I was thinking and widened his smile. "You've got nothin' to worry about, Miss Hazel. You're polite, and pretty. They should be glad for your company up there."

My mum used to say that anyone who wished to fit into high society needed three traits: intelligence, charm, and wealth.

"But," she'd added, "you don't need all three. Two will be good enough. If you are intelligent and have charm, they may forget you aren't wealthy. Or if you have charm and wealth, they won't care about your brains. And you can be as rude as you wish if you have both intelligence and wealth."

"But what if a person has all three?" I had asked.

Mum had smiled. "Then you may become anything you want in this world. Choose well, Hazel."

I thought about the people I'd met so far. Mrs. Abelman seemed to be a person with all three. I wondered if anyone would care if she ventured into first class. Sylvia probably had all three as well, though no one would question the daughter of Edgar Thorngood about anything.

They would question me. There was a hole in the hem of my dress, torn by a stick in my path as I'd walked to Southampton. I wasn't fit to dine on the upper decks. "Charlie, I can't—"

He bumped a fist to his forehead. "Didn't I tell you? Miss

Thorngood already had me deliver a dress to your room. She's taken care of that for you."

Then I thought again about the Mollisons, that horrid couple. If their plan caused any harm to Sylvia or her family, Miss Gruber had to be warned.

I would have to be careful to avoid Officer Kent since he had already warned me once to stay away from the first-class promenade. But it would help if I was wearing a different dress. Maybe I could get away with it, just this once.

"So?" Charlie urged.

My heart began to pound. If Mum was right, that I had premonitions, I was having one right now. But once again, I ignored it. "Tell her I would love to go."

Charlie smiled. "I'll give her that message. By the time you're dressed and ready, I'll be back and can show you a better route upstairs."

I stood and hurried back to my cabin, eager to make myself as presentable as possible.

"Intelligence, charm, and wealth," I whispered aloud. "You've got no wealth, Hazel, and charm has never been your strongest trait. It looks like tonight, you'll have to slide by with a little intelligence."

And for that, I'd need my notebook.

R.M.S. "TITANIC"

FIRST CLASS PARISIAN MENU
A là Carte

<u>Hors D'Oeuvres</u>
Oysters
Warm Baquettes and Butter

<u>Soup</u>
Cream of Barley

<u>Main Course</u>
Poached Salmon with Cucumbers
Roast Duckling
Pâte de Foie Gras

<u>Fruit</u>
Peaches with Chartreuse Jelly

<u>Dessert</u>
Chocolate or Vanilla Éclair
French Ice Cream

Tea or Coffee for All Meals

R.M.S. "TITANIC"

THIRD CLASS MENU

<u>BREAKFAST</u>
OATMEAL PORRIDGE & MILK
BROILED CAMBRIDGE SAUSAGES
IRISH STEW
FRESH BREAD & BUTTER
MARMALADE   SWEDISH BREAD
TEA   COFFEE

<u>DINNER</u>
BARLEY BROTH   BEEF À LA MODE
LIMA BEANS   BOILED POTATOES
FRESH BREAD & BUTTER
RICE PUDDING   ORANGES

<u>TEA</u>
FRESH BREAD & BUTTER
COMPOTE OF APRICOTS & RICE
LEICESTER BRAWN
PICKLES
TEA

<u>SUPPER</u>
GRUEL   CHEESE

Any complaint respecting the food supplied, want to attention or civility, should be at once reported to the Purser or Chief Steward. For purposes of identification, each Steward wears a numbered badge on the arm.

CHAPTER
TWELVE

My Second Chance Faltered

An hour later, Charlie came to my door with an awkward smile, holding a bit of white hair ribbon.

"Now don't go and get any ideas with the ribbon," he said. "Someone must have dropped this earlier today. I picked it up and it's been in my pocket. I thought it might match the dress . . . if you want it."

It was exactly what I needed to look more upper-class. "It's perfect, thank you!" I tied it into my hair, finishing it off with a neat bow. "How's that?"

Charlie smiled and maybe blushed a little. "Don't you worry about fitting in tonight, Miss Hazel. You look as first-class as any of those rich girls."

I hoped he was right. I was beginning to feel nervous.

Charlie led me through the gates into the first-class areas, but once there, he shifted his weight, becoming nervous.

"I've got to leave you now. Miss Thorngood paid me to get you into first class, but I can't risk my job by taking you any farther."

"No, indeed," I said. "And if I'm caught, I'll say I crossed over by myself."

He winked at me. "I can trust you, then. The Parisien is on B Deck, starboard side near the aft staircase. You'll find it well enough."

It shouldn't have been any trouble to find the Parisien, but I had to take a different stairway to avoid Officer Kent, and at one point I walked toward the port side of the ship because I thought I spotted the Mollisons.

By the time I finished avoiding everyone I didn't want to see, I had explored much of the upper decks of the ship. Every part of first class was beautiful, but the Grand Staircase that wound up through the center of the ship took my breath away.

Glancing down from the top, I could look over the rail and see the stairs descend through several decks, or gaze upward at a dome of glass and iron. I doubted even the finest chapels in Europe could compete with this.

Eventually, I located the Café Parisien. It was long and narrow with large windows to allow an easy view over the ocean.

The interior was styled to look like a café in Paris itself. White latticework framed the walls and ceiling, with the occasional piece of greenery climbing a trellis. The tables and chairs were made of white wicker, and a red carpet rolled out along the center aisle.

Miss Gruber was waiting at the entrance to greet me, though her greeting was hardly friendly. She looked me over, clearly determined to find at least one flaw in me. I was equally determined to impress her.

"Why did you say you were traveling to the United States?" she asked.

"To stay with my aunt," I replied.

She harrumphed. "Will your aunt provide you with a servant at her home? Someone to brush your hair and set out your clothes?"

My aunt lived in a crowded apartment with other women from the factory. She had no servants. At best, she was the servant.

"No, ma'am," I said.

Miss Gruber turned to enter the café. "Then you had better learn how to brush out your own hair."

I ran my fingers through my hair. Sure enough, there was a knot I had missed in the back.

"Come along." Miss Gruber waved me forward. "Heavens, child, didn't your parents teach you any manners?"

Manners hadn't been the highest priority of my education as a farm girl. I didn't know why the plates in this café had so many forks and spoons when only one of each should be enough. I didn't know how to address a countess or a duchess, nor could I describe the difference between them. But I knew which breed of cow produced the best milk, and how to coax a chicken into producing more eggs. I doubted that any duchess in England knew how to properly coax a chicken.

I held my head high as I walked over the red carpet, its bold color seeming to remind me that I was breaking a serious rule on board, and that the meal I was about to enjoy was likely worth more than my family could earn in a month off our farm.

Yet that all passed when I saw Sylvia waving me over to her table. She had changed into a formal dress for the evening and looked very pretty. I took a small comfort in the fact that Miss Gruber's outfit was even more boring than when I'd seen her yesterday.

A handsome gentleman in a formal suit was also seated at the table. He stood to greet me and even held out a chair for Miss Gruber. He appeared to be in his mid-twenties and had a kind smile.

"This is Mr. Emerson Waddington," Sylvia said. "He is a student, studying to design ships just like the *Titanic*."

"Better than the *Titanic*, if you'll forgive me for boasting," Mr. Waddington said. "What you see here is only the beginning of what will be possible one day."

"Have you been studying the *Titanic* while on board?" Sylvia asked.

"Indeed, I have. I had a tour of the ship yesterday, and today I spent most of the afternoon in the engine rooms."

That caught my interest. Mr. Waddington must have seen the fire, or heard about it. I reached for my notebook, hoping to ask him about it, but Sylvia touched my arm.

"I'm so glad you could come," she whispered. "It took a long time to convince Charlie to bring you the invitation."

"Thank you for having me here, and for the dress," I replied. It was the prettiest dress I'd ever worn and probably would ever wear in my life.

"Miss Thorngood insisted on inviting you," Miss Gruber said. "This was not my idea."

That had already been perfectly obvious. Miss Gruber was staring at me as if I were diseased.

Sylvia brought my attention back to her. "How has your first full day on board been?"

"Exciting! I have learned so much." I immediately wished I had not answered that way. Most of my learning involved Captain Smith crashing the *Titanic*'s sister ship, and a fire somewhere in the single hull of this ship. But there was one thing I had learned that was extremely important, the very reason I had agreed to come to dinner. In a quieter voice, I added, "I need to talk to you and Miss Gruber about two people I—"

"Ah, and here are our next guests." Miss Gruber's face lit up and I turned, feeling the blood drain from my face.

Walking toward our table was the very couple I had wanted to discuss with Sylvia. Mr. Mollison was dressed in the same suit as yesterday, but his wife was in a different gown, a yellow one that hung awkwardly on her frame. I suspected that dress wasn't made for her, any more than Sylvia's dress was made for me.

Miss Gruber said, "Mr. Waddington, this is Mr. Clyve Mollison and his lovely wife, Letha Mollison. I believe you all have met my ward, Sylvia Thorngood."

Mr. Mollison was all smiles as he offered to shake Sylvia's hand. "What a pleasure to see you again, Miss Thorngood. I trust you have had a good afternoon."

Sylvia shrugged. "Miss Gruber has done well at keeping me hard at work on my lessons, even while at sea."

What she was really saying was that the last thing she wanted while on board was to work on her lessons. But she said it in such a way as to compliment Miss Gruber. Maybe that was how good manners worked.

Sylvia gestured to me. "This is my new friend, Miss Hazel Rothbury."

"That is a lovely dress," Mrs. Mollison said to me, and then her tone soured. "Very different from the dress you were wearing yesterday on the promenade."

My heart skipped a beat. They had seen me there? This meant they knew I had overheard their conversation.

If I was going to warn Sylvia and Miss Gruber about the Mollisons, it was better to do that now, before the dinner began. I turned to Sylvia, wondering what I dared to say with the Mollisons right beside us.

"Manners, Miss Rothbury," Miss Gruber said. "A conversation should be for everyone at the table."

A long silence followed until Mr. Waddington pointed to the notebook in my shoulder bag. "Are you a writer, Miss Rothbury?"

"I want to be." I pulled out the notebook and pen. "The *Titanic* holds many secrets and I wish to discover them all.

About the ship and"—I eyed the Mollisons—"the secrets of some of its passengers."

"That is an expensive notebook," Mr. Mollison said. "Where did you get it?"

"It was loaned to me by a friend on board," I said. "Mrs. Abelman offered it to me yesterday, in return for a favor."

"But you have written in it already, so it cannot be borrowed," Mrs. Mollison said. "Did you steal it?"

"Come now," Mr. Waddington said. "There's no reason to accuse the girl. I wish to hear more about her writing." He leaned toward me. "That sounds very interesting. What will you do with all this information?"

"I'll write it into a news story. I hope to sell it to a newspaper after we reach New York."

His smile widened. "My governess taught me that the job of a good journalist is to ask questions. So I wonder, what questions do you have about the ship?"

Forgetting the Mollisons, I opened the notebook and said, "What do you think of the *Titanic* having only a single hull on the sides?"

Mr. Waddington tilted his head. "That is a very big question for someone as young as you are."

"It is a silly question," Mrs. Mollison said. "Why should anyone care about that?"

Mr. Waddington chuckled. "Are you a writer too, Mrs. Mollison?"

"Hardly." She squinted back at him. "My father believed

that unless a person had something new to say, writing was a waste of ink."

"Ah, well, perhaps Miss Rothbury will have something new to say, if we can answer her very thoughtful question." Mr. Waddington turned to me again and spoke as if he was actually taking me seriously. "The *Titanic* has a double hull on the bottom. That is because the greatest threat to a ship is crossing through a shallow area with rocks. But the sides are only a single hull, because there is little risk to them in an open ocean."

"Unless there's an iceberg." Mrs. Mollison stirred her finger around the rim of her goblet, looking utterly bored.

I, however, was fascinated.

"It is true that a ship could encounter icebergs," Mr. Waddington said. "But the *Titanic* has two lookouts in the crow's nest at all times. They'll give the warning long before any trouble comes. Even if a problem did occur, the ship is protected by a series of bulkheads."

I wrote down that word, then repeated it as a question. "Bulkheads?"

"The hull of a ship is not one large hollow space," Mr. Waddington replied. "It is lined with bulkheads—tall walls that strengthen the shape of the ship's hull. Here on the *Titanic*, the bulkheads can be sealed off from each other so that, even if one section floods, the other sections can remain afloat."

Mr. Mollison leaned forward, finally looking interested.

"You are telling us that if the ship's hull is scraped open, water might fill one bulkhead section, but it cannot get into the other sections?"

"Exactly," Mr. Waddington said. "So the *Titanic* will stay afloat, even if water gets into one or two bulkheads, or perhaps even if three or four bulkheads flood."

Miss Gruber said, "Then I assume the bulkheads are kept watertight at all times."

"That's not possible," Mr. Waddington said. "Doorways between the bulkheads allow the crew to move from one area to another to work. But if needed, the bulkheads have watertight doors that can be closed within seconds. Once those doors close, it is impossible for water to get from one bulkhead into the other. The design is really quite genius."

I was scribbling notes as fast as my pen could move. "How many bulkheads does the *Titanic* have?"

"Fifteen, which means there are sixteen compartments."

I paused there. He had said we'd stay afloat, perhaps even if three or four compartments flooded. We were perfectly safe, then, even with a single hull. Nothing would breach the hull enough to sink us.

Mr. Waddington continued, "A dozen ships must be crossing the Atlantic right now, and they do so every week. A ship hasn't foundered in open water for nearly forty years. I declare that we are safer here than on any other ship currently crossing the Atlantic."

"Then let's be finished with such a dismal conversation,"

Miss Gruber declared. "I see that oysters are offered for hors d'oeuvres this evening. Shall we have one order or two?"

Oysters.

I hated oysters.

That should have been my first clue to how the rest of the evening would go.

CHAPTER
THIRTEEN

Then It Fell Apart

I didn't care how nutritious oysters were—to me they tasted like swallowing slime. Everyone else at the table was enjoying them, so it would look bad if I spat mine out onto my plate.

But I wanted to. I wondered how many courses still remained and if the food would get any better. I wondered what they were serving in third class.

The conversation had turned toward Sylvia, which was fine by me. She was the guest of honor at this table.

"So, Edgar Thorngood is your father," Mr. Waddington was saying. "I hear he is building the future of this world."

"He has invested thousands of dollars to advance the design of airplanes. Papa says that one day, airplanes will cross the ocean faster than any ship can travel."

Mr. Mollison laughed. "Then he must have been joking. The *Titanic* is a very fast ship. I defy anything in the air to be faster or safer."

Sylvia's tone sharpened. "My father was not joking, sir."

Mrs. Mollison quickly cut in, saying to Miss Gruber, "If a father with such a great vision for the future trusts you with the care of his daughter, you must be an excellent governess."

"He has indeed trusted me with Miss Thorngood," Miss Gruber said, then more pointedly added, "And with much of her family's future."

"Perhaps we could all meet again tomorrow for lunch," Sylvia suggested.

Miss Gruber shook her head. "I'm afraid not. You must attend to your lessons. There is no time for fun."

I chuckled, thinking at first that Miss Gruber had to have been making a joke of her own. Yet I quickly got a fresh glare and Miss Gruber's sharp tone became aimed at me.

"Life is not to be enjoyed," she said. "It is a time to make the most of oneself. Miss Thorngood is preparing to enter society. She must be trained in the arts and the classic languages, and in proper manners." Her right eye twitched as she stared down at me. "Perhaps you cannot understand why that is so important."

Miss Gruber's stare lasted so long that I realized I must be breaking some rule of manners, yet I had no idea what it was. Sylvia pointed at her elbows. Mine were resting on the table. Hers were not. I couldn't see why this was a rule of manners, but I lowered my hands into my lap anyway. Miss Gruber seemed to relax afterward, which meant that the disapproval shifted from her full expression merely to her pursed lips. That wasn't as bad.

"If Miss Thorngood is busy with lessons, I'd be happy to keep you company this week," Mrs. Mollison said to Miss Gruber. "I've heard there is a lovely salon on board where we might have our hair done."

Miss Gruber returned her version of a smile, a crease in one corner of her mouth. "I should like that very much."

"No!" I said, then watched as all eyes turned to me. I felt the heat of anger coming from both Mollisons. Maybe I'd misunderstood the conversation that I'd overheard. They hadn't admitted to being thieves or con artists. What if I was wrong about them?

"No," I repeated, adding, "No, you should not miss the chance to get your hair done."

To my relief, the awkwardness lifted when a waiter appeared with bowls of a green-colored soup. "I'll bring your third course soon," he said. "Please enjoy."

Third course? How many would there be? Never in my life had I eaten a meal served in courses. I worried that by the time the final course arrived, I would be so full that I'd pop open. And that would be a very bad show of manners.

"What kind of work does your father do?" Mr. Waddington asked me.

"My father passed on two years ago," I replied. "Before then, he was a—"

"Her father's work would have no interest to us," Miss Gruber quickly said.

But it was too late. I finished my sentence: "Fisherman."

"Ah!" I saw the shift in Mr. Waddington's expression. The daughter of a deceased fisherman would have no chance of being a first-class passenger—and he knew it.

"She has no place at this table," Mrs. Mollison said. "I'll call for a porter to escort her back where she belongs."

"She's my guest here," Sylvia said firmly. "And just you wait. One day she will be a famous journalist, one of the first female journalists in the world. How lucky we all are to know Hazel Rothbury now, before all her wealth and fame."

I felt myself blushing as I smiled back at Sylvia. She seemed to believe in me, even more than I believed in myself.

Mr. Mollison crushed that dream as quickly as Sylvia had built it. "A child journalist? There's no such thing."

I pressed my lips together and stared back at him, determined not to flinch. "There's no such thing . . . yet."

Both Mrs. Mollison and Miss Gruber gasped, but Mr. Waddington raised his glass to me. "Well said."

"On your best behavior now," Miss Gruber warned. "Captain Smith has just entered the café."

We all turned to look at a man in his sixties or perhaps even older. He had white hair and a neatly trimmed beard. His roughened skin was evidence of the years of facing salty ocean air. He was not as tall as I had imagined the captain of such a grand ship to be, yet something about his presence commanded respect.

He shook hands with a few of the men as he passed by

them, including Mr. Waddington, aware that nearly everyone in the café was watching him. Once he was within view of most of the passengers, he held out his arms and said, "To my old friends, and my newest friends, welcome on board the *Titanic*."

Everyone applauded, so I did too. Once it faded, he continued, "Since many of you have asked, I thought it best to answer a few of your questions all at once. We have more than twenty-two hundred souls on this ship. Thirteen hundred are passengers, and the rest are officers and crew, or a select few who were hired by our company to make the visit even more delightful. Our every wish is to make this the finest overseas journey you have ever enjoyed, so if we can improve your time with us, please just ask."

This announcement was met with more applause, but this time, I did not share in it. Instead, I opened my notebook again and glanced at the notes I had made earlier that day. I'd promised Charlie not to say anything about the fire, but I did have other questions, including some that only the ship's captain could answer.

A gentleman near the back of the room stood up. "Say, Captain, a few of us were wondering if there is any danger to the ship from icebergs?"

Captain Smith nodded as he considered his answer. "If there is any risk at all, we will know of it well in advance. I assure you, there is nothing to worry about."

Though the other passengers applauded yet again,

his words troubled me. Mrs. Mollison had mentioned icebergs too. I wondered if they were a serious threat to a ship like ours.

By then, Captain Smith was shaking hands with guests and preparing to leave. If I didn't ask my questions now, I knew I might never have the chance. So, I stood and in a firm voice said, "Captain, how fast is the *Titanic* traveling now?"

"Miss Rothbury, you will apologize and sit down," Miss Gruber hissed.

I glanced over at her, but I would not sit down, and I certainly wouldn't apologize. If another guest could ask a question, why not me?

He smiled politely. "Excellent question. The *Titanic* crossed nearly five hundred miles yesterday, and we expect an even greater distance by the end of today. Our plan is to gradually increase speed, perhaps reaching our maximum of twenty-three knots by Monday. That will make us one of the fastest ships currently in operation."

Again, his answer was met with applause, and I took that time to write that down in my notebook, though now I had a second question.

"Captain?"

"Hazel."

I glanced down at Sylvia, whose cheeks were flushed with embarrassment. I couldn't understand why. That gentleman had asked the captain a question and no one objected. Why should they object to my question?

Then I understood. They weren't embarrassed by my question. They were embarrassed by *me*.

"Yes, child?" the captain asked, still as polite as before.

"I, uh . . ." I felt heat on my cheeks. All I wanted now was to sit back down and become invisible, but I had the captain's attention, so I would have to ask the question. "I only wondered, if the *Titanic* had to turn to avoid a hazard, how quickly could that happen?"

Captain Smith stared at me for what felt like a very long time, and his smile faded. He said, "Open water stretches out around us. There should be no reason for any sudden changes in course. We have two sailors stationed at all times in a crow's nest ninety feet above our top deck. Their only job is to watch for potential trouble ahead. I assure you, we will have plenty of warning before we need to slow down or change course."

"But—"

"Thank you very much, ladies and gentlemen. I must return to my duties now." The captain gave us a respectful nod, then quickly left, likely before I could ask any more questions.

I felt the eyes of every diner in the restaurant on me as I slowly sank back into my chair. Sylvia's head was down, and Miss Gruber was staring at me through narrowed eyes.

Mrs. Mollison leaned over to Miss Gruber. "That young lady of yours ought to be better trained in her manners."

"She is not *my* young lady," Miss Gruber said. "She doesn't belong here with us."

"No, I really don't," I said. "Excuse me." I paused long enough to look at Sylvia. "Thanks for the invitation, but I should go."

Then I escaped from the restaurant as quickly as I possibly could.

CHAPTER
FOURTEEN

As Seconds Became Minutes

With tears clouding my eyes, I took a wrong turn from the restaurant and ended up back on the Grand Staircase. I stared up again at the dome of glass and iron. If the *Titanic* was the queen of the seas, then that dome was her crown.

And I was the court jester. How could I be anything else but a joke now? How could I ever have thought I belonged up here?

I knew better now, yet I felt stranded on the stairs. If I went downstairs, I would enter the elaborate dining room, where even more judging eyes would fall upon me. But if I went upstairs, I'd be farther from third class. That was the only place I truly wished to be at the moment, to be back where I belonged.

My decision was made when I heard voices coming up the stairs. Unsure of what to do, I turned and began hurrying up the staircase, hoping to stay ahead of them. I ran out a set of doors and onto the first-class promenade.

To my surprise, I saw a familiar face. Mrs. Abelman was only a few steps away, seated in a deck chair and casually waving me over to her.

I wiped my eyes, then walked forward. After a polite greeting, I said, "I thought you were traveling in third class."

"And why would you have thought that?"

The answer seemed so obvious that the question confused me. I finally said, "Well, I believe it's because you were in third class when we met."

"And so were you, but look at us now."

"You're a first-class passenger, then?"

Mrs. Abelman smiled. "You are assuming that for the same reason you assumed I was in third class."

Perhaps so, though by this point, I wasn't entirely sure what we were talking about. "What class are you in, Mrs. Abelman?"

"Why does that matter?" She clapped her hands together and drew in a breath as if she was about to say something important. "Who invented class anyway, other than a few elites at the top who wished to be sure someone would always be at the bottom to serve them?"

I sat beside her. "Whether any of us likes it or not, we are in classes here on the ship. Surely you have noticed the differences."

"Indeed, I have, and I feel sorry for the wealthy. Why, in first class, the family very often bunks alone, in separate compartments, simply because they can afford to do so. Those people must be miserable with no one to talk to but each other. But in third class, as many as ten passengers are allowed to sleep in one room, ensuring a lifetime of friendship."

I smiled but shook my head. "That's not the way they think of it. No one in first class envies anyone in third."

"Are you sure?" Mrs. Abelman tilted her head. "Then what are those gates I keep seeing? I thought they were to prevent those rich snobs from sneaking down to spend time where the real fun happens."

Now I laughed. "You know very well the gates are there to keep the third class separated from the rich."

She sniffed. "If you and I are both here, then they don't do a very good job of it."

"Did you go past those gates?" She only smiled back, much entertained by herself, and I added, "When we last met, you needed my help just to go down some stairs."

"I *asked* for your help. I didn't need it," she replied. "There's a difference. You were an excellent helper, though. I imagine your parents will miss your help very much."

"She has my brothers there," I said, as a more somber mood overtook me. "I wouldn't have needed to leave home if my father were still with us."

"What happened to him?"

I brushed one hand across the folds of my skirt, remembering him again, remembering the day that his captain had come to our house with an apology and a fist full of flowers that would die within the same week.

"A storm at sea ran the ship onto rocks," I said. "Papa could have saved himself, but instead, he went belowdecks to save the other sailors."

"Your father must have been a very good man," said Mrs. Abelman.

"But he had the choice," I said. "He could have saved himself and come home to us that night. I don't know why he didn't."

Mrs. Abelman let that moment pass in silence before she asked, "Does your mother still grieve his loss?"

"Very much. Some days I wonder if she'll ever get past it."

"Grief is like the flu," she said. "It brushes by some, barely leaving its mark. For others, it will take hold, perhaps for a very long time before a person finds healing."

I barely dared to look over at her. "Sometimes, the flu wins."

"Sometimes," Mrs. Abelman echoed, her voice more faint than before.

A long silence passed before I said, "You told me that you lost a daughter."

"Yes, in a factory fire." Mrs. Abelman's gaze softened, as if she was thinking of another time. Finally, she said, "I hadn't seen her in years, didn't even know she worked in a factory, poor thing. I later heard that my daughter stayed back to help others get out first. I will forever admire her courage." Now she sniffed. "But I am learning to smile again." As proof of that, she looked over at me. Her smile looked genuine enough.

"Do you think my mother will learn to smile again too?"

"What does your gut tell you?"

I squinted over at her. *Gut* seemed like a very unladylike word.

She smiled, completely unoffended by my reaction. "You seem to have good instincts, Hazel. Trust your feelings. If something feels off, then act on it. Maybe you'll be wrong, but that's far better than realizing later on that you were right. So, tell me, what does your *gut* tell you about your mother?"

I smiled and nodded. Mama would be all right. But my mind lingered on the rest of what Mrs. Abelman had said, that if something felt off, I should act on it.

Something had felt wrong to me this very morning. It had happened twice, actually. First, the impulse came to leave the ship. Second, I knew it was a bad idea to accept the invitation to dine with Sylvia.

I said to Mrs. Abelman, "I embarrassed Sylvia Thorngood at supper just now." I sat on the chair beside her, feeling utterly defeated. "All I did was to ask the captain some questions. I still don't see how that was wrong."

For a while, Mrs. Abelman was silent. Finally, she said, "When I was young, my family was poor. To earn money, we rented out rooms in our home as lodging for travelers. Many of them came from very old money, which they believed made them more important than those of us who had come from old poverty."

A corner of my mouth turned up. My family had come from old poverty too.

She continued, "I was curious about these travelers, who had come from faraway places, and longed to ask them questions. But the travelers preferred to sit around our kitchen table and gamble away their wealth in games of cards. They complained about not having enough money, when they should have complained about not having enough good sense." She brushed a hand over the carving of the eagle's head on her walking stick before adding, "It is questions that keep us alive, Hazel, questions that keep us moving forward."

I nodded and felt my eyes grow hot. "I can't help it. There are so many questions in my mind, all the time. This is a miserable problem."

"It's only miserable if you see it as a problem. I think curiosity is a gift, and if you are to be a journalist, it's an absolute must."

I pulled Mrs. Abelson's notebook from my bag and held it out to her. "At supper, they laughed when I said I wanted to be a journalist. You should take this back."

"Do you think that would make the curiosity go away?" Mrs. Abelman lifted her cane and sharply tapped the floor, prompting me to look up at her again. "Who would you be without your questions? Perhaps a girl easily led around by others, with no thoughts of your own? I would rather be curious than beautiful, for a girl without curiosity is only beautiful on the surface. I would rather be curious than wealthy, for a girl with a mind full of questions is more valuable than a girl with jewels on her empty head. I would wish to be the kind of person to ask questions more than I would wish to be anyone with no questions worth asking. You should keep the notebook awhile longer."

I smiled back at her. "Thank you."

"Now, what horrid questions did you ask to cause such

embarrassment at the supper? Did you ask the captain if he was going bald?"

"Of course not."

"At any point, did you ask whether his undergarments fit him properly?"

"Mrs. Abelman!"

"I assume that means no. Well, then, your questions could not have been too offensive. Did you get them answered?"

"I think so, but now I have a new question. It's a difficult one."

"Ask me. Perhaps I can answer you."

"A gentleman in the café asked the captain about any risk to the ship from an iceberg. The captain did not seem to believe there was any great threat to us, because he said the lookouts would see the iceberg in time. Two of the *Titanic*'s bulkheads could flood and the ship would still stay afloat, but could an iceberg cause three or more bulkheads to flood?"

Mrs. Abelman sat back. "I confess, I was not expecting *that* question out of someone as young as yourself."

"Mum says I'm an old soul."

"Do you know what that means?"

I shrugged. "I think it means that I ask big questions."

"Close enough." She looked me over a moment, then asked, "How much do you know about icebergs?"

"Very little. But I want to learn."

"Then you shall. Tomorrow morning after breakfast, meet me in the library on C Deck. You'll find it overlooking the well deck."

I knew exactly where it was. "That's for second-class passengers."

Mrs. Abelman shook her head. "That's where the books are that you need, and books should be for everyone." She stood and leaned on her eagle's head walking stick. "By then, I expect you to think of at least a dozen more questions worth asking. Can you do that?"

"Yes, and thank you!"

She passed me the newspaper that she had been reading. "If you wish to create the news, then you should be reading it. I will also expect to hear a report from you about Captain Scott's expedition to the South Pole. Front page."

My eyes widened. "We've reached the South Pole, then?"

Mrs. Abelman only smiled back. "Read first, *then* give me your questions."

CHAPTER
FIFTEEN

Did Threats Matter?

Someone wiser than me might have left the first-class promenade as soon as possible. However, someone exactly like me decided to explore this deck while I had the chance.

More than anything, I wanted to see the view from the bow of the ship. I knew it was a risk. That's where the officers would be, and the wealthiest passengers who would know in a single glance that I had no business being there.

Unless I could fool them.

I looked at the other women up here and decided to carry myself as they did, with my chin up, my eyes forward, and with a very slight smile, like I was happy, but not too happy.

I held that pose until I reached the bow. I was struck by the simplicity of it—just four railings that came to a rounded point. Yet a thrill rushed through my whole body. If only my family could see me now!

As I stared out over the dark ocean, I suddenly felt very

small. Who was I compared to all of this? How arrogant I had been to come to the bow, as if I were the queen of this very small world at sea.

But of course, the *Titanic* itself was arrogant, a challenge to the heavens and everything below it, and to nature itself.

If I had learned anything from the death of my father, it was that nature would have its way. Anyone who refused to accept that reality would one day have to face it. Perhaps even on this mighty ship.

When I'd had my fill of the view, I turned and noticed the lifeboats on the deck. They weren't on the first-class promenade, where the wealthy might object to a view tainted by large boats. But they were here, in the area reserved for the ship's officers.

One of those officers was approaching me now. It wasn't Officer Kent, but he could get me in trouble just the same.

"My name is Quartermaster Rowe," he said, treating me with perfect respect. "May I help you, miss?"

"No, thank you." I turned to leave, then sighed. I might not get another chance to ask my question. "Sir, I did wonder how many lifeboats are on this ship?"

His brow furrowed. "You understand, I hope, that it is not likely we will ever need them. Is there a reason for your question?"

I thought of Mrs. Abelman and answered, "Curiosity is a good thing, is it not?"

"It is good," he said. "Very well, then. We have twenty lifeboats, eight on each side of the ship. Four of them are collapsible, so you won't see them placed out in the open like the others."

I thanked him, then walked closer to the boats, estimating how many people could fit inside each one. It wasn't an exact count, of course, but I believed each one could hold sixty people, more or less.

Captain Smith had said that this ship held more than two thousand people. If the *Titanic* ever faced a problem serious enough that the passengers would need to abandon ship, at most, those lifeboats could hold only half that number. Why weren't there more lifeboats?

"Women and children first." That's what Charlie had said to me.

If the *Titanic* had a problem, it would be women and children *only*. Or, with so few lifeboats, it might be only *some* women and children. How was this possible?

Once more, my mind flew back to the Irish wife whose mother had worried about her boarding the *Titanic*, then of my own *gut feeling*, as Mrs. Abelman would call it, to leave the ship in Ireland.

Perhaps I should have listened to that feeling.

I sat on a deck chair against the wall, pausing long enough to record the number of lifeboats into my notebook. It seemed like an important detail to include for my future readers.

Because I wanted to sell this story, almost more than anything in the world. And what if they liked it enough that they asked me for another?

Maybe that was a silly dream, but it was the most important dream of my life. It was the only chance I had to escape working in some dangerous factory once we reached New York.

If I could write newspaper stories, I might even earn enough money to bring my family over to America too. I'd book them passage on the *Titanic*, so they could experience the same luxuries as I'd seen thus far.

On the other hand, the *Titanic* was on fire.

And like that, my dream ended.

"You are a foolish girl, Hazel," I muttered to myself. Obviously, nobody else on this ship was worried, not even the captain, so why should I have been?

Because my *gut* told me that something was wrong. I just didn't know what it was.

"Obviously, our plan has become more complicated now."

That was Mr. Mollison's voice, and hearing it sent a shudder through me. I quickly sat back in the deck chair, then opened Mrs. Abelman's newspaper, spreading it out wide in front of me.

"Because of Hazel Rothbury?" Mrs. Mollison snorted a laugh. "She's a child, and she's alone on this ship. She won't be a problem for us."

"She wants to discover secrets on this ship. My dear, we have far too many secrets. What if we end up in that notebook she carries?"

I glanced down at the notebook in my bag. At the supper, I probably shouldn't have hinted that I knew about the Mollisons' plan, and I definitely shouldn't be wishing now that I did know something.

By then, the Mollisons had come around the corner. They stopped speaking when they were nearly in front of me and I worried that they might have suspected I was here.

I held the newspaper as silently as possible, annoyed by the evening breeze that rustled the pages. I wanted to hear what the Mollisons were saying.

Mr. Mollison said, "We must stay focused on the plan. That's all that matters."

His wife grunted. "The plan has changed. We need to stop Hazel Rothbury."

A gust of wind had rattled the newspaper halfway through her speech. Had Mrs. Mollison just said that they needed to stop me? Stop me from what?

Mr. Mollison seemed to disagree. "Hazel doesn't matter. She'll write a line or two in those pages, then get bored with it. By the time we reach New York, nobody will give her a second thought."

Yes, they would. I had made up my mind on that.

As they moved on, Mrs. Mollison said, "My dear, please don't go to play cards again tonight. You lost so much money last night."

"Last night was important," Mr. Mollison replied. "Money comes so easily to these rich snobs, they think they don't have to work for it. I can use that against them. I'll lose a little money again tonight, then by tomorrow, I will begin to use the special cards that I keep hidden in my sleeve."

I rolled my eyes. *Special* cards? Now I could add cheating to the growing list of things I disliked about these two.

Mrs. Mollison raised her voice. "This is such a beautiful ship. Can't we spend time together to explore it?"

"Another time, my dear. I believe I can hear the sound of cards being shuffled nearby. They are calling me tonight."

"At least see me safely to my room. You wouldn't want to see me falling over the rails now, would you?"

"If you should fall, my dear, I would ask the captain to lower one of these lifeboats and search for you."

"You'd ask the captain? You wouldn't go yourself?"

"With my shoulder injury? I'd be of no use in a lifeboat."

By then, they were walking on, too far for me to hear them anymore, but that might have been for the best. I needed a few moments to think about what I'd just heard.

I still didn't know their plan, but I did know it was big enough that they were worried about anyone finding out about it, including me.

I also believed that part of their plan involved Mr. Mollison's gambling, although his wife was clearly unhappy about that.

Somehow, I had to figure out why they were so interested in a friendship with Miss Gruber, and why stopping me had become so important.

This was going to be fun.

I walked back to my room, my mind racing with thoughts of the Mollisons and Miss Gruber and the snobbery of first class. Then thinking about my plans to meet with Mrs. Abelman tomorrow morning. Before then, I had a newspaper to read, and a dozen good questions to write for her.

Without a doubt, my evening would end far better than it had begun.

CHAPTER
SIXTEEN

Did Tea Matter?

Friday, April 12, 1912

Mum always said there was no excuse for bad manners, but I disagreed. Mrs. Abelson would be in the library, waiting to answer some of my biggest questions. It would be rude *not* to gulp down my breakfast as quickly as possible, so that I wouldn't keep her waiting.

I was wearing Sylvia's dress once again. I'd spent part of last night washing my usual dress and it was still drying in my room. But that wasn't the real reason for wearing Sylvia's dress today. I needed it to pass for a second-class passenger.

As I entered the ship's library, I passed a five-piece orchestra playing in the vestibule. The music was fun and full of joy, a bit of a contrast to the library itself, decorated with light and dark wood paneling, which gave the room a serious feel. There weren't many women here yet, but those who had come were seated at tables playing games or writing letters.

I wondered about the people here in second class. These were wives of shopkeepers and teachers and scientists, educated but not wealthy. No doubt some people here longed to have power and wealth one day, but they hadn't quite made it yet.

A woman seated across the room was staring at me, and at first I thought she must have seen through my thin disguise. I'd properly combed my hair and my face was clean. I wondered what gave me away. When she caught me staring back, however, she merely smiled and returned to her writing.

My eyes then drifted toward the bookcases, filled with more books than likely existed in my entire village.

I had expected to see Mrs. Abelman here already, but until she came, I wandered over to the bookshelves and began scanning the titles. There were books about history and geography and some of the great classics of literature, but for now, I only wanted books that answered my questions about the *Titanic*.

"... the *Titanic*." A woman near me had finished with the same words I had thought to myself. I wondered what she had been saying.

So, I leaned toward the group. Over the past few days, I had broken several rules of good manners, but the worst of them was eavesdropping. One day I would have to learn to behave better. However, today was not that day.

The woman who had been speaking before continued, "My husband was on the boat deck yesterday when Mr. Astor himself walked by in conversation with Captain Smith. Mr. Astor was concerned about the number of lifeboats on board."

"So am I!" Judging by the way they stared back at me, I knew I'd done something worse than eavesdropping. But I'd already interrupted the conversation, so I was committed now.

Stepping closer to the women, I added, "I counted the lifeboats myself. There are twice as many people on board as there are lifeboat seats."

"Which would only be an issue if the *Titanic* were in serious trouble," another woman said. "But it won't be."

"Nobody ever expects trouble," the first woman said. "But even on a ship such as this one, trouble is not impossible."

"On the *Titanic*, I believe it is impossible," her friend replied. "My husband spoke with the *Titanic*'s engineer last evening, who said that every possible danger has already been anticipated. They designed the ship to avoid those dangers. That's why the lifeboats won't be needed."

"But if danger is impossible, why have lifeboats at all?" I asked.

"Only because the law requires it. Nothing out in open water should concern us."

"What about icebergs?" came a voice at the entrance to the library.

We all turned and there stood Mrs. Abelman, balanced on her cane. I smiled back at her and she nodded politely.

Without a word, she walked forward, her eyes scanning the books just as I had done earlier. She pulled one book from the shelf and brought it over to me.

While she flipped through the pages, I angled my head to see the title: *A Traveler's Guide to Ocean Voyages*.

Finally, she found the page she wanted, then set it in my hands. Chapter six began with, *There is more to understanding icebergs than you might think.*

That was enough to get my attention. I dove into the rest of the chapter, letting the women I had been speaking to earlier fade away.

"I hope you will like it," Mrs. Abelman said. "I read it yesterday afternoon. Most interesting."

"Thank you," I said, then glanced around at other women who were entering the library, some who seemed to be watching me with suspicion. I leaned in closer to Mrs. Abelman. "Would it be all right if I read this book in my room? I can . . . concentrate better there."

"Of course you may," Mrs. Abelman said. "Just remember to return the book when you are finished."

I nodded, then quickly left the library. From there, I crossed the promenade toward the stairs, my eyes glued to the book's pages, which meant I didn't see Sylvia until I had nearly bumped into her.

"Hazel, I've been calling your name," she said.

"Oh, hello." At first I had been happy to see her, but my smile faded once I remembered how the supper had ended last night. She probably wanted an apology, but I couldn't offer one, not until I understood exactly what I had done that was so wrong.

But she spoke first. "I'm so glad to have found you. All I've thought about since you left last night is what a horrible friend I was. I should have defended you, especially after Miss Gruber was so rude."

I wasn't sure how to respond, for that was hardly what I had expected. I shifted my weight from one foot to the other before saying, "Miss Gruber only spoke the truth. I don't belong in first class. I never should have accepted that invitation."

Sylvia's eyes moistened, as if I'd hurt her feelings. "I don't have many friends, you know. Miss Gruber always pushes away anyone she feels is beneath my family, and I have no siblings as you do. I had hoped that maybe we could be friends."

"I don't have many friends either," I replied. "There's always so much work to be done on the farm, as I'm sure you know."

Sylvia glanced away and I realized my mistake. No, she knew nothing about farmwork.

"I'm sorry that I embarrassed you last night," I added.

"What you did was . . . unexpected," Sylvia replied. "But they were good questions. I wish I had thought of them."

I lifted the book in my hands. "I hope to find the answers here."

Sylvia giggled. "What kind of answers?"

"I want to know more about icebergs."

Sylvia's smile fell. "Icebergs? Do you think we'll encounter any this week?"

"I don't know. But I can read this book and tell you what I've learned!"

Now her smile returned. "Would you come to tea this afternoon? You can tell me and Miss Gruber about icebergs then." I hesitated and she added, "Mrs. Mollison has become so friendly with Miss Gruber, I haven't seen one without the other since last night. But it would only be the three of us this afternoon, and it's really important to me that you come. Please, Hazel."

I would have said no, until she mentioned Mrs. Mollison. I never had properly warned Sylvia and Miss Gruber about their plan.

"I don't think you should trust the Mollisons," I said.

"Why not?"

I sighed, wishing I had any proof against them. "I think . . . the Mollisons are after money, and your family has a lot of it."

"There's no reason to worry," Sylvia said. "It's true that we are coming home with nearly five hundred pounds of my father's money. But it's all perfectly secure, though. We put it in a safe deposit box."

"What if the Mollisons are being nice to Miss Gruber in hopes of getting the key to that box?" I asked.

Sylvia considered that for a moment. "Perhaps I'll check on the safe deposit box later today. I'll tell you what I find out when we meet for tea."

Miss Gruber ducked her head out of one doorway. "Miss Thorngood, I was looking everywhere for you. You are supposed to be at your lessons!"

Sylvia winked at me before saying, "I might've snuck out for a quick walk along the promenade."

I giggled and Miss Gruber repeated, "Miss Thorngood!"

"I'll see you at tea this afternoon," Sylvia said. "Though you may wish to wear one of your other dresses, perhaps a dress you would use while staying with your aunt. Miss Gruber thinks you cannot fit in with first-class society. You can prove her wrong."

"I don't—" I protested, then gave up. "I'll see you this afternoon!"

Sylvia hurried over to Miss Gruber, but I wished I had finished my sentence while I could.

I didn't have a dress appropriate for the first-class areas.

I didn't have the manners or money to fit in with anyone there.

I wasn't sure I even wanted to fit in with most of the people there, but that didn't seem to matter. I had agreed to come for tea.

My sigh was heavy and hung in the air. When I had said I'd be delighted to join them, that really meant there was literally nothing in the world I was dreading more.

SEVENTEEN

I Was Falling Short

If I was going to meet Sylvia and Miss Gruber for tea, then I knew how important it was that I spend the day finding a dress or remaking a new one with whatever scraps I could gather on board.

And I had no idea where to begin with that plan.

Until I could think of something, I wandered to the third-class general room and there found a comfortable chair where I could read the book Mrs. Abelman had given me. I began with a chapter on the bulkheads that protected the hull of a ship.

Until reading about them, I had never imagined that bulkheads were so important. When necessary, they could be sealed off so that water cannot enter from any direction, including water that may come in from above.

I stopped there. Yesterday evening, Mr. Waddington had

said that the doors connecting each bulkhead could be made watertight. But could water come in from above?

My room was on E Deck. The long corridor known as Scotland Road ran the entire length of the ship, so the bulkheads could not rise any higher than E Deck.

That became my next question to write down:

Are the Titanic's bulkheads watertight from above?

Then I continued reading. Time seemed to melt away with each page that I turned. My notebook was filling with questions that needed answers, and with answers in search of the right questions.

Eventually, I reached the chapter on icebergs, which was the most fascinating of all. I wrote down pages of notes and made drawings as the different forms of icebergs were described.

Once I had finished, I looked up and saw Mrs. Abelman seated at a table near me, smiling widely. Pinched between her fingers was a key, which she placed in a pocket of her coat; then she said, "I wondered when you'd pull your head out of those pages."

"Were you here for long?" I asked.

"An hour perhaps, but I could see you were concentrating, so I had no wish to disturb you. I hope you have learned a few things since we last spoke."

I certainly had. The excitement to share what I'd learned welled in my chest. Eagerly, I picked up my things and joined her at her table. "I hardly know where to begin! Before today, I knew icebergs existed, but not much more."

"You've never seen one, then?" I shook my head and she continued, "I've seen only one. It was wide, but very low on the water. What does that tell you?"

"That it was probably a growler," I replied. These were smaller icebergs, chunks that floated low in the water. "They can be dangerous because they are difficult to spot."

"But if they're small, why should it matter if a ship of our *Titanic's* size crosses its path?"

Mrs. Abelman already knew the answer, but if she was testing me, I was happy to respond. "It might look small on the surface, but most of its mass sits below the waterline. So, a lookout may not see the growler as a threat. Instead, the commanding officer might try to use the ship's hull to bump the growler aside. He'd realize too late how dangerous that is." I stopped there and looked up at Mrs. Abelman. "Are there growlers in these waters?"

"There are. But a good lookout in the crow's nest should be able to spot it. Even more so if he has a pair of binoculars in hand."

I breathed easier, then showed Mrs. Abelman my notes. I pointed to the first iceberg I had described. "This is a white iceberg. It's newer so it's filled with air pockets, and isn't as packed together. It poses the least threat to a ship because the ice is softer and easier to break apart."

"Very interesting." Mrs. Abelman's tone made me think she really did find this interesting. I knew I did.

I turned the page and showed her the next drawing. "The older icebergs are more dangerous because the ice is harder and has fewer air holes. There are blue icebergs, and worse, the dark icebergs."

"Why would a dark iceberg be dangerous?" Mrs. Abelman asked.

"Because there's almost no air left inside it. If you stared at it beneath the water, it would have a dark color, but above water, it's nearly clear, sometimes almost impossible to see."

"Ah, then you must also know about refraction," Mrs. Abelman said.

"Refraction?"

Mrs. Abelman smiled. "That is a conversation for another time. I believe you promised to have other questions for me."

"I have one, but it's a newer question." I turned to that page of my notes. "What do you know about the bulkheads on this ship?"

"Almost nothing," Mrs. Abelman said. "But I will help you find someone who does. Come with me."

I followed her out into the corridor, though it wasn't long before I realized she was leading me to the purser's office. I absolutely could not go there.

I tugged on her arm, urging her to stop. "Please, ma'am, he'll know we don't belong here."

"Nonsense. The purser is there to help with any needs a passenger may have," she said, continuing on without slowing. "We have a question that needs to be answered, do we not?"

"Yes . . . but . . ."

But it was too late. We were there. The purser's office was located at the landing of the Grand Staircase. Two booths were set up, each with a gentleman inside to assist the passenger next in line.

We took our places behind a husband and wife discussing whether to send a telegram.

"My dear, must we send this message?" the husband was asking. "If you want to tell your sister that we are having a lovely time, why not wait until we are home to write the letter yourself? Telegrams are expensive."

"Yes, but think of what fun it will be for her to receive the message while we are still at sea. What a wonder of technology this is!"

Her husband sighed and pulled out his pocketbook as they stepped forward.

When it was our turn, Mrs. Abelman approached the purser, a middle-aged man with a thin mustache and hair slicked straight back with a strong-smelling pomade.

"Are you here about your safe deposit box?" he asked Mrs. Abelman. "I only need the key."

"No indeed." She pointed to me. "This young woman has a question for you."

The purser arched a brow. "Does she?"

I cleared my throat, suddenly nervous. "I, uh . . . wanted to know how far the bulkheads rose above the waterline."

He looked around, obviously confused by my question, then said, "I'm sure there are far more interesting things for a child of your age—"

"I don't think they go any higher than E Deck," I said.

"Hmm. And why does this matter?"

Now I pulled out my notebook. "I want to write the story of the *Titanic*."

"For your school studies?"

"For the newspaper. Maybe one in New York."

He chuckled, as if I'd been joking. "Simply adorable," he said. "You'd best run along now. There are other passengers with real questions."

"I don't believe you've answered her question yet," Mrs. Abelman said firmly.

"Very well." The purser's face sharpened. "I'm afraid I don't know that answer. But I'm happy to find out if you wish to check back in a day or two."

Disappointed, we thanked him, but as soon as we turned around, I heard a man say, "Hello, Miss Rothbury, the young journalist. I see you are still at it."

I smiled, recognizing Mr. Waddington from last evening's supper. He was carrying some rolled-up papers beneath one arm and appeared to have been on his way to somewhere else.

I thought it best to begin with an apology. "I should not have left the supper that way. It was poor manners."

He grinned. "To be honest with you, I wish I'd had the courage to leave. I enjoyed Miss Gruber and her ward, but that other couple—the Mollisons . . ." He cleared his throat. "Well, I would be impolite if I said anything further."

"They're horrid," I said.

Now he laughed. "Yes, they certainly are." His attention

turned to Mrs. Abelman behind me and his eyes lit up with happiness. "But can I believe my own eyes? Is this my former governess before me? My dear Mrs. Abelman, how long has it been?"

She held out her hand for him, in the genteel style of the upper class. "My husband died fifteen years ago, and you were the first ward I took on after that. I believe it must be ten years since our last meeting."

"Then it's been far too long. How have you gotten along?"

Mrs. Abelman sighed. "I wanted to carry a lighter burden. Instead, I was given stronger arms."

He nodded in solemn understanding, then said, "You are strong because you have spent a lifetime helping others carry their burdens. Now, where is your cabin? I am surprised that I have not seen you on the promenade or in the dining rooms before now."

"I am on D Deck, but I dine wherever it suits me."

I shook my head, curious again. If Mrs. Abelman's room was on D Deck, she could be traveling in any of the classes. Yet she dined wherever she wished. Why would she dine anywhere but in first class?

Mr. Waddington smiled. "I would be delighted if you joined me for dinner this evening so that we could catch up on old memories."

"I accept, provided that I am able to get Miss Rothbury's questions answered first."

"That is the very reason I spoke to her just now." Mr. Waddington looked down at me. "You asked me about bulkheads last night, and I have something that I think will help you."

For the first time, I realized he had been holding something else in his hand, a small metal box, with a hinge on one end for the lid. He lifted the lid to show the box was empty, then said, "Imagine this is one of the *Titanic*'s sixteen compartments that sits inside the hull. Each wall of this box is a bulkhead. Now tell me your question again."

I pointed to the lid. "Do our bulkheads have anything like that? Are they watertight from above?"

He shook his head. "I'm afraid not. If water were to pass over a deck above the bulkheads, it would eventually drip down inside them, like filling a bathtub."

"Where do the bulkheads end?" I asked. "On which deck?"

He shrugged, as if he was not happy about what he was about to say. "The *Titanic*'s bulkheads stop at E Deck. But E Deck is at least six or seven meters above the ocean level, higher than the water will ever rise, so there is nothing to worry about."

"What if the ship sinks six or seven meters lower?"

Mr. Waddington tilted his head, deep in thought. His brows pressed close together until he slowly shook his head. "If the *Titanic* did sink that low, then the crew would have much bigger problems to think about." He paused a moment and his brows pressed together. "Are you worried about this ship sinking, Miss Rothbury?"

I shook my head. "I don't see how that would be possible, but . . ." I hesitated, unwilling to say the next part.

"But what?" he coaxed.

"If you believed it was impossible for you to trip and fall, would you be careful about walking?"

He frowned. "No, there would be no need for it."

"If everyone on board believes this ship is unsinkable, then I wonder if they are watching for problems as carefully as they should."

Mr. Waddington considered that for a moment, then said, "I assure you, this crew is very watchful. Out here in open water, without a single obstacle in sight, how do you imagine this ship would sink seven or eight meters into the water?"

"An iceberg, sir."

He arched a brow. "Go on."

"The sides of the ship are a single hull, so if an iceberg scraped open a hull, water would fill that bulkhead."

"Yes," Mr. Waddington said. "But the *Titanic* won't go under, even if four bulkheads fill."

That was my point. "It doesn't have to go under, sir. The *Titanic* only has to fill with enough water to sink seven or eight meters. Then water would run across E Deck, and—"

"And fill every other bulkhead." Lines formed on Mr. Waddington's forehead until he finally shrugged. "But for that to happen, everything that might go wrong would go wrong. Real life is rarely so awful."

"But is it possible?"

His eyes met mine, all humor gone from them now. "Yes, Miss Rothbury. That is possible."

I nodded back at him, wishing he would have given me any other answer. Suddenly, all I could picture in my mind was water flowing across the long corridor on E Deck, from one end of the ship to the other. I thought of what I would do if I was in my cabin and saw water seeping in below the doorway, and how I'd react if I heard other passengers scrambling for higher ground.

I could imagine that so well that I could practically hear the sound of an iceberg scraping along a metal hull of a ship.

A single hull, like the *Titanic* had on its sides.

If the *Titanic* ever did have a problem, it would come from the side of the ship.

And the problem would come from a dark iceberg.

CHAPTER

EIGHTEEN

While Minutes Became Hours

Mr. Waddington and Mrs. Abelman exchanged a long look before he said, "I can see that this still troubles you, Miss Rothbury, but you needn't worry. The ship's designers and the officers who run this ship have thought about all of this before."

That was true enough, and something I needed to remember. Obviously if I could think of these questions, then those in charge of this ship would have already planned for any such problems long before we set sail.

I smiled back at Mr. Waddington, genuinely relieved. "You are right, sir." Or at least, I hoped he was right.

The clock behind the purser's office chimed out the time. I counted five bells. Five o'clock.

Five o'clock?

Sylvia!

I turned to Mrs. Abelman. "I'm so sorry, but I'm late to meet my friend!"

I started upstairs, then realized I hadn't found a new dress, nor tidied my hair or washed my face. I would have to go to tea in Sylvia's dress once again, which was beyond humiliating, but I had no other choice.

I ran down to my room, pushing past other passengers or skirting around them as they strolled across their promenades. I threw off my shoulder bag, then pulled my hair out of its braids and quickly finger-combed through any knots. I splashed a little water on my face, then started back out the door.

Only after I'd left did I realize that I'd left my bag behind. I never went anywhere without it, but there was no time to go back for it. I was far too late already.

I flew back up the stairs, taking care to slow down when other passengers were around who would disapprove of a girl racing through the corridors.

Finally, I made it up to the Parisien, but Sylvia was not there, nor was Miss Gruber. I checked the clock on the promenade nearby. Five thirty. That was ninety minutes after I should have met them for tea.

A waiter was passing by, and I said, "Pardon me, but did you see a girl here about my age?"

He frowned down at me. "If you are speaking of Miss Thorngood, she and her governess left about forty minutes ago."

My shoulders slumped. Sylvia had told me how important it was that I be here tonight. And she had been so excited when I'd said I would come.

But I had completely forgotten about it. I really was a terrible friend.

"I told Miss Gruber you wouldn't show up."

Recognizing Mrs. Mollison's voice, I tried my best not to groan out loud, though it didn't work, and I groaned much louder than usual. She had been seated on a deck chair, but now she stood and said, "Take a walk with me, child."

"No, thank you."

Her tone turned nasty. "Take a walk with me, you little stowaway, or I'll report you right now."

My breath locked in my throat. I didn't know how she knew the truth, but that didn't matter. All that mattered was she did know.

"I had you figured the first time I saw you," she said. "I told my husband later that evening that you had to be some kind of fraud."

"What gave me away?" I asked.

"One fraud can always spot another."

If I had been worried about the *Titanic* before, that was nothing compared to the worry spreading through my chest as I began following her down the promenade. "Are you going to tell anyone?"

"I might. That depends on you."

"I overheard you and Mr. Mollison last night. You were saying that you had to stop me."

She smiled crookedly. "Hiding behind that newspaper, were you? What we said wasn't personal, dearie. I know how it is."

My brows pressed together. "How *what* is?"

"I used to be poor, like you. I was a housekeeper before

boarding this ship, so I know what it's like to have big dreams and no hope of ever reaching them."

I stopped walking. "No hope? Mrs. Mollison, one day I *will* be a journalist."

"Sure you will, darlin'." Mrs. Mollison continued to stroll along the promenade as if she didn't have a single care, while everything I cared about was slipping out of my reach.

Finally, I caught up to her. "What are you trying to stop me from doing, Mrs. Mollison?"

We paused as the *Titanic*'s whistle blew, signaling the start of another mealtime. She gestured toward the bridge. "That's a loud whistle, probably disturbed a few people who were taking their afternoon nap, and now they're shaking a fist at it for waking them up. But that's not the whistle's fault. It's just doing what it was meant to do." Now she looked at me once more. "I reckon you're doing what you're meant to do too."

I stopped again. "I'm meant to . . . be loud and disturb people?"

"Exactly!" Mrs. Mollison folded her arms and looked at me. "But I think we can help each other."

"Oh no." I began backing away. "I see you pretending to be so friendly to Miss Gruber, like you're the oldest of friends. You are using her to take money from the Thorngoods. I won't help you do it."

I turned to leave, but heard Mrs. Mollison behind me. "I'm sure the penalties for stowaways are very serious. Who knows, maybe they'll even lock you up in prison for this. What will your poor widowed mother do then?"

I stopped where I was. What would Mum think if she found out what I'd done? The news would surely break her heart, and after Papa's death, I doubted her heart could take any more awful news.

It would break my entire family beyond repair.

My hand flew to my mouth. I could not allow Mrs. Mollison to tell anyone about my crime.

"So, what do you think now?" Mrs. Mollison asked. "Shall we help each other or not?"

What did I think? I couldn't think at all. I only knew that my knees had become so weak, I wondered why they didn't give out. I felt my heart pounding, and my palms had become clammy with sweat.

I also knew that I couldn't help her take money from any other passengers, especially not Sylvia. My only choice now was to warn her that I could talk too.

So, I said, "All I need is evidence against you. Then I'll write everything down about your plan and sell the story to the newspapers!"

Her eyes narrowed. "And *that*, Miss Rothbury, is why you must be stopped. I always get what I want, and that is true now. So here's our agreement. I know you suggested that Sylvia Thorngood should count the money in her safe deposit box. You'd better talk her out of it, because if she does count that money, and if anything is missing, I'll make sure you get blamed for it. Do you understand?"

I understood perfectly. Mrs. Mollison must have already stolen Sylvia's money. "I'm going to tell Sylvia," I said. "She'll believe me."

"Are you sure?" Mrs. Mollison asked. "Who will they believe, a respectable lady in first class, or a stowaway?"

"Mrs. Mollison?"

I turned to see Charlie behind me. He had a silver tray in one hand, so I thought he must be out on some sort of errand. It must have been by sheer luck that he saw me here now, and his eyes were darting about as if he wasn't entirely sure what to say next.

"What is it?" Mrs. Mollison asked impatiently.

"There's a, uh, message for you at the purser's office."

"A message? While we're this far out at sea? And why would it come for me and not for my husband?"

"I don't know, ma'am. I was only told to come and find you."

Mrs. Mollison turned to me, eyes blazing, then said, "I have some unfinished business here, then I will get the message."

"Ma'am, they said it was extremely urgent."

Now Mrs. Mollison sighed, defeated. "Very well." She glared at me again. "You'd better remember your place. And make sure Sylvia doesn't count . . . or I'll see that you are placed in the brig of this ship."

"Pardon my interrupting," Charlie said. "The *Titanic* has no brig."

Mrs. Mollison's face reddened as her glare shifted to him. "Go warn your captain he'd better start building one soon. Maybe for the both of you!" She scowled, then stomped away.

I waited until she had left for good before finally collapsing onto a deck chair. "Thank you," I whispered to Charlie.

"You'd better not stay here." He frowned. "There is no message for Mrs. Mollison at the desk, and it won't take her but a few minutes to figure that out. She'll be back soon."

"Would they really put me in a brig, if I'm caught?" I asked.

He sighed. "Just don't get caught doing anything wrong. There's still a long way to New York."

I nodded, feeling a weight settle on my shoulders. For the first time, my only concern about the speed of the *Titanic* was that we weren't traveling fast enough.

I took Charlie's suggestion and hurried back down to E Deck, though I paused there, looking both ways along the long corridor of Scotland Road. The top of the bulkheads would rise to just below my feet. But I had bigger problems to worry about now.

My room key was in my hand, but as I came closer, I noticed the door was already open. I knew I had been in a rush when I left my room earlier, but I was certain I had locked the door and closed it tight.

Hadn't I?

I entered my room and instantly knew something was wrong. Everything in my room was exactly as I had left it, with one exception.

My shoulder bag was gone.

It contained all the money I had in the world, money I would need once we reached New York.

And my pen and the few other small items I'd brought along.

And the notebook was gone.

I looked beneath my mattress and even beneath my bed, all in hopes that I'd hidden it and forgotten where.

Except I knew that was not the case.

Mrs. Mollison had said she always got what she wanted, and what she wanted was to stop me. By taking the notebook, she had obviously succeeded.

Tears welled in my eyes, and I nearly choked on the first cry to erupt from my throat. I fell on my bed, burying my head in the pillow to mask the sound of my sobbing. Everything was gone.

NINETEEN

I Had to Learn Fast

Saturday, April 13, 1912

It was still early on Saturday morning when I entered the saloon. I had missed supper last night, so of course I was hungry for breakfast. But mostly I was here in hopes of seeing one of the passengers parading about with my notebook in hand. I hoped for that so intently that the worry was beginning to feel like rocks in my stomach.

At this point, no matter who had taken it, I wouldn't report the theft to any officers. How could I when I had stolen my way onto this ship? I didn't care about justice now. I only wanted my bag back.

So, I sat and watched and waited and studied every passenger who came and went from the saloon, trying to ignore the voice in my head that insisted I already knew who had my bag.

The Mollisons.

They knew I planned to report on their crimes, so, of

course, they would want my notebook, to see what I'd written about them. And they'd be all too happy to steal my money while they were stealing the notebook.

My thoughts were so focused on them that I barely registered my own name when I heard it spoken aloud.

"Hazel?"

I glanced up to see Mrs. Abelman standing near my table, but I barely smiled. "Good morning."

She sat across from me. "What a sour face you have. Why is that?"

The faint smile I'd managed so far faded away. "The notebook you let me borrow was stolen last night. I'm so sorry."

"That isn't for you to be sorry. If it was stolen, then that wasn't your fault."

"Then I'm sorry for myself." I laid my chin on my hands. "I'll never sell my story now."

"I'm sure you're right."

That was not the answer I'd expected, nor the tone of voice I'd expected. She didn't seem to understand that my entire world had collapsed into utter hopelessness and that I would likely never find happiness ever again.

She added, "Obviously, when your notes were stolen, everything you've learned about the *Titanic* disappeared too."

I glanced up. "No, I remember everything."

"Ah, and so this is the only notebook you will ever own. Its paper is so unique, so rare, that no other notebook can possibly take its place."

I shook my head and even managed a slight smile. "It was a beautiful notebook, but there are others. It's just that all of my questions and answers were in there."

"Do you have memory problems, Hazel?"

"My memory is fine." Now I understood. "You're telling me that I don't need the notebook to be a writer."

"You need something to write on, I agree. But you were writing before I gave you that notebook, so get another one."

"I have no money for a notebook," I said. "That was stolen too."

"Ah, well, that is a problem. But do not worry too much for it. What is lost can always be found."

I wanted to point out that my bag was stolen, not lost, but then I remembered what I had truly lost last night.

"There's another problem," I said. "I was supposed to meet Sylvia Thorngood for tea, but I completely forgot. She had said that it was very important to meet her. I feel awful about that."

"That truly is a problem." Mrs. Abelman clasped her hands together. "You will have to find her and properly apologize and assure her that you value your friendship. But for now, I am ready to answer a question that you have not yet asked me . . . if you are not too sad."

I lifted my head. I still was very sad, but now I was sad *and* curious.

Mrs. Abelman reached for a pitcher and began pouring water into the goblet in front of her, stopping when it was half-full. "Last night, I used the word *refraction*. Do you know what that means?"

I shook my head. I'd never even heard that word before last night.

Mrs. Abelman smiled. "The ship's lookout sits in a crow's nest ninety feet above the deck. His only job is to look ahead on the water, watching for danger."

"I heard he is given a pair of binoculars, to bring everything close again," I said. "So he should be very good at spotting problems when they are still far away."

"You are correct," Mrs. Abelman said. "Yet there is one challenge the lookout might face, and that is when the light bends."

I sat up. "Light can bend? How?"

"And there is the question I hoped you would ask!" Mrs. Abelman lifted her glass of water in front of her. "Can you see through this glass?"

"Yes, ma'am, of course."

"That is because of the light that passes through it. However, both the glass and the water inside it change the speed that the light travels. When the light slows down, it is forced to change direction to a slightly different angle. That is called refraction."

I repeated the word, wishing once again I could simply write it into my notebook. "Refraction."

"You have seen refraction many times, even if you didn't know the word for it. For example, if you looked into a pond and saw a fish, what would happen if you reached down to grab it?"

I smiled, because I'd actually attempted that very thing. "I'd miss. The fish wouldn't be where I think it is."

Mrs. Abelman set the glass back on the table, then picked up her knife from her place setting. She raised it directly behind the cup. Above the level of the cup, the knife was straight, but the part behind the glass looked distorted and was even more distorted behind the water.

She continued, "Telescopes and binoculars use refraction to magnify images that are very far away. The lookout in the crow's nest of the *Titanic* will have a great advantage with a pair of binoculars in his hand."

"Then why would the bending of light—the refraction—create a problem for the lookout?"

Mrs. Abelman smiled, ever patient with me. "It would only cause a problem in a specific kind of weather."

"Such as?"

She motioned for me to look closer at the glass of water. "What if the ocean was as still as that water? And what if it is also the night of a new moon, so that everything is dark?"

"Could the lookout still see if there was trouble ahead?"

"He could, yes. But what if the water is very cold and a warm air happens to pass over it? That would create a fog in the air."

"Then any light that passes through the fog would bend." Now I understood. "So, the lookout may believe he sees an obstacle in one place and it might be in a slightly different place."

"Exactly. And if the water was very calm, the light will stay bent, so the obstacle will remain hidden—"

"Until it is too late." Then my eyes widened as I made another connection. "When I was telling you about the icebergs yesterday, you told me that the risk is refraction."

Mrs. Abelman arched a brow, apparently pleased with me. "Yes?"

"Even if the iceberg could be seen, in the right conditions, refraction would make the iceberg seem like it was in a slightly different place in the water. That might make it truly impossible to see." A rush of fear flowed through me. "Could that happen to us?"

"As I said, that would be a very rare thing indeed, and certainly this ship has safeguards against problems like that. Furthermore, a good pair of binoculars would help, or better still, a strong spotlight. If the night was dark and a fog arose, they could turn on the spotlight and see everything clear as they'd like."

Since I couldn't write the questions into my notebook, I repeated them aloud, hoping to lock them in my memory: "Do the lookouts have binoculars? Does the *Titanic* have a spotlight?"

When I looked up, Mrs. Abelman was folding her arms, looking quite pleased with herself. "You see, I am an excellent teacher, and you are a wonderful student. If I were younger, I would have thought it a great honor to be your governess and teach you everything I know."

"I would have liked to learn it too." I felt proud of myself for understanding the concept, and happy to know there was a word for such a fascinating idea. Refraction.

"I like that smile." Mrs. Abelman clasped her hands together. "Now that we have managed that great scientific question, I think you must go and apologize to your friend."

My sigh was heavy, but I knew she was right. "Yes, I believe that I must. Wish me luck!"

Mrs. Abelman smiled instead. "Luck may not be enough to help you. I know you will find a way to keep that friendship."

I hoped she was right. I wanted to keep Sylvia's friendship.

Refraction

CHAPTER
TWENTY

Tell the Hard Truths

For the next few hours, I kept a steady watch from the poop deck, waiting until I saw Sylvia on the first-class promenade, and hoping she'd be alone. Miss Gruber seemed determined to disapprove of me, no matter what I did. I was beginning to think nothing I could do would ever change her mind.

But then, it didn't help that I had failed to meet them for tea. How could I blame Miss Gruber for having such a low opinion of me when I had made such a serious mistake?

Despite that, I still hoped I could save my friendship with Sylvia. Especially now.

It was nearly noontime before I spotted Sylvia near the rails. There was a chance she would head to lunch before I could get up to her. If only they had built a ladder from the poop deck to the promenade. That would have made it much easier for me to properly sneak into first class. As it was, I had to race through several different corridors inside until I emerged onto A Deck.

Sylvia saw me coming and hesitated, making me wonder if I shouldn't have come. I couldn't blame her for being angry with me. But she waited in place, right in the center of the promenade, as I approached. I started by saying, "I'm so sorry."

"Where were you?" she asked. "We waited for almost an hour."

"I know. I was busy reading about icebergs, then Mr. Waddington was explaining to me about bulkheads, and by the time I remembered, you were already gone. I really am sorry, Sylvia."

"Icebergs and bulkheads?" She frowned. "Were those more important than a friendship?"

"No, but . . ." I hesitated, wondering how to say the next part. "But they are easier, because they are simply facts. Friendships are not so simple."

"Friendships matter far more, or they should. Except to you. I think you only care about your questions, about what you can write down in your notebook. You seem determined to find the smallest flaw with this ship, or to create scenarios in which everything might go wrong. You are inventing problems because somehow that is more important to you than real people."

I lowered my eyes, not sure what else I could say to make her understand how much I regretted my mistake.

Sylvia added, "Miss Gruber is asking you to return my dress. I'm sure you have other dresses you can wear while on the ship."

I only had the dress I'd worn on my back the day I boarded

the ship. I felt ashamed to be wearing Sylvia's dress in front of her again. This dress did not belong to me, nor did I belong here on this deck.

"I will return it today." I turned to leave, but stopped myself. My chest felt tight and I wondered if that was because it was full of words I still needed to say to her, so I added, "I do care about the questions, Sylvia, but it's not because I want the *Titanic* to fail. It's just the opposite. If this ship does have flaws, then hopefully I can ask the right questions to help them fix any problems before the next voyage."

"Nobody will listen to you," she said. "Nobody at White Star will care what some young girl from third class thinks about the finest ship in their fleet."

"Then I'll ask the questions for myself! I always have. At home, I wanted to know everything about our farm, about the way our house was built and if it could've been done better. I want to know how automobiles work, how airplanes fly. Everything."

Sylvia glanced away, a touch of anger still in her eyes. "My father designs airplanes. I could have explained all of that to you, had you come for tea."

I lowered my head. Maybe she was right, that I was putting my questions above people. If that was true, then I felt even worse than before.

I said, "I really am sorry, Sylvia. If you still want to be friends, I'll do better."

"But is that what you want?" she asked. "After all, we'll likely never see each other again after we reach New York.

Miss Gruber will keep me busy with lessons and you'll be with your aunt, having the best of times, I'm sure."

My heart ached. It was time to tell the truth. "I'm not going to America for the best of times. My aunt works in a garment factory, and I'll start work there too. That factory might be the best I can do in life." I drew in a deep breath, dreading the look on her face when I told her the rest. "So, you can see, I don't need manners and proper behavior. I only need a strong back and two good feet to stand on."

Sylvia blinked at me, and for a moment I was certain she would walk on and leave me where I was, on my two good feet fit for nothing but the workhouses. When she spoke, she only said, "Oh. I didn't—"

I sighed, relieved to finally be sharing my true feelings with someone. "Once I begin work in the factories, there will be no time for my own dreams. This week is probably my last chance to prove that I can make something of my life. I need to sell my news story, and I need to do it as soon as we reach New York."

Kindness returned to Sylvia's eyes. "Then I should apologize to you, Hazel. I didn't realize why this dream was so important, but now I do. No wonder you risked so much to be on this ship."

That gave me pause. I leaned toward her, not wanting to ask, but knowing I had to. "What do you mean by that?"

"It's obvious that your mother doesn't have much money, but when I thought your aunt did, I assumed she must have paid for your ticket to America. If she didn't, and your mother couldn't . . ."

Sylvia let her words drop there, but my heart slammed against my chest. She knew. Somehow she knew.

Sylvia continued, "You snuck aboard the ship. Didn't you?"

I heaved out a sigh, dreading this confession. All I could do was to nod, and even that caused me intense shame.

After a moment in which neither of us spoke, I said, "You won't tell Miss Gruber, will you? She already thinks so little of me, this would only make it worse."

"I won't say a word to anyone," she said. "And if you do sell that newspaper article, perhaps some of the money you earn can be used to pay for an honest ticket."

"That was my promise to Charlie Blight—the porter," I said. "I want to make something of my life, but I want to do it honestly."

She smiled. "Then you shall. Come with me."

I tilted my head, confused once more. "Where are we going?"

"We're friends. So, I'm going to give you a story that all the newspapers will want." As she walked, she continued, "I tried to check on my family's money in the safe deposit box, as you suggested, but the purser told me I needed the key. Maybe you can help me find it!"

I paused, remembering Mrs. Mollison's offer . . . or threat to me. I had to stop Sylvia from checking the safe deposit box, or she'd turn me in.

On the other hand, if we did find the key and saved Sylvia's money, that would be a news story I could sell!

My mind lit up with excitement. Sylvia was right. Anyone

on board could write about the *Titanic*, but maybe I could write about a crime happening on the *Titanic*.

As we walked, I asked, "Where is Miss Gruber?"

"She is with Mrs. Mollison at the hair salon. I'm supposed to be studying my lessons."

More happily now, I continued following Sylvia through a carpeted and wood-paneled passageway, but when we reached the rooms, I darted around a post to hide. Farther down the passageway, I had seen Mr. Mollison exit a room, placing his pocketbook in his suit jacket before he walked away.

Sylvia noticed me stop and came back around the corner. "What's wrong?"

"Is he gone?" I whispered.

She looked back around the corner, then nodded. "Didn't I tell you that the Mollisons' cabin is right across from ours?"

No, she hadn't. I peered around the corner myself, then noticed an important detail. The Mollisons' door had been left slightly opened.

Somewhere inside that room was my stolen notebook, I was sure of it.

"We can find your key next," I said. "But first, I'm going to get my notebook back."

TWENTY-ONE

Take the Risks

Sylvia was clearly horrified by my suggestion. She crossed in front of me. "You can't go into someone else's room like a thief!"

"They're the thieves, Sylvia. One of them went into my room last night. They stole my bag. Everything I have in the world was in there."

"How do you know it was them?"

"Because nobody else would have done it. Please don't stop me. This might be my only chance to get it back."

Sylvia sighed, then nodded. "All right, but be quick about it. If you are caught, you'll be in terrible trouble."

"I'll be in terrible trouble anyway if I don't have my bag," I said.

Despite how firmly I had spoken to Sylvia, my hands were shaking as I approached the Mollisons' room. I stopped at the doorway and looked around, but the corridor was empty.

Only Sylvia was looking back at me, her mouth pressed in a disapproving frown.

"Just hurry," she said.

Hurrying was my plan as well. Unless my bag was very well hidden, I could get in and out in less than a minute.

I held my breath, then darted forward, pushing open the door no more than I had to and quickly shutting it behind me.

In a brief glance, I understood that this would not be the one-minute search I had hoped for. The room was smaller than I had expected for first class, though it was certainly bigger than mine and much finer in its furnishings. The carpet was dark green with light green flowers. The bed, table, and wardrobe were made of dark-stained oak. The room had both a heater and a ceiling fan, and a small panel near the bed had buttons on it for electric lights or to call a steward to the room.

All of which meant only one thing: A search of this room could last longer than it would take to style Mrs. Mollison's hair in the salon.

I began with the luggage rack posted to the wall above the bed. A traveling bag was set in there, but when I went through it, I saw nothing of any interest to me and certainly not my stolen bag. Nor was it in the wardrobe. Then to my delight, when I lifted the mattress, there was my notebook! That was a start.

With my heart pounding, I pulled it out, only to realize that this was not my notebook after all. This one was darker in color and smaller, and when I went to put it back, several papers fell out that had been stuck between the notebook pages.

"Oh no," I breathed, then knelt to pick them up. I began stacking the pages, then stared at the one on top, a paper with a handwritten list of debts alongside various addresses throughout England, and the total amount below: four hundred and twenty pounds. That was a great deal of money. At the bottom, someone had written the words *Paid in total*, with the date April 9, 1912, beside it. The day before the *Titanic* left Southampton. Beneath that was another note that read, *To be repaid April 17, 1912*. The day we were supposed to arrive in New York.

So the Mollisons had found a way to pay their debts before leaving England. Now they had one week to replace that money.

And they would do it by stealing from Sylvia's family!

I stuffed the papers back into the notebook, hoping they were in the same order as before, though that couldn't possibly be the case. I replaced the notebook where I'd found it, then lowered the mattress. With the seconds ticking by far too quickly, I began looking around the room for any other possible place where they could have hidden my bag.

Except there really was no other place to look and I was becoming frustrated, and the frustration quickly turned to fear. I was in the very center of the room when I heard a key being fitted into the door to the cabin.

I first turned to the wardrobe, but I couldn't hide there. The chances were far too great that one of the Mollisons was returning to change their clothes for supper.

In one desperate dive, I slid under the bed just as the door opened. The bed skirt gave me cover, but I barely could move because of baggage stored under here. I worried that even breathing would give me away.

"The door was already unlocked," Mr. Mollison said. "You must be more careful, my dear."

"You were the last one in our room," she replied. "The fault is yours. Perhaps if you hadn't been so eager to get to the game tables."

"Perhaps if you weren't so eager to spend my hard-earned winnings at the beauty salon—" he retorted.

Mrs. Mollison's mood immediately changed. "There are winnings?" she asked. "You won a game?"

"I won a very big game! Nearly twenty pounds."

Once again, the mood shifted. "Only twenty pounds?" The disappointment in Mrs. Mollison's tone was clear. "That wouldn't cover even one of our tickets."

As they spoke, my eyes drifted to a paper lying halfway beneath the bed skirt. It had to be one of the papers I'd dropped. If they looked down, they'd see it. Then they'd see me!

Meanwhile, Mr. Mollison continued. "It's more money than you've earned today. What about the plan?"

Mrs. Mollison humphed, then sat on the bed above me. "I made progress. The papers we want are in a safe deposit box. Now all we need is the key."

Papers? I had thought Sylvia's safe deposit box contained only money. Were there also some important papers inside?

Mrs. Mollison shifted one foot, nearly touching the paper that had fallen beneath her bed. I feared she'd step on it, then hear the paper crackle. As carefully as possible, I put my hand on it and began slowly pulling it beneath the bed with me. Once I had it closer, I realized that I had seen this paper before. It was the same rose-colored paper as the Mollisons had with them when I first saw them on deck. This time it was unfolded, though I wouldn't be able to see all the writing at this angle.

At the top, I read:

Step One: Repay debt.

Step Two: Book tickets on the ~~Californian~~. *Titanic*.

Step Three: Get the safe deposit key.

Step Four . . .

That was as far as I could read without moving the paper again, but this was obviously the outline of the Mollisons' plan. I wished it had more details, but I hoped there was enough here that I could report them for any crimes.

"What about that Hazel Rothbury?" Mrs. Mollison asked.

That got my attention. I forgot about the letter and listened more intently.

"She definitely complicates this plan, which makes it far more dangerous for us," Mr. Mollison said. "I will have to get everything we want with a game of cards."

"There's too much risk of you losing."

"Not if I cheat." He chuckled. "Set up the game tonight in the main dining room. I will impress the entire ship with my skills."

Mrs. Mollison sighed. "Very well, my dear. I'll see what I can do. But is gambling really a skill?"

They continued to bicker until they had left the cabin. I waited a full minute with my mind like a sponge, absorbing every thought and worry and fact around me, and there was plenty of it to be absorbed. Then I slid out from under the bed to leave as fast as I could. My notebook was still missing, but I didn't dare to remain here a second longer. The danger was far too great that one of them might return, and besides, I needed to tell Sylvia what I had overheard.

I knocked on the door directly across from the Mollisons' room, then whispered, "Sylvia, it's me!"

The door opened and there was Miss Gruber staring down at me. With a stern frown, she said, "I thought you would come here sooner or later."

I stared back at Miss Gruber, with no idea what I should say now. All that squeaked out of me was, "May I see Sylvia, please?"

"Certainly not! You are a bad influence on my ward."

I could hardly disagree with that, but I was trying to help Sylvia now. I said, "Miss Gruber, it's about the Mollisons. I just heard—"

I stopped there and clamped my mouth shut. If I told Miss Gruber what I'd heard, she would know that I'd been in their room, and I absolutely could not let anyone find out about that.

But they would eventually figure out that someone had disturbed the papers in the notebook I'd found, and one of them was now beneath their bed.

Once they discovered that paper, they would know some-one had been in their room.

And without a doubt, they would know it had been me.

I would have to warn Sylvia another time. So, I turned on one heel and ran. Once again, I'd failed to prove myself as her friend.

Once again, the Mollisons had won.

TWENTY-TWO

Find New Hope

On my way belowdecks, I spotted Charlie with a paper in one hand. He beckoned to me, so I hurried over to him. "I think I've crossed this ship twenty times already today to pass messages from one person to another," he said, then glanced sideways at me. "No more notebook? Have you given up the excitin' world of journalism?"

My smile at seeing him quickly fell. "I'm sorry for what happened yesterday, with Mrs. Mollison."

He lifted a finger, more serious than I'd expected. "Once again, I'd like to tell you that it was no trouble at all, but in fact, that turned out to be quite a bit of trouble, didn't it?" Now he found his smile. "And it was worth every minute. She's a terrible person, Hazel. I'm happy you got away from her."

"I didn't get enough away. She stole my bag with all my money in it, and my pen and notebook."

Charlie let out a low whistle. "You don't say? I knew the

Mollisons were low-life swindlers, but I didn't have them pegged as shoulder bag thieves. Do you think they wanted your money, or your notebook?"

"It must be the notebook. I overheard them talking about needing to stop me. Maybe they think I will write about them."

"Why would they think that?"

I blinked back at Charlie. "I do plan to write about them. Sylvia is going to help me."

"I see." Charlie shifted his weight, which was probably the alternative to rolling his eyes at me. "So maybe you shouldn't write about them, and they'll leave you alone."

"What kind of journalist would—"

"You're not a real journalist, Hazel!" Charlie pushed a hand through his hair. "Maybe you will be one day. I hope you will because I think you'd be brilliant at it. But for now, leave this to the adults. You should warn Miss Gruber, then let it go."

I was still stinging from what he'd said, so my tone was sharp as I replied, "Miss Gruber would never believe me. She dislikes me too much."

Charlie shrugged. "I think Miss Gruber dislikes everything and everyone. I think sometimes hard things happen to people, and a few of 'em forget how to smile."

That gave me pause. "You think that's the reason she wears black, and always frowns?"

"Maybe." A long silence followed before Charlie said, "Listen, when I said you weren't a real journalist, that doesn't mean you can't write your story. In fact, I just heard something

I reckon you'll want to know. The . . . trouble . . . down in the boiler room is over."

I leaned toward him. "You mean the fire?"

"Shh. Yes, it's out."

"Is there any damage?"

"From what I'm told, it's still too hot for the firemen to get close to it. I reckon we'll know more in the morning. But that is a spot of good news, eh?"

It was a lot of good news, especially compared with how the rest of my day had been.

"Hazel!"

Charlie and I both turned. There was Sylvia, hurrying toward us, nearly breathless.

"I'm so glad I found you," she said. "I wanted to apologize for not warning you about the . . ." She paused, her eyes on Charlie. "Hello again."

"I haven't seen you since you had me invite Hazel to dinner," he said cheerfully. "Have you enjoyed the trip so far?"

"Nearly every minute," Sylvia said. "And I have seen you on the deck. They keep you moving, don't they?"

"I can always go a bit faster," he said. "It's what I'm paid to do, and I'm happy to do it."

"You can trust Charlie," I said. "And you don't need to apologize for anything. I know you would've warned me if you could."

Charlie grimaced. "This sounds like one of those conversations a crewman of the ship shouldn't hear. If you'll excuse me as I go to deliver this note, I'll try to find you again soon."

He ran off in one direction while Sylvia and I simply leaned against the ship's rails, staring out at the ocean.

I wanted to begin first, to say everything that I needed to before Sylvia shifted the conversation in another direction. "I shouldn't have lied to you about why I was going to America, but I didn't want you to think of me as some common factory worker."

Sylvia smiled. "If I were to think of you that way, then I would think of someone who is working hard to help her family, and someone who is taking charge of her life to get ahead."

I saw her smile, and she seemed to believe what she was saying, but she made the factory work sound far more noble than it would be. Mum had warned me that I might be working as long as ten hours a day, often in some of the most dangerous areas of the factory. Whatever Sylvia pictured for how my life would be in America, it wouldn't be nearly that nice.

Sylvia continued, "Does your mother want you to work in the factories?"

"No, but I need to find work somewhere, at least until my brothers are old enough to build up our farm or to find work themselves."

Sylvia thought for a moment, then said, "After we return to New York, there is a good chance my father will dismiss Miss Gruber as my governess."

"Oh?"

"We went to England to visit my grandparents. My grandfather gave Miss Gruber five hundred pounds to bring back home to my father—that's what is in our safe deposit box now. But Miss Gruber has been acting strangely ever since, changing our travel plans at the last minute, leaving me with lessons to complete while she disappears for hours and gives no explanation. She's still acting rather odd."

"Is it possible she is helping the Mollisons to steal your family's money?"

Sylvia's eyes widened with shock, and I immediately regretted making the accusation.

"Why would she help them?" Sylvia firmly shook her head. "They only met because our cabins are so close. Miss Gruber wouldn't turn on my family for them."

"No, of course not."

"There is something unusual in her behavior, though," Sylvia said. "I will find out what it is. Until then, do you remember when I told you that there is a way you wouldn't have to work in the factories?"

"So I could write the story about the Mollisons? I don't think I can—"

"Actually, I've had a better idea. What if you worked for my family instead?"

My nose wrinkled. "As a servant?"

"No, as my companion. You'd assist me with my hair and wardrobe, and if I'm at a dinner or a dance, you would be there to help, should any problems arise."

"That sounds like a servant."

"It's different. You would be treated almost as a member

of the household, and you would be paid as well." Sylvia stared directly at me. "Much better pay than you would ever earn in the factories. And much safer."

My eyes widened. I scarcely dared to ask the next question, for fear I had misunderstood. "Why would you want *me* to be your companion?"

Sylvia smiled. "Because we're friends, Hazel. And this is only if you're interested."

Of course I was. It sounded a thousand times better than working in a garment factory.

But still not as good as becoming a journalist. And I'd never get there if I accepted Sylvia's offer.

I said, "May I think about my answer?"

"Of course! But I do hope you will say yes!"

"Until then, I need to tell you what I saw when I snuck in—"

"Snuck in where?" Miss Gruber asked as she walked up behind us.

My heart sank and I slowly turned to face her. Miss Gruber was folding her arms, with her mouth pinched in disapproval.

Sylvia said, "I offered Hazel a position as my companion."

"You will withdraw your offer at once." Miss Gruber eyed me. "Hazel is a liar and a thief. She let herself into the Mollisons' room and, from what I am told, stole a highly valuable paper from them."

I shook my head. "I didn't steal anything, I swear it!"

"But you don't deny breaking into their room."

"I didn't break in. The door was left partially opened."

That detail was hardly the point of her complaint, but I needed every bit of help I could get.

"It's still a crime, Hazel. And when Mrs. Mollison reported her suspicions to me just now, she added one other detail. Is it true that you are a stowaway aboard this ship?"

I looked down, tears filling my eyes.

Miss Gruber turned her attention toward Sylvia. "I told you it was a mistake to befriend this girl. She has come from nothing, and her life will amount to nothing."

"I'm going to become a journalist," I said between gritted teeth.

"A girl who comes from poverty should know better than to have such a big dream. When word of your crime spreads, you will never work as a journalist. You will never be hired to work anywhere."

"When word spreads?" Sylvia asked. "Miss Gruber, did you tell anyone?"

"As an honest woman, I had to report the crime." Miss Gruber gestured to a ship's officer coming toward us, someone I had seen before. This was Officer Kent, the man who had warned me away from the first-class promenade when we first set sail from England.

I was running out of time, but I had to speak quickly. I turned to Sylvia and whispered, "You need to find out how much money is in your safe deposit box. If I'm correct, then you will be missing four hundred and twenty pounds of it."

"Speak up, child," Miss Gruber said. "What did you say?"

I stared back at her with as much defiance as I could muster. "The *Titanic* has many secrets, Miss Gruber. So do I."

That was as far as I got before Officer Kent reached us. He looked down at me as if I were a thorn he had plucked from his foot.

"Hazel Rothbury?" he asked. "You will come with me."

"I will," I said, "but first let me explain to Sylvia—"

"She is Miss Thorngood to you," Miss Gruber said.

Officer Kent took my arm, but I pulled it away. "One more minute, please, sir," I said.

"This way, Miss Rothbury." Officer Kent gently took my arm again.

As he led me away, I looked back at Miss Gruber. "Didn't you ever have a dream so big that you were willing to risk everything for it? If you never have, I feel sorry for you."

Miss Gruber seemed to flinch.

Officer Kent continued to lead me away. He said, "This is one risk you should not have taken, even for a very big dream. Stowing away aboard a ship is a very serious matter, young lady."

By then, we had moved out of sight of Sylvia and Miss Gruber. I hung my head and followed Officer Kent toward whatever punishment awaited me.

Whatever it would be, the stocks or a dungeon, or sending me back home to my family in shame, I doubted anything could make me more terrified than I was at this moment.

TWENTY-THREE

Before It Was Over

There was no getting around it. I was in serious trouble. A stiff punishment was surely headed my way, but no matter what it was, even worse would be the consequences for my family if I was unable to find work.

I needed to think of a plan to help them, but as I trudged behind Officer Kent toward the boat deck, all I could think about was that I had dozens of unanswered questions, and a ship's officer was certain to have all the answers.

I had to ask. I had to try.

"Sir, in this area of the ocean, could there be dark icebergs, or even blue icebergs?"

Officer Kent gestured toward the ocean. "I see no icebergs anywhere, do you?"

I looked, but saw only an endless stretch of water. "No, but *could* there be?"

"I suppose."

That was two questions successfully answered. Why not a third question, then?

"Do the lookouts in the crow's nest always have binoculars, or is that only on nights with bad weather?"

"I don't know anything about the binoculars. I'm not a deck officer."

My heart skipped a beat as we passed near Captain Smith, walking along the promenade with another officer, his arm pointing out to the sea as if giving orders.

I turned back to Officer Kent. "Would you mind if I asked the captain about that?"

"I would mind very much, and so would he. You do remember why you are up here, correct?"

"Yes, sir, but I can explain."

Officer Kent barely slowed his step. "For your sake, young lady, I hope it is a good explanation."

From the boat deck, he walked me up a short flight of stairs to the bridge. He gestured for me to follow him, but I didn't move. How could I care about my punishment when I was *here*, in the command center of the greatest ship on earth? Slowly, I turned in a full circle, watching senior officers in close conversation, occasionally giving commands, and with a snappy "Yes, sir," the sailors immediately obeyed.

What an extraordinary gift, that I should be able to see all of this.

Of course, I was only here because I was in serious trouble—but at least I was here! Questions flooded my mind so fast, I hardly knew where to begin.

As it turned out, the questions would have to stay in my head for a while longer.

"You'll wait in here, Miss Rothbury." Officer Kent opened a door marked as an officers' lounge, leading me into a room with fine wood paneling and comfortable chairs and desks for writing. It seemed to be a place where the ship's officers could relax or hold private conversations, or apparently, where they could punish a girl who had stowed aboard their ship.

On one of the desks was a chart with notepads and hand-written messages marked with a code, many of them prefaced with the letters *MSY*.

I pointed to it. "What do those letters mean?"

"That's the call sign for the *Titanic*, the letters that identify us," Officer Kent said. "Now, Miss Gruber has accused you of—"

"Why those letters?" I asked. "They have nothing to do with the name of this ship."

"And *you* should have nothing to do with this ship," he said. "Is the accusation true? Are you a stowaway?"

I drew in a deep breath. "Yes . . . and no."

He arched a brow. "Oh?"

"A stowaway is someone who sneaks onto a ship with no intention of buying a ticket. I do plan to pay for my ticket, sir. I just don't have the money yet."

Officer Kent frowned. "It doesn't matter what you planned to do."

My tone became more urgent. "How can it not matter? Sir, I already promised to pay for the ticket as soon as I have the money."

"To whom did you make this promise?" Officer Kent asked.

"It was . . ." I stopped there, realizing my mistake. I couldn't involve Charlie in this. "It was a promise to myself, sir, and I intend to keep it."

"And *how* do you intend to keep it?"

"I did have some money with me, but . . ." Now I had nothing. No money. No notebook. No future. "I don't know how I'll pay for the ticket, but I will pay, I promise."

"Does your family know what you've done?"

I shook my head. That was the worst part of this. Mum would be horrified when she heard, and deeply ashamed of me.

"I hope you understand that stowing away on a ship is not only illegal, it is very dangerous. Believe it or not, you should consider yourself lucky that you were caught."

For the record, I disagreed on this point. But he wasn't finished.

I slumped into my chair as he said, "You need to provide me with your family's address. I must send them a telegram to explain the trouble that you are in and ask them to send the money."

That's when I sat up again. This was not an option. "We have no money, sir. I can stay on board and work for the price of the ticket, clean cabins or wash linens or whatever is needed. I want to make this right, if I can. But please don't ask my mother to pay."

He clicked his tongue, then slowly nodded. "I will speak to the captain about this. He is a fair man, but he is also an honest man who will not look favorably upon what you have done. You had better prepare yourself for the most serious of consequences."

I gulped. In a rare moment for me, I had no interest in asking the question that was now framed in my mind: What were those serious consequences? I thought I had prepared myself to deal with any possibility, but now that the time had come, I was frightened.

A knock came at our door. Mr. Kent turned that way and said, "Please enter."

A younger crewman opened the door. "Sir, there is someone out here who thinks she may have information involving that girl sitting behind you, a woman from first class. She wishes to speak to the girl alone."

That had to be Miss Gruber. I rolled my eyes, dreading another scolding from her.

After casting a curious look in my direction, Mr. Kent stepped outside, slightly closing the door. Despite that, I heard a whispered conversation asking what sort of information this woman had and why we needed to speak in private first. He must have been satisfied with the answer because I heard him say, "You may have five minutes, no more."

I stood again, determined to withstand anything she wanted to say to me. But it was not Miss Gruber who came through that door. Mrs. Mollison entered instead. My gut twisted.

She eyed me as the door closed behind her. Thin creases of anger lined her mouth, which was pinched into a tight circle. I imagined that was not so different from what the kiss of death might look like.

When she was satisfied that we were alone, she said, "Didn't I warn that you'd end up in the brig?"

I wasn't going to let her intimidate me. "This is an officers' lounge, Mrs. Mollison."

"It's still your brig. Didn't I also say that you and I could help each other?"

I shook my head. "Help you steal money from Sylvia Thorngood's safe deposit box?"

Mrs. Mollison's eyes widened. "Sylvia Thorngood's box? I haven't taken a single farthing from that box, nor will I do so."

I frowned back at her. "You told me that if Sylvia checked the box and if money was missing, that you'd blame me for it."

"That is still my plan if you don't cooperate. But Mr. Mollison and I have much bigger plans."

Bigger than the Thorngoods? If she wasn't planning to steal their money, then whose safe deposit box did she want?

Before I could ask, she continued, "The reason I've come is that a paper is missing from our room. Don't bother to deny taking it. We know you were in there. We want it back, you little thief."

"*You* are the thief," I said. "I don't know whose money you're after, but I do know you're trying to get it from someone on this ship. When I figure out who it is, I'll tell them all about you."

"Why would they believe you? If there is a criminal in this room, my dear, then it is you."

My face hardened. "I'm no criminal."

She began counting off on her fingers as she spoke. "Stowaway. Impersonation of a first-class passenger. Fraud. Breaking into another passenger's cabin."

Well, when she put it like that, I could see how bad it sounded for me. But I wasn't a criminal, or a bad person. I still knew I was in the right.

So, all I said was, "There were good reasons for everything I did."

"Let's not add lying to your list of crimes." Mrs. Mollison took a step across the room before she continued. "I have come to offer you a trade, and if you are smart, you will accept."

"What trade?" I asked.

"The way I figure things, once you got on board this ship, someone must have helped you find a room where you could stay."

My stomach twisted. I knew exactly where this was going.

"Last evening when you and I were talking out on the deck, that young porter came forward and told me a lie of his own. I think he intended to protect you, correct? Now why would he involve himself in your interests unless he had already involved himself in your interests before? I believe that boy helped you get a cabin down in third class."

"You keep Charlie out of this," I said. "It was my decision to stow away on the *Titanic*. No one else's."

"I asked around about him," she continued. "Poor thing. He has five younger brothers and sisters and a mother who can't possibly feed them all. Charlie Blight sends home every farthing he earns on this ship. He might be the only chance his family has of surviving. Helping a stowaway is a serious offense. If he loses his job—"

"Don't tell them anything about Charlie," I said. "Don't get him in trouble too!"

"Here is the plan," Mrs. Mollison said. "Return the paper that you stole from our room and swear to keep quiet about anything you might think you know about me and Mr. Mollison. If you do, I will keep quiet about Charlie."

I stared back at her as my mind twisted into knots. I could not agree to her plan because I had not taken the paper that I had seen in her room.

But I could not refuse her plan either. Otherwise, Charlie would get in trouble and probably lose his job, which would ruin his family.

"I . . . I . . ." I genuinely did not know what to do.

"My husband has an important card game tonight, and when he wins, our plan is complete," Mrs. Mollison said. "All my life I have struggled for every coin I ever earned, working as a housekeeper for a family so wealthy, they never lifted a finger a day in their life. Tonight, everything will change for me. All I want to know, Hazel, is if you are willing to help me, and I'll help you."

The door handle began turning.

In that very moment, I knew who was the target of her plan. It was so obvious that I couldn't believe I had missed it before. Mrs. Mollison used to be a housekeeper. I knew of a passenger on board who was dismissed from her job as governess after a housekeeper accused her of theft.

Step two of the plan I had seen on the rose-colored paper was to book travel on the *Californian*, later changed to the *Titanic*.

Mrs. Abelman had told me that she had originally planned to travel on the *Californian*. The Mollisons changed their plans because of Mrs. Abelman!

And Mrs. Abelman must have a safe deposit box, because I'd heard the purser ask her about it. I didn't know what was in that box, but I was willing to bet that inside that box was a stack of papers that were valuable in some way. I needed to find out what those were.

I looked at Mrs. Mollison, my jaw set forward in determination. "I know what you're planning to do, and I will stop you."

"No, you won't, dearie."

The door opened and Officer Kent poked his head in. "Well?"

Mrs. Mollison's mouth pinched tightly together before she said, "Sadly, the situation is just as I had thought. She confessed everything to me. The boy was involved in her crimes." Mrs. Mollison glared back at me as she left the lounge.

"No, it was only me!" I rushed to the door to continue my protest, but stopped, seeing Charlie facing me.

I backed up as Officer Kent directed him to enter the lounge. Charlie only stared at me. His glare wasn't half as severe as Mrs. Mollison's, but it felt ten times as harsh.

"The captain will come to speak with both of you soon," Officer Kent said, then closed the door.

I started to say Charlie's name, to apologize to him, but he only sat back and folded his arms. "So, you confessed every-thin' about me? I thought you were a better friend than that. Maybe you're not my friend at all."

"Charlie, I didn't—" He looked over at me, his eyes filled with something between anger and hopelessness. "You told me that you can always take a little more. Is that still true?"

"No." He turned away. "There is nothin' more, not after this."

CHAPTER
TWENTY-FOUR

In a Small Moment

For the next two hours, I did my best to speak to Charlie, to apologize to him, to get him to even acknowledge that I was there in the room.

"I know this is entirely my fault," I said for the hundredth time. "I understand that."

Finally, he answered, though it began with a long and very sad sigh. "Not entirely. You didn't ask me for a cabin on the ship. I made that decision."

"Only because I begged for your help."

"I thought it was the right way to help you out of a bad situation." He looked up at me. "I know that I should say this isn't a problem, that I would gladly do this over again. But it is a very big problem, and if I could do this again, as soon as I found out you were a stowaway, I would have taken you directly to the captain."

My heart sank further. I thought about the bargain that

Mrs. Mollison had offered me. If there was any way I could have agreed to it, I would have done so, for Charlie's sake.

He added, "When the captain comes, he'll dismiss me for sure. I'll never work on another ship again. I might never work anywhere again if future employers find out what I did." He lowered his head further. "I'll have nothin' to send my family when we reach America. They'll starve."

If I had felt awful before, I felt even worse now, but the hardest part was that nothing I could do would fix this.

Charlie said, "As for you, once back onshore, they'll report you to the authorities. Since you're young, you probably won't see the inside of a jail, but they may require you to work off the debt to the ship before you're allowed to return to your family."

That was bad news too. I had been worried about Mum getting by until I could begin sending her money from the factory job. Now, it could be months before I worked off the debt to the ship, and I likely wouldn't be able to get a job afterward. A fine family like the Thorngoods would never allow me to work as Sylvia's companion. Even the factories wouldn't have me now.

We sat together, both of us equally sad, until Charlie finally pointed up at the clock in the lounge. "Pity that there's no aft windows here. There'll be a shift change for the lookouts soon. You'd want to see that for your news story."

"It doesn't matter," I said. "I'm not a journalist. You told me so yourself."

"Maybe one day, when you are a journalist, you can write about us being in here. So, ask me a question. That's better than sitting here feeling sad for ourselves."

"Fine. How often do the lookouts change shifts?"

"There's six men total, and they rotate in two-hour shifts. It's nitherin' cold up there, so any longer, and we'd bring them down frozen."

"Oh." I tried to care. I wanted to care, but I still didn't see the point.

Charlie added, "I mentioned the shift change so you could see for yourself how attentive the lookouts are."

"I'm sure they are," I mumbled, then added, "Do both lookouts have binoculars?"

"I don't know, but there's some paper on the desk if you want to write down your question for later."

"I won't do that." I knew how childish I sounded. I wasn't trying to be difficult. I just didn't want to write anymore.

Charlie's sigh was louder than it had to be. "Was your dream so small that you're giving up on it already?"

"No, my dream was too big. It could never happen."

"And how do you know if you give up now? Write your story and send it to White Star. Maybe they'll read it and make the *Titanic* safer than it is already. If your story could save lives one day, then you have to write it."

I turned to him, stunned that even here, when he was in so much trouble because of me, he spoke as if we were still friends.

I started to ask Charlie about his family, but we were interrupted by Officer Kent reentering the lounge. We stood to greet him, and I tried to read his expression, but that proved impossible. Officer Kent looked to Charlie first.

"The captain has given orders concerning the two of you. Mr. Blight, you will return to your quarters this very minute, and you will remain there until the captain summons you to speak with him tomorrow morning. Dismissed."

"Yes, sir." Charlie quickly glanced at me before he left.

I would have felt better with Charlie still here, but since I was alone again, I had to stand tall and accept my own punishment. I doubted it would be as simple as what Charlie had received.

"As for you," Officer Kent said, "your ticket for passage on this ship has been paid. You are free to return to your room, and it is your room now, but I warn you not to get into any further trouble. You will remain in the third-class areas only. You will stop asking questions to make the passengers nervous. And if you did enter the room of Mr. and Mrs. Mollison, then you will . . . er . . . not enter it again."

My heart had skipped a beat with his first sentence, and still wasn't back to normal. "I can leave, just like that?"

"You are now officially an honest passenger on board."

"Yes, sir, thank you . . . but . . . who paid for my ticket?"

"It was done anonymously. I cannot say."

"Oh." I couldn't imagine who that would have been. Miss Gruber never would have allowed Sylvia to pay it, and that's the last thing Mrs. Mollison would have done. Even if she had the money, Mrs. Abelman didn't know I was here. I did not know who I was supposed to thank for literally saving me.

I started to leave the lounge, then glanced up at the crow's nest one more time. I turned back to Mr. Kent. "Sir, do the lookouts have binoculars?"

His answer was not what I had expected.

"Binoculars are not necessary for the lookouts," he replied. "Their job is to spot a problem, not to identify it. If the lookout sees a problem, he will call down to an officer on deck. The deck officer does have binoculars, and he will pass on whatever orders are necessary to protect the ship."

"Oh. But—"

"Miss Rothbury, if you insist on asking questions, I will have to return you to that lounge."

"No, sir." I started to leave, then turned back to him. "Do you know about refraction, sir?"

He arched a brow. "Refraction? I'm a low-level officer on this ship, Miss Rothbury. I have no need to know what refraction is."

I grinned. "If you tell me who paid for my ticket, I'll tell you all about refraction."

Unexpectedly, he smiled back at me. "I don't know the name of your benefactor, but I can tell you that she said she wished someone had believed in her dream when she was your age."

I wrinkled my nose as I thought about that. Mrs. Mollison had spoken of her dreams when she was younger, but the last thing she'd want was for me to go free. She knew if I did, the first thing I'd do was find Mrs. Abelman.

I had to find Mrs. Abelman and warn her about the Mollisons!

"You've asked your questions," he said. "Now, return to third class, or else I'll—"

I was already headed straight toward the Grand Staircase,

hoping to find Mrs. Abelman somewhere between here and my room on E Deck. I hoped there was still time to stop the Mollisons.

Yet as I came closer to the main dining room, I paused at the top of the staircase, noticing a crowd below, most of them huddled around a single table.

At first I couldn't see what everyone was so interested in. I only knew that with so many people here, I'd have difficulty getting past them all.

A gap finally opened up, and once through it, I saw Sylvia across the room. She pointed me out to Miss Gruber, who frowned and rolled her eyes, obviously irritated. But Sylvia ignored her and pushed her way through the crowd toward me.

"How did you get out?" she asked. I had no time to answer before she said, "I'm so glad you are here. You must see this!"

"See what?" I craned my head to discover the answer, which came when a gentleman moved just enough for me to see two people seated across from each other at the table, with playing cards set out between them.

On one end was Mr. Mollison, the card sharp and someone who had earlier told his wife he intended to cheat in order to get his win.

On the other end was Mrs. Abelman. My heart slammed into my throat. I was too late.

TWENTY-FIVE

All Was Lost

"Why is Mrs. Abelman playing cards?" I asked Sylvia. "They must have tricked her!"

Sylvia looked as worried as I felt. "I only know that Mrs. Abelman and the Mollisons met on the deck a short time ago. Next thing I heard was that they were all here."

As the crowd pressed in, I was better able to see the game from my position on the stairs. Both Mrs. Abelman and Mr. Mollison had a stack of chips in front of them, though his stack was far greater.

Between them, thirteen cards were laid out in two separate rows, all faceup. Mrs. Abelman was moving her chips around, then with each move, Mr. Mollison would lay down another card.

"I don't understand the rules," I whispered.

"She must guess whether the next card will be higher or lower than the card her chips are on," Sylvia said. "But he's already taken most of her chips. He's going to ruin her."

In an impatient voice, Mr. Mollison said, "It's your turn, Mrs. Abelman. What would you like to do?"

Mrs. Abelman looked up and spotted me standing on the stairway. She gave a brief smile and I tried to smile back, though I wanted to shout out a warning for her to leave the game before it was too late. Maybe it already was.

After giving me a quick wink, she shifted some of the chips around. Mr. Mollison played a new card and the crowd groaned when he took those chips from her and added them to his pile.

She sighed. "I may have gotten myself into trouble by agreeing to play this game with you. When your wife and I used to work at the same estate, she often said that you were not very good at gambling."

He flinched. "My wife was mistaken. I am an excellent player."

"Indeed, I have underestimated you." Mrs. Abelman paused and looked around the room again, and then in a strong voice, asked, "How well do you know your mythology, Mr. Mollison?"

He blinked back at her, obviously confused, but said, "I know it well enough."

"Then you know about the Titans, the twelve children of Sky and Earth. They were powerful; they were gods. But their strength made them arrogant. They believed nothing was capable of defeating them, certainly not their children, the Olympians."

Mr. Mollison snorted. "Why are you telling me this now?"

"Because I believe too often in my life, I have been arrogant. Too certain that my strength was enough to control my fate. But I am older now, and my life has become fragile. I have learned the lessons of the Titans. We must live the best we can until we gracefully accept our fate."

I thought back to the story my father used to tell me, that of the Viking king Canute, who showed his people that despite all his power and greatness, he could not command the tide.

"Are you playing the game or preaching a sermon?" Mr. Mollison growled. "Your move."

"Very well." Mrs. Abelman shifted her chips around again. Her opponent laid down a new card, then gave a smug smile as he pulled the rest of her chips toward him. Another win for him.

"I have all of your chips now," Mr. Mollison said. "Unless you have something more to offer, the game is over."

"I believe that I do have one more item," Mrs. Abelman said.

I held my breath as she reached for her handbag, praying she wouldn't add to her losses. I didn't know how much money was in the chips on the table, but I did know it must be nothing compared to whatever was in her safe deposit box.

Sure enough, when Mrs. Abelman withdrew her hand, pinched between her fingers was a small key, the same key I had seen earlier.

Mrs. Mollison must have seen it too. She pushed her way forward through the crowd, her eyes fixed on that key with such intensity, I wouldn't have been surprised if drool started foaming at the corners of her mouth.

Worse still, in her hands was a familiar item: my shoulder bag. I gripped the staircase rail even harder than before. Only hours before, she had accused me of being a criminal, even while having possession of my stolen bag!

Mrs. Abelman must have spotted it too. She looked from the bag, down to the key in her hand, and then up at me again. I tried to read her expression. Was she nervous, in a worried panic?

I certainly was and shook my head back at her. This was awful.

Mrs. Mollison returned to her place in the crowd, but Miss Gruber was at her side by then. I saw a flash of metal in Miss Gruber's hand, then she dropped what she had been holding into her pocket.

"She keeps the safe deposit key in her pocket." I turned to Sylvia. "You've got to get it. If the Mollisons did take your family's money, you'll have no chance of getting it back after we reach New York."

Sylvia nodded back at me. "I saw that too."

At the game table, Mr. Mollison's eyes were still focused on Mrs. Abelman's key. "If I win, then the contents of your safe deposit box will be mine?"

"Yes, *if* you win," Mrs. Abelman said. "One round of our game remains."

"You see the cards," Mr. Mollison said. "We both know how this will end."

In a full panic by now, I turned to Sylvia. "Is there any way to stop this game?" But Sylvia only shook her head.

"So, you are a Titan, then?" Mrs. Abelman asked.

Mr. Mollison looked at the crowd, fully aware of how many eyes were on him, and said, "You make me think of this great ship upon which we travel. The *Titanic* truly is the greatest ship on the seas. Indeed, we sail on an unsinkable ship. So, you ask whether I am a Titan. Yes, for I too am unsinkable."

A few members of the crowd applauded him, which was all that he needed to continue. "I know something about you, Mrs. Abelman."

"Oh?"

"I know that you are a Jew, born into such poverty that your family had to rent out their rooms to strangers. Eventually, you were lucky enough to marry into extreme wealth, all of which you inherited upon the death of your husband. And then, when you could have afforded every luxury this world could provide, you became a governess, lowering your own station."

"Teaching children raised my station, I assure you," she said. "But you are correct: In my life, I have been part of every class."

"And from this moment forward, I shall only live among the wealthy. It has been a pleasure to play this game with you, Mrs. Abelman."

"And you as well." She glanced up at me a third time, very briefly, but this time I was sure I saw a spark in her eyes. "It's a pity that you do not know more about me. My father did indeed rent out our rooms, to travelers who gambled every night. From my earliest days, I watched carefully. I learned their games . . . and their tricks." She leaned forward, her eyes bright with anticipation. "Please turn the last card, Mr. Mollison."

He glanced at the card, then bent toward Mrs. Abelman and said something to her, so quietly that she had to lean forward herself to hear it. When he'd finished, their gazes met, and I was sure I saw tears in her eyes. Whatever he'd said, it had hurt her.

Then he lifted the final card, and slowly, his face drained of color. He turned it, and though I couldn't see the card, it was obvious who had lost.

Mr. Mollison stood and threw the card onto the table. "Impossible! That is impossible!"

The remaining crowd applauded for Mrs. Abelman, who merely sat there, staring at the stacks of chips on the table and her precious key. Once the applause died down, she said, "I propose an exchange."

Mr. Mollison turned toward her. "What sort of exchange?"

Mrs. Abelman pointed to Mrs. Mollison. "Everything on that table, in exchange for the bag your wife is holding."

All eyes turned to Mrs. Mollison, whose jaw dropped open. But no more than mine did. I wanted to cry out that this was a terrible offer. Mrs. Abelman herself had assured me that the loss of the notebook was a small matter, and the money in my bag couldn't be as much as Mrs. Abelman's chips, still on the table. Certainly not as much as the valuables she kept in the safe deposit box.

I began to stand, to hurry over to her, but Sylvia grabbed

my arm. "Don't interfere," she whispered. "You shouldn't even be here. You'll get in trouble."

I continued walking forward anyway, but I was already too late. Mrs. Mollison tossed the bag toward her husband, who passed it to Mrs. Abelman and said, "It has been a most excellent evening. Thank you for the game."

"Thank you for the trade." Mrs. Abelman folded the bag under her arm, then walked my way. When she was close enough to speak to me, she merely said, "Come with me."

Sylvia squeezed my hand and whispered, "It will be all right, Hazel," though I wasn't sure that I agreed. Mrs. Abelman had won the game, but had still lost everything.

I followed her up the stairway, out of the dining room and onto the promenade, then we continued walking until we were alone. She turned to me and said, "I thought you might take the risk to come watch the game."

"Why did you do that, Mrs. Abelman? You won the game!"

"I did, and what a relief that was. Mr. Mollison cheats, you know."

"What did he say to you before he turned that last card?"

The light in her eyes dimmed ever so slightly. "Ah, well, that is a story for another day. At least you have the notebook again."

"The notebook is only papers that can be replaced. You told me that."

"And you told me that what you had written in the notebook was valuable." She smiled and passed the bag over to me. "Your words are here, Hazel, your questions. This will become your news story."

My shoulders fell. "There won't be any story. When I spoke about being a journalist, that was just childish talk."

"And what's wrong with childish talk? I daresay that if more adults could speak with your enthusiasm, we would not have so many broken dreams and crushed souls. If you are giving up so easily, then the problem is you are thinking too much like an adult."

"Even if I did write the story, no one would ever buy it."

"How will you know if you do not write it? Besides, if the value of your words is found in what someone pays for them, then consider how much I paid to retrieve your notebook."

I shook my head, tears filling my eyes. "I don't deserve this, Mrs. Abelman."

"Sometimes life gives us better than we deserve, and we repay that by making the most of the gift. Hazel, write your story. This notebook is yours now, and everything in it."

I beamed up at her. "Thank you, then. But I promise not to ask you for anything else while on board."

"You are young, and I am an adult," she said. "You have the right to ask for anything that you need."

Now my smile widened. "I need you as my friend. That will always be enough for me."

WEATHER REPORT
Sunday April 14, 1912

The mild temperatures in the mid-Northern Atlantic over the past week will begin to cool by mid-morning, with brisk northwest winds of 20 knots.

A new cold front from the west will bring a further drop in temperatures. Air temperatures in the late evening could reach near freezing.

Overnight, expect still winds and calm seas with a possible low-lying haze. Lookouts are warned that potential hazards will be more difficult to spot, as they will not create ripples upon the water.

Moon Phase — Waning Crescent
Clear Skies
Atmospheric Pressure of 1035 hPa

CHAPTER
TWENTY-SIX

On That Final Day

Sunday, April 14, 1914

I awoke early on Sunday morning with a heavy feeling in my gut that I couldn't quite identify. There shouldn't have been any reason to worry. I was an honest passenger now, freely able to move about in third class as any other passenger might.

Eager to relieve the restlessness I felt, I dressed and headed toward the saloon to wait for breakfast. Maybe I was just hungry.

Maybe not.

Once inside the saloon, a good breakfast sat before me. My notebook was opened on the table in front of me. I should have been deep into my writing, and yet, my stomach was churning.

I finally figured out why: Charlie. I hadn't heard anything from him since leaving the officers' lounge up on the boat deck. I remembered how worried he had looked when I left, and I could imagine his conversation with Captain Smith had not been an easy one.

And perhaps it had been a terrible one.

I'd hoped to distract myself by starting to write the *Titanic*'s story, but I'd gone through my entire breakfast and three glasses of milk and still the page was blank.

I needed to write it. If I started now, there was a chance I could finish before we arrived in New York. Then, whether for better or worse, I could try to sell what I'd written.

But I had no idea where to begin. Mostly because I had no idea what the *Titanic*'s story was.

Yes, of course there were some problems with the ship's design, some concerns that White Star ought to address, but that was hardly enough for the newspapers. No ship was perfect, and who was I to criticize the designers and builders who had spent years creating every piece of this ship, down to each single rivet in the metal?

Who was I to write anything at all?

I closed the notebook, looking around at the crowded saloon full of hundreds of people gathered for breakfast. They spoke different languages and came from different places on the map. They were young and old; some were travelers and others immigrants, seeking a better life ahead. Yet there was a great sense of unity here, all of us bound by the hope of what tomorrow might bring.

Sylvia said I spent too much time thinking of my questions and not enough about people. So maybe that was where I ought to begin, with the people here who surrounded me. With their stories.

I picked up my pen again.

"You've begun your story, then?"

I cried out with delight. What did my story matter compared to the joy of seeing Charlie again? "They let you leave your room?"

"Captain Smith came to my quarters late last night. I told him what I'd done wrong, and why I'd done it. I hoped that if he could understand my reasons, then he'd agree that I'd made the right decision."

"So, he agreed with you?"

"Oh no. He told me I'd shown poor judgment, that I wasn't to be trusted, and that I'd lose my wages for this entire trip."

"I'm sorry."

"He was angry, chewed me up dearly, but it was nothin' I didn't deserve. I took it and apologized and swore it would never happen again." Charlie grinned and sat down at the table across from me. "After that, he said that I wasn't doin' any good shut up in my room, and that they were already short-handed, so if I worked my hardest for the rest of the trip, he might give me a second chance."

"Then he's letting you stay on the crew?"

Charlie nodded eagerly. "He's givin' me the chance to prove that I should stay on. If I can earn back his respect, he'll let me stay on for the return to England."

My nose wrinkled. "I think that's good news, isn't it?"

"It's very good news, considerin' what he might have done. Though he's goin' to keep me closer than before. No more helpin' the passengers. I'm only to deliver messages between the captain and deck officers today."

"What kind of messages?"

"Any messages that come in, I reckon. All ships in the area regularly send out messages, warnin' each other of any dangers. We receive them in the Marconi Room." His eyes brightened. "You've seen that room—it was on the bridge, across the passageway from the officers' lounge."

"I did see some of those messages," I said. "Why were they marked with MSY?"

"Those are messages sent directly to the *Titanic*, and could be about anything. If the message is very important, it will begin with a CQD. Those messages are immediately delivered to the captain."

"Have any messages come in with a CQD heading?"

Charlie looked around to make sure no one was listening. "No, and let's be glad for that. However, we did get a message a little earlier this morning marked with MSG. That code means the captain should see it, but it's not an emergency."

"Do you know what the message said?"

"It came from a ship about a day ahead of us, warning of growlers in the area."

I turned the pages of my notebook to the drawings I'd made of the growlers. These icebergs were far more dangerous than they appeared since most of their mass was beneath the water. A ship might believe they were approaching a minor threat, without realizing that the true threat lay hidden far below.

"Will Captain Smith adjust course now?" I asked.

"Of course he will," Charlie replied. "I wanted you to see that the captain is aware of everythin' happening on the ship and solvin' problems long before any passengers know they exist." He winked at me. "That includes journalists, I'm told."

I was sure he was right, yet deep inside, something tugged at my mind. When Captain Smith had commanded the *Olympic* last fall, he had courted danger by allowing his ship to come too close to that warship. And despite a direct collision that had created a gash in the *Olympic*'s hull, a gash taller than Captain Smith himself, the ship remained afloat. What if the captain decided that these reported growlers weren't a threat to the *Titanic* either?

"Ah, there's that worry line on your forehead again," Charlie said. "I shouldn't have told you."

I shook my head, determined to have a good day. "Not at all. Now that the warning has come, the officers will make the right decisions."

Yet even as I said the words, I felt a prickling in my gut. Along with that came new questions.

Would the new course be any safer than our current direction?

Would Captain Smith take this warning seriously?

Did the warning need to be taken seriously? Or yet again, was I looking for problems just to write a more interesting story?

"I'm glad you're not worried," Charlie said. "Sunday services will be starting soon. Are you planning to stay?"

I looked around and noticed people filling the saloon, most of them dressed in nicer clothes than I'd seen in here before. At the front of the room, a Catholic priest was setting his Bible out on a table.

"I want to find Sylvia and apologize again for any trouble I caused," I said. "I owe her that much."

"She'll be in Sunday services in the dining room," he said as he stood from the table. "But I can give her the message if you'd like. I'm headed upstairs anyway. Lifeboat drill for all crewmen."

"Now? But we're halfway to New York already!"

"It's a routine exercise—makin' sure that in an emergency, we'd all know exactly what to do."

"Do your best, then," I said. "Hopefully the captain will see how hard you work and promote you to first officer!"

Charlie laughed. "I'm just happy not to be scrubbin' the decks with my toothbrush! But I'll get that message to Sylvia for you."

"Thank you. And if you see any exciting messages for the captain, be sure to tell me."

At that, Charlie became serious again. "I can't share a message with a passenger, you know that."

"What about a journalist?"

One corner of his mouth turned up. "Especially not with a journalist. But . . . if it is very important, perhaps I can give you a signal from the promenade. If I tip my hat to you, then you will know that somethin' interestin' is happenin'."

I lifted my notebook. "I'll be waiting!"

Once he left, I settled in to listen to the priest. He referenced Scotland Road, the passageway that we all had become familiar with by now. He clasped his hands and said, "You may have heard one of Scotland's finest songs, 'The Bonnie Banks o' Loch Lomond.'"

I had heard of it. Only two nights ago right here in the saloon, a trio of Scottish brothers performed it for all of us, the song of two lovers who are separated by fate and unlikely ever to be reunited again.

The priest continued, "The chorus says, 'Ye'll take the high road and I'll take the low road, and I'll be in Scotland afore ye.'" He glanced heavenward before adding, "In life, we have that same choice to make, whether to take the high road or the low road. You see, my friends, the noblest among us choose the high road. They do what is right simply because it is right. Those who choose the low road act only for themselves. Join me, my friends, on the high road."

I wondered which road I was taking. Since boarding the ship, I'd taken the low road far too often. But no more. From now on, it'd be the high road for me, and I'd get there by writing the best news stories I could. I would write them so well that the newspapers would have to take me seriously.

And they would. I was determined to find the *Titanic* story the entire world would want to hear.

Now if I could only figure out what that was.

To:	Origin Station:	Time and Date:	Via:	Remarks:
MGY	Caronia	__ H __ M __ 19 __ 14 APR		

Apr 14, 1912
7:12 am New York / 9:12 am Titanic
Prefix: MSG
Office of Origin: 'Caronia'
"Captain, 'Titanic.' West-bound steamers
report bergs, growlers, and field ice in 42
degrees N., from 49 to 51 W. April 12.
Compliments. Barr."

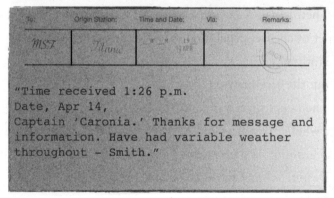

To:	Origin Station:	Time and Date:	Via:	Remarks:
MST	Titanic	__ H __ M __ 19 __ APR		

"Time received 1:26 p.m.
Date, Apr 14,
Captain 'Caronia.' Thanks for message and
information. Have had variable weather
throughout - Smith."

TWENTY-SEVEN

Warnings Came In

I promised myself that before the sermon ended, I would figure out what I wanted to write about the *Titanic*.

I broke my promise to myself.

Then I made a new promise, to find my idea during our
supper of cheese, gruel, and cabin biscuits.

Nothing.

But the biscuits were delicious.

Then, as I peeled my orange after the supper, I decided to
start where all stories did: at the beginning, or at least, with
my beginning. Which meant I needed to write about the fire.

Despite what Charlie had said, I couldn't believe that two
or three weeks of a coal fire would have no consequences.
There had to be some level of damage to the bulkheads. No
crewman would ever admit that to me, but maybe I could get
the information for myself. This was going to require some
sneaking around.

I began by walking to the far end of the corridor. There, I stared up at a sign that clearly stated only crew members were allowed past this point. The boundary was marked by a thick metal door on wheels. This had to be one of the watertight doors that could be closed in an emergency.

The story that Charlie told me of the ship *La Bourgogne* came to mind. If the *Titanic* were ever in danger, closing this door could prevent the crew from coming onto the deck and taking the lifeboats meant for the passengers.

I shivered at that thought and wondered if the crew did too when they were down here, knowing that if that door ever closed, they would have no way of reaching the lifeboats.

I looked around to be sure I was alone, then drew in a deep breath and crossed through the opened door.

Nobody appeared to be on this side of the door either. Likely, most of the employees were either up on the decks with passengers or else they were getting a little sleep between shifts. Turning the first corner, I spotted the same alcove beneath the stairway where I'd hidden after sneaking on board. This was where I'd first heard about the fire. Hopefully, with some patience, the firemen would come this way again.

While I waited, I opened my notebook once more. I wanted to write something about the crew. I needed to mention the people who washed the linens each day and baked the bread and polished the rails. It was their work that gave the *Titanic* its regal feeling. But the firemen were the most interesting to me. They were the invisible crew, who somehow kept this ship running each day, though I knew so little about what their work involved. I did know they left each shift covered in soot and ash, so I imagined theirs was not the kind of job most people were even capable of doing.

Such as putting out a fire on board a ship.

Once again, I felt torn between the responsibilities of a journalist to tell the truth, and the real people who would face the consequences of what was written. If I wrote about everything I'd learned, Charlie would be in trouble, possibly Officer Kent. And likely, the firemen here.

So was taking the high road telling the truth, or was it protecting decent people?

Until I decided for sure, I lowered my notebook, leaned back, and closed my eyes. I could be waiting here for a long time, so it was a good thing I had such a big question to figure out.

After nearly a half hour, I finally heard voices approaching from the far end of the passageway. A quick peek around the corner revealed two men with coal-blackened trousers coming this way, just as I'd hoped. I'd seen one of the men before, the fireman who'd told me to get out of the crew area. He seemed to be upset about something now.

". . . he thinks it'll be good enough to cover the bulge in bulkhead six with some oil?" the fireman was saying. "He can pour oil all over that wall but it won't fix the damage."

"We need to report it," the second man said. "If the fire was hot enough to cause a metal wall to do that, the bulkhead can't be watertight anymore."

"That'll be our first order of business for repairs once we reach New York," the first man said. "I wouldn't trust my life to that wall, nor ask any of you to do so."

While they spoke, I kept as still as I could, though I wanted to write down every word while it was fresh in my mind. The instant they passed by, I grabbed my notebook and wrote down what they had said, adding to it one more question:

Can bulkhead #6 be trusted?

Because if the answer was no, until the wall could be repaired, then that was the one place where the ship must not be damaged. Because if it did and the wall failed, two compartments would instantly flood.

I sat there only a moment before I decided to return to the boat deck and ask one of the officers about their repair plans. Surely even a third-class passenger had the right to ask a question as important as this one. Charlie had said there was a lifeboat drill. Hopefully the ship's officers were there for it too.

The problem was that the easiest route to the boat deck required me to use the Grand Staircase. The Sunday services for first class were still happening, so the entire dining room was filled. Even Captain Smith was there, and some of his officers.

I kept my head down and skirted around the bend in the staircase, hoping nobody would notice my presence. Or at least, I hoped no one would care enough to stop me.

Once I reached the boat deck, I hurried toward the bridge. There didn't seem to be any lifeboat drill, so either it had ended sooner than I'd expected or else it had never happened. I'd have to ask Charlie about that.

"Mr. Blight," an officer somewhere behind me said.

"Yes, Mr. Murdoch." I turned and saw Charlie hurrying over to a man I'd seen last night in conversation with the captain. Officer Murdoch was tall, with thoughtful eyes and sharp features, and seemed to be in his late thirties. He was the first officer of the ship and second-in-command. He and Charlie had a brief conversation, too low for me to hear, then Officer Murdoch gave Charlie a paper and pointed toward the stairs.

I recognized the shape of the paper and my curiosity sparked. It was the same size as the other messages that came from the Marconi Room. I wondered who this message was for.

Somehow Charlie found me among the other passengers and his eyes locked on mine. He subtly gestured for me to follow him, and I eagerly did.

By the time I caught up with him on the stairs, he was leaning against one wall, reading the message. His body was tense and one hand was curled into a fist. Something was wrong.

Charlie looked up at me, and I knew from his expression that I was about to get an answer to a question that I had never wanted to ask.

"What does it say?" Even as I spoke the words, I wasn't entirely sure that I wanted the answer.

Charlie looked down at the note again, slowly shaking his head. "I can't show this to you—that would violate the ship's rules. But if you were to ask me about the note, in very specific terms, maybe I could at least nod."

My brows furrowed. What did he want me to ask?

I stepped closer to him. "Is there a problem with the ship?"

"Of course not," he replied. "The *Titanic* is in clear water, at least *right now*."

"Right now? Does that mean the weather is going to change?"

"I don't know about the weather. It is right chilly today, though, and we are about to move into some very cold waters."

Very cold waters. A pit formed in my stomach.

I kept my voice low. "Charlie, are there icebergs ahead?"

He nodded.

"A lot of them?"

Without my asking, he added, "We got another warning note while you were in Sunday services. This is the third message to come in the last few minutes. All of them are reporting ice. I'm supposed to take this note directly to the captain."

"May I come with you?" Then I could ask the captain about the fire damage as well.

Charlie shook his head again. "You're not even supposed to be up here." My hopes fell flat until he added, "I suppose that I can't stop you from following me. Just don't make it obvious. Wait at least a minute."

I nodded my agreement, but only managed to wait ten seconds after he left before I followed.

When I caught up to Charlie on A Deck, he had already found the captain, who was now visiting with guests inside the first-class lounge. I waited outside the door, watching Charlie pass him the note. The captain briefly glanced at it, then slid it into his pocket and said a few words to Charlie. He nodded, then left, motioning with his hand that I should not follow.

My attention was briefly diverted when Mrs. Abelman passed by the captain, leaving the lounge with a woman near her own age. That woman was elegantly dressed in a black satin dress with a white sash and a pearl necklace. Mrs. Abelman was in a lovely emerald-green gown with her usual carved eagle's head cane in hand.

Mrs. Abelman paused in front of me. "Are you well, Hazel?"

My eye was still on the captain. He was now in conversation with a second man, tall and lean with dark hair combed straight back and a mustache a little wider than his mouth and turned up at the ends.

The captain pulled out the note that Charlie had just given him and showed it to this man, who read it, and the two of them began quietly speaking to each other.

I said, "Mrs. Abelman, who is that gentleman speaking to Captain Smith?"

She said, "You are looking at Mr. J. Bruce Ismay, the chairman of the White Star Line. He is the captain's boss and the owner of the *Titanic*."

Mr. Ismay glanced over at me, as if he sensed that I was asking about him. He frowned, then excused himself from the conversation with the captain and left.

"Is there anything else you need?" Mrs. Abelman asked.

I looked in the direction Charlie had gone. "How does the Marconi Room receive messages?"

Mrs. Abelman only smiled. "If you truly want to know, then meet me in the library in ten minutes."

I thanked her and hurried on, hoping to find Charlie again. After a few minutes, I found him on his way back up to the boat deck.

"Charlie!" I called.

He stopped when he heard me, but was already shaking his head before I'd started my question. "I can't tell you every-thing, Hazel."

"Tell me this. You gave the captain that message. Why would he then give it to Mr. Ismay?"

"He gave it to Mr. Ismay?" Charlie shrugged. "That doesn't make sense. There are rules on this ship that even the captain must follow. All warning notes are to be posted so that every officer on deck can see them. I hope Mr. Ismay will get that note posted soon."

"I hope so. I also wondered about the emergency drill today. How did it go?"

Charlie hesitated, then said, "It was canceled. But every eve-ning at six, they have a boat drill to be sure that each lifeboat has a lamp and its supplies. So, all will be taken care of then."

I hoped for that too, though by now I was late to meet Mrs. Abelman. When I reached the library, she was already seated with a book in her hand, opened to a page with the alphabet in one column and a series of dots and dashes beside each letter.

"Morse code," Mrs. Abelman said as I sat down beside

her. She turned the book to face me. "Messages are tapped out by an operator. Anyone within range of the signal can receive the code and translate that into words."

As she spoke, I was already copying the code into my notebook, my mind racing with possibilities. If I could get near enough to the Marconi Room to hear the messages, I wouldn't have to wait for Charlie to tell me what they said.

"I believe this will hold your interest for some time," Mrs. Abelman said. "So if you will excuse me, I will find something to eat for lunch."

I nodded, but in truth I barely heard her. I wasn't only hoping to understand Morse code. I intended to memorize it.

To:	Origin Station:	Time and Date:	Via:	Remarks:
MGY	MBC	13 H 57 M 19 12 14 APR		

Apr 14, 1912
11:42 am New York / 1:42 pm Titanic
Prefix: MSG
"Greek Steamer Athinai reports passing
icebergs and large quantities of field ice,
today in latitude 41° 52' N, longitude 49.9°
W. Wish you and Titanic all success.
- Commander"

To:	Origin Station:	Time and Date:	Via:	Remarks:
MGY		19 12		

1:47 pm Titanic
"Amerika Office. 14 April, 1912.
Time sent at 11:45 am. 'Amerika' passed two
large icebergs in 41 27 N., 50 8 W., on the
14th of April. [Captain] Knuth."

CHAPTER
TWENTY-EIGHT

Time Was Running Out

I wasn't sure how much time had passed since I'd last looked up from the book, and I only did so because I heard someone calling my name.

"Miss Rothbury!"

There stood Miss Gruber in the entrance, arms folded, lips pursed. I heaved a sigh. Once again, I had been caught in an area where I was not supposed to be.

What would it be now? I wondered. She'd already reported me to Officer Kent once. Maybe she had reported me twice.

The frustration I felt at being caught was nothing compared to the irritation of being interrupted. Although I knew some of the simpler codes, the more complex letters were still confusing me.

For the past half hour, I'd turned my attention to memorizing the code patterns that might be heard more frequently on board.

CQD, the most important of messages: -•- --•- -••

MGY, messages meant specifically for the *Titanic*: -- --• -•--

And SOS, a new code, one that some people wanted to be used as an international signal. From my reading, I didn't think it was much used yet, but I memorized it anyway since it was the easiest of them: ••• --- •••

I would have loved to continue studying the codes, if not for Miss Gruber standing impatiently at the doorway. I closed the book and replaced it on the shelves, then picked up my bag and dragged myself over to meet her.

Her face was as stern as ever as she looked down at me. "May I ask what you were reading just now?"

"It's the code ships use to communicate. They call it—"

"Morse code. I am familiar with it. Mr. Thorngood taught the code to his entire family, so naturally I learned it too." She arched a brow. "Why does it interest you?"

"Everything interests me, Miss Gruber."

"Hmm." She turned to leave. "You will please come with me, Miss Rothbury."

I gave one final sigh, then began walking at Miss Gruber's side. At first, I had hoped that maybe our meeting would be friendlier. After all, I had a ticket now. I belonged on this ship as much as she did. Just not . . . in this part of the ship. As we walked, she said, "Do you understand the difference between first, second, and third class, Miss Rothbury?"

I was in no mood for another scolding. Truthfully, I was in no mood for anything that involved Miss Gruber, so my tone was less than polite. "Yes, ma'am."

"And can you explain it to me?"

My answer was less than polite as well. "Third class is for hardworking people who are trying to make something of their lives, and most of them will if they get the chance. Second class is for the people who already got that chance. First class is everyone else."

She frowned down at me. "If your opinion of first class is so low, I wonder why you have taken the trouble to be among us at every possible opportunity."

So, it was clear. She disliked me as much as ever.

I stopped walking, realizing we were headed toward Sylvia's room, with the Mollisons' room directly across the corridor. I shook my head, refusing to take another step forward. When Miss Gruber turned to see why I was no longer following, I said, "If you have something to tell me, please do so here. The Mollisons have caused me nothing but trouble."

"They are belowdecks at the moment, so please do not waste my time with your stubbornness." Miss Gruber opened the cabin door and held out her arm to me. When I still refused to move, she added, "I did not bring you here for a punishment. Will you join me or not?"

I finally gave in, though I was cautious about going inside. I still wasn't sure if I could trust Miss Gruber.

Sylvia and Miss Gruber's room was larger than the Mollisons', and nicer in its decor. But there was no obvious reason why I should be here, so I turned to Miss Gruber again.

"Where is Sylvia?"

"At supper, waiting for me to join her, but this is important. I wish to tell you a story."

I squinted back at her. All this fuss so I could hear a story?

She motioned for me to sit at the desk, which I did. A small frame was on the desk, and inside it was a sketch of a father and mother, surrounded by four boys and two girls. Miss Gruber pointed to one of the girls, quite pretty and smiling wide. "That's me."

I looked at the drawing more carefully. The smile on that girl's face looked so natural and easy. Could someone that happy ever have been Miss Gruber?

"I grew up very poor," Miss Gruber said. "Like you, I had only one dress. Like you, I had no education, no manners. I saw the way you were studying that book back in the library. You remind me of myself."

That was hardly good news. I felt she had just condemned me to turning out like her, sour and disapproving of everyone and everything, and with an entire wardrobe full of black clothes.

She continued, "You think that I am so hard on you because I disapprove of you, but that is not true. I am hard on you because many years ago, I *was* you. I did have dreams, Miss Rothbury, but my parents said they were foolish dreams and told me never to speak of them. So, I put them away, locking them deep inside my heart. I suppose that when those dreams died, so did that piece of my heart."

When Officer Kent told me about the person who paid for

my ticket, he'd said it was a person who wished they'd had someone in their life who believed in their dreams.

Had Miss Gruber paid for my ticket? Why would she do such a thing . . . for me?

Miss Gruber continued, unaware of the new questions filling my head. "I know you dream of becoming a journalist, Miss Rothbury. So do what it takes to become a journalist. You must not give up."

"Is that what you wanted, to become a journalist?" I asked. "Was that your dream?"

Miss Gruber smiled . . . a little. "Oh, I never had anything new to say. Anything I wrote would have been a waste of ink. I would have liked to be a cartographer—to make maps. But I became a governess, which was far more practical."

"Have you liked being a governess?" I asked.

"Very much. And after so many years, this is all I know." Miss Gruber sniffed, and the tone of her voice softened. "I think it is quite likely that when we return to New York, I shall be dismissed. I don't know what I will do then."

I wanted to ask why she believed that, but I already suspected the answer: Miss Gruber knew money was missing from the safe deposit box. The question that rose in my mind was why she was continuing to be friendly with the people who had stolen it.

Miss Gruber went on, "I know that Sylvia has asked you to be her companion. I wish to know how you intend to answer her."

I looked up at Miss Gruber and saw sadness in her eyes. Despite her unfriendly nature, I was beginning to feel sorry for her.

"I . . . don't know my answer yet," I said.

"You should accept her offer." This time, I studied Miss Gruber more carefully. The lines on her face were deep, probably the same lines that appeared on my forehead when I worried, except she must have been worrying for much longer than me. Miss Gruber was afraid.

"It seems that you have things to teach her that I cannot," Miss Gruber continued. "I have taught her to listen, but you ask questions. I have taught her the privileges of being in first class. You have opened her eyes to the possibilities for all people, even those from third class." She pointed to my notebook, still in my hand. "And rather than accept a job fitted to your station, you truly believe it is possible to make something of your life. I can only teach Sylvia reality, but you can teach her to dream. And as I said, my time with her will end once we reach New York."

I truly did pity Miss Gruber now. Maybe I could help her. I replied, "Your time doesn't have to end. If the Mollisons stole the money from Sylvia's family, I can help you get it back."

Miss Gruber arched a brow. "How do you know about the money?"

I grinned. "I'm a journalist!"

She still didn't smile. "Can you prove any of this?"

Before I could answer, the door opened and Sylvia walked

through, asking, "Prove what?" She saw me first, then looked over at Miss Gruber. "Is this about the Mollisons?"

Miss Gruber sniffed and wiped at her teary eyes. "We were discussing Hazel's future."

"You were?" Sylvia turned to me, so excited that I wondered if she had failed to notice how sad Miss Gruber was. "I hope that means you are still thinking about my offer."

"To be your companion?" Even before Miss Gruber had brought me here, that had been very much on my mind. It was much better work than I'd find in the factories, and I thought Sylvia and I could become the best of friends in time. Beyond that, if I was to be treated as a member of the household, then there was also a chance they'd educate me, not only on the basics of reading and doing numbers, but really learning about the world. Of course I wanted that.

But if I accepted the position, would Miss Gruber have to lose hers? Despite everything she'd said or done, I was sure now that she had paid for my ticket. I could not repay that by causing her to lose her job.

I turned to Sylvia, though it broke my heart to have to say what I did. "I'm sorry, I cannot accept your offer. It's just . . . not right for me."

"Oh." The disappointment was thick in Sylvia's voice, which made me feel even worse. She turned to Miss Gruber, her expression now one of anger. "You told Hazel to say that, didn't you?"

Miss Gruber's eyes widened, and I said, "No, she told me to accept!"

But Sylvia didn't seem to have heard me. She pulled a key out of her pocket and held it up. "The Mollisons are up to something and maybe you are helping them. I'm going to check my family's safe deposit box right now. Do you have anything to confess?"

Miss Gruber paled. "I . . . I don't know what you're talking about."

"You will. Hazel was right about them, and I'm going to prove it!"

She turned and ran from the room with Miss Gruber following. I stood there a moment, wondering what I should do now.

Sylvia was going to prove that the Mollisons had stolen her family's money. It was up to me to prove they were after some valuable papers in Mrs. Abelman's safe deposit box and save them from the Mollisons.

Mrs. Mollison had said she wanted to stop me. I intended to stop them first.

I drew a deep breath and left Sylvia's room. The idea turning in my head was a terrible plan, but I already knew I was going to do it.

TWENTY-NINE

Hope Faded

I sat in the general room for some time, working out every detail for how to get back inside the Mollisons' room. It wouldn't take more than a few tense seconds to retrieve that paper beneath their bed. In and out, they'd never know.

The problem was the first half of the plan: getting *into* the room. That had worked for me before only with a spot of good luck. I couldn't count on that again.

I did have one idea, but it would involve Charlie. As his friend, I knew I should keep him out of this. But as Sylvia's friend, I needed Charlie's help.

I truly did not know what to do. So after a long debate, I decided to go looking for Charlie, to ask his advice.

He wasn't on the boat deck, nor were there many passengers on this chilly day. However, I did spot a small group ahead, talking with Captain Smith. I heard the word *warning* and decided to press in closer, hoping to catch a little of their conversation.

As I did, I heard one of the men say, "The weather has turned much colder today, Captain. Do you expect we will see any icebergs soon?"

Captain Smith's smile was as casual as if he'd been asked about ice cream rather than icebergs. "We might have, on our original course. But we have been going south for a few hours, so I believe we are far removed from where the icebergs would be." He pulled out his pocket watch. "In fact, if you will excuse me, I am late to give the order to turn west. After all, we are going to New York, not to Florida!"

The passengers around him laughed and Captain Smith strode onward. I stopped walking, thinking about what he had said. He must have taken the iceberg warning seriously, because it was true that we had been moving southward, entering warmer waters.

"Why have we come so far south?" That was Mr. Mollison's voice, just around the corner from me.

I ducked low as he and his wife entered the promenade, then took cover by squatting behind a crate on the deck.

"This will delay us getting to New York," Mrs. Mollison said. "The stock certificates from Mrs. Abelman's safe deposit box are worthless until we get them to a bank."

My ears perked up. So that was what they had taken from Mrs. Abelman's safe deposit box! What were stock certificates?

"We'll go to the bank as soon as we reach New York," her

husband said. "But we still have one problem on this boat to take care of."

Mrs. Mollison nodded. "Hazel Rothbury. She'll be stopped, don't you worry."

I grinned. They wouldn't stop me now.

They continued walking, and after that I could hear no more of their conversation. I would have followed them, but Officer Kent was on deck, so I needed to be anywhere else. When it was safe to leave, I crept out from behind the crate and went back inside the entrance to the Grand Staircase.

Once in the dining room, I passed by Mr. Ismay once again, in conversation with two ladies who seemed to have arrived a little early for supper. He was standing beside a chair with one foot on the seat, rather disrespectful of his own ship, I thought. Then from the stairs, I watched as he pulled out the same note that I had seen him receive from Captain Smith earlier.

"And what is that?" one of the women asked.

"Ladies, this message means we are in among icebergs." His tone surprised me. This was not a humble warning, nor one of caution and concern. Rather, he seemed to be boasting, as if he dared the icebergs to get in the way of his ship.

Like the Titans against their children.

Like King Canute's warnings against the tide.

The two women seemed as shocked as I was. One of them said, "Of course you are going to slow down."

"Certainly not," Mr. Ismay replied. "We are not going very fast, twenty or twenty-one knots, but we are going to start up some extra boilers this evening."

Extra boilers? Did that mean he planned to push us to travel even faster?

Maybe they had to. Charlie had told me that the ship was low on coal. Since we had been forced to go south to avoid the icebergs, maybe the *Titanic* needed to go faster in hopes of getting to New York before it ran out of coal.

Charlie entered the dining room, moving toward the stairs. He said, "I figured you'd be somewhere close by. Officer Kent spotted you up on the deck just now. I've been ordered to escort you back to third class."

"Yes, that's perfect!" I said. His brows lifted, curious about my enthusiasm to be in trouble once again. Yet this would give me time to talk to him about the Mollisons with some level of privacy. So, as we walked downstairs, I said, "I need your help to solve a problem."

He sighed. "No, Hazel. Whatever you've got in mind, it's not worth it."

"It is, Charlie. The Mollisons have Mrs. Abelman's stock certificates." I took a breath. "What are stock certificates?"

He frowned. "They talk about them in first class. It's proof of ownership in a company. They can be sold for money, sometimes quite a lot of money."

"Then we have to get them back!" Before Charlie could protest again, I quickly added, "There's a paper under the bed in the Mollisons' cabin. That could be evidence of their plan. Besides that, they're talking about doing something to stop me."

Charlie turned to me. "Stop you from what?"

"I don't know. Maybe they want to stop me from stopping them." I huffed. "But if I can find that paper, I could stop them from stopping me from stopping them."

"You're making me dizzy," he said. "Let's just report this to the captain."

I shook my head. "What will happen when he asks how I know that paper is there?"

Charlie stared at me, weighing his next question. Finally, he kicked at the floor, then asked, "Do you think it's still under their bed?"

"I don't know, but I want to sneak in again and look. I was thinking about that closet of spare keys."

Charlie sighed. "So was I. Come with me."

THIRTY

Danger Loomed

Charlie and I hurried down to the stairway where I had slept my first night. As we did, he said, "There's a closet behind the stairway. It holds spare keys for every room on this ship. As a porter, I can access those keys, although of course we are forbidden to take any key unless it's to help a passenger." He frowned over at me. "How important is it to get that paper?"

I knew how much he did not want to do this, and understood how much I was asking him to risk for my sake, but I still had to ask. "It's very important, Charlie. But I can go in. You don't have to be anywhere near the Mollisons' room."

He shook his head. "It won't matter. If you're caught, they'd still know I gave you the key. You put an eye on that room, find out if they're inside. Once I have their key, I'll meet you there."

I did as he suggested, arriving near the Mollisons' cabin

soon after the bells sounded for dinnertime. I darted around the corner, expecting them to leave, but instead, even from this distance, I heard raised voices coming from within their room. I couldn't hear what they were saying, but I did hear the anger. Several minutes later, the door opened.

"You must not play cards tonight," Mrs. Mollison said as she followed her husband out of the room. "We don't have the money yet."

"I don't even know how much money we will have, because you won't let me open the envelope. Give it to me. Then I'll know how much I have to gamble with tonight."

"If I do, that money will be gone before we reach New York." Mrs. Mollison humphed as she marched away, now with Mr. Mollison following. "I'm keeping the envelope sealed and with me."

A minute after they were gone, Charlie tapped my shoulder from behind. I nearly leapt out of my skin until I turned and saw him holding the key in one hand. "Don't worry," he said, "this won't take but a few seconds."

Of course I would worry. Ever since boarding this ship, I seemed to have become an expert in worrying. "Be careful in there, Charlie."

"I will!"

My heart pounded as I watched him dart forward, stick the key into the lock, then enter their room, closing the door behind him.

The seconds he had promised seemed to become hours,

and I barely breathed through any of it. What was taking him so long? He only had to grab the paper and leave.

The doorknob turned. He was coming out. It seemed to turn in slow motion, yet in that same moment, I heard voices coming this way. *Their* voices.

I had to do something. I had to stop this!

"I don't see why it's so important to have your gloves tonight," Mr. Mollison was saying.

"It's much colder this evening." Mrs. Mollison was following her husband, both of them still clearly irritated with the other.

Maybe I could dart out and distract them. Charlie was counting on me. I tried to force myself to move, but I felt frozen stiff. And I was already out of time. If time had crawled by since Charlie entered their room, the next three seconds passed in a single blink.

Mr. Mollison pulled out his key in the same instant that Charlie opened their door. Their eyes locked, with an immediate understanding of what this meant for each of them.

"What are you doing in our room?" Mr. Mollison asked.

Mrs. Mollison pointed a finger of accusation in Charlie's face. "Did Hazel put you up to this?"

"I only—" was as far as Charlie got before Mr. Mollison grabbed his shirt and yanked him from the room.

"Come with us, you little thief!" he said.

I started forward, but Charlie shook his head, perhaps as a warning that I should keep myself out of this one. I watched as both Mollisons half dragged, half pushed him down the passageway, completely unaware that I was behind them.

Charlie's right hand was around his back, in a fist. Before he was taken around the next corner, he let a half-crumpled paper drop to the floor.

A rose-colored paper.

I immediately darted forward and picked it up, and for the first time was able to read all of what had been written there.

As I'd seen before, the note began:

Step One: Repay debt.
Step Two: Book tickets on the ~~Californian~~. *Titanic*.
Step Three: Get the safe deposit key.
Step Four . . .

And now it continued.

Step Four: Find stock certificates.

They had the certificates now. Only one step remained in their plan.

Step Five: Repay new debts.

New debt? If they had paid all of their debt before boarding the *Titanic*, how could they have more debt already?

At least I understood now that they had followed Mrs. Abelman on board with a plan to steal her stock certificates.

This was it, their entire plan!

I could fix this, though, for Mrs. Abelman and for Charlie. All I had to do was show this paper to the captain. He'd know what to do!

I turned to run toward the bridge deck, but stopped when I saw Mrs. Mollison directly in front of me. She blocked any chance I had to escape, but I was ready to shout for help if she took another step forward.

"I know everything now." I raised the paper to show her. "When Captain Smith sees this—"

"Hush!" Mrs. Mollison's eyes darted around. "A party is about to begin in honor of Captain Smith and I must be seen there. If you want to help your friend, you will meet me on the boat deck at seven fifteen. Bring that paper."

I didn't want anything to do with meeting Mrs. Mollison anywhere, but I had failed to help Charlie before. I owed him this much.

We exchanged a nod, then she returned upstairs. I waited only a minute to be sure she was gone, then hurried up to the boat deck. I didn't want to take any chances of missing Mrs. Mollison if she came early.

Despite my worries, and despite the chill in the air, I had to admit this was a beautiful night. The stars were already out, but no moon had risen yet, and everything was so quiet.

Another cold gust of wind rushed through me, leaving a shiver behind. Remembering the warnings of icebergs, I walked to the rails, expecting to see us surrounded by them. But that was not the case at all. Within the area of the ship's lights, the ocean seemed as calm as if we were drifting on glass. It was strangely calm, really.

And there were no icebergs.

Hoping to distract myself, I pulled out my notebook. Using the deck lights, I wrote:

Sunday evening. The cool weather we have enjoyed thus far has turned. Soon, I fear even our blankets and the heavy fur wraps for the wealthier women will not be enough for warmth. Yet with the arctic air has come the most beautiful starry sky I have seen in my life. Never have I imagined there were so many stars, more than I could count in a lifetime. There is no moon out yet, and the ocean is as calm as glass. This great ship barely makes a ripple as we sail on. A slight haze has begun to rise as well.

I stopped there as my heart leapt into my throat. The *Titanic* had traveled south for much of today. We were in warmer waters than before, yet the wind was colder than ever. What had Mrs. Abelman told me about cold air moving over warmer water?

When cold winds roll over warmer waters, a haze will begin to form.

The haze might play tricks on the eye, making it seem like an iceberg ahead was in another place than it truly was, or it could hide the iceberg entirely.

Refraction.

I stood again and peered ahead, then breathed a sigh of relief. There was nothing at all on the horizon, just open water. That was a great relief, but I also knew that hundreds of miles of ocean still lay ahead of us.

And we had been receiving iceberg warnings all day long.

THIRTY-ONE

For the Last Time

The more I thought about the iceberg warnings, the more my thoughts began to fly apart. I wanted to find a ship's officer, to ask whether they knew about refraction, whether they had any plan for it.

But I knew there was no point. Of course the officers would know all about refraction, but would that be enough? I understood about bees, but I could still be stung by them.

Once again, my gut was stirring. I wished I knew what it meant. Maybe I was just inventing reasons to make people worry once again, like Miss Gruber said I did.

Or maybe there were real reasons to worry.

But I couldn't leave the deck. I had to remain here to meet Mrs. Mollison. I wished she would hurry. The bells on board signaled that it was now seven o'clock. My breath had become visible in the night air, steadily growing colder. I looked ahead to the bridge and saw Captain Smith speaking to two of the officers on watch. They gave him a salute, and as he walked away he called back, "Should you need me, I'll be in the dining room."

I nearly said something to the captain as he passed by me, wanting to ask him about refraction, but as I stepped forward, from the corner of my eye, I also saw Mrs. Mollison approaching, shaking her head as a warning to remain silent. I obeyed . . . for now.

Once the captain was gone, Mrs. Mollison approached, taking my arm to pull me into the shadows of the ship, away from the lights on the deck. I readied my courage, determined to win this, once and for all.

"Where is the paper you stole?" she asked.

"Hidden." I'd put it between the pages of my notebook to keep it safe out here on the open deck. "If you want it, then you'll have to give me something too."

She cocked her head. "Such as?"

"Mrs. Abelman's stock certificates."

Mrs. Mollison laughed so hard it sounded like the bray of a donkey. "Ha! Absolutely not."

"The note I found is proof that you were trying to get those papers from Mrs. Abelman all along. That was your plan."

"Nothing on that paper is a crime, dearie. Besides, Mrs. Abelson traded those certificates away to get that notebook of yours."

I stood up as straight as I could, hoping it would help me feel more courageous. "I also want you to drop any complaint against Charlie Blight for being in your room. Let him go free."

Mrs. Mollison scoffed. "We can drop our complaint against that boy. But it's the captain's choice whether to release him."

I stepped back. "I want the stock certificates, and Charlie's release, and I want you to return the money you stole from Sylvia Thorngood's family."

Mrs. Mollison's eyes narrowed to thin slits. "I already told you once, if Sylvia's money is missing, we didn't take it. Besides, I happen to know that money was only borrowed. It'll be paid back and Sylvia will never know the difference."

Then someone had taken Sylvia's money, but who?

When I had been in the Mollisons' room and grabbed their notebook, several pages had fallen from it. One of the pages showed that the Mollisons had a debt of four hundred and twenty pounds, which had been paid the day before the *Titanic* left Southampton.

Another note indicated that same amount of money had to be repaid before we arrived in New York.

The Mollisons hadn't taken Sylvia's money to pay off their debt. Miss Gruber had, and she was expecting them to repay the money into Sylvia's safe deposit box before New York, before she could be discovered.

The Mollisons planned to get that money from Mrs. Abelman's stock certificates! If they were valuable enough, they might become wealthy, even after repaying Miss Gruber.

"How did you know that Mrs. Abelson had stock certificates on board?" I asked.

"Always the curious one, aren't you?" Mrs. Mollison

scoffed. "I was the housekeeper at the estate where Mrs. Abelman worked as a governess. I found the certificates in her room one day and took 'em for myself. Mrs. Abelman caught me and turned me in to the master, so I had no choice but to blame her for some missing silver pieces, which I also stole. I even put the pieces in her room, so he'd be sure to believe me. They had no choice but to dismiss her once they were found. I heard Mrs. Abelman say as she left that she planned to go to New York. We figured she'd bring the certificates with her."

"You thought she'd board the *Californian*, but instead she bought a ticket for the *Titanic*."

"Which cost us a pretty penny more. But it will be worth it once we cash in the certificates." Now she held out her hand again. "I want that paper."

I stepped back, maintaining my distance from her. "You said if I came, you would tell me how to help my friend. So drop the charges against Charlie."

"That is not the friend I thought you'd want to help." Mrs. Mollison grinned. "What about Sylvia Thorngood?"

A lump formed at the back of my throat. I didn't like the way Mrs. Mollison was smiling. "What about her?"

"We're not going to repay Miss Gruber. We're going to let Sylvia be missing for a while, ask a ransom of four hundred and twenty pounds. Miss Gruber can tell Sylvia's parents that she had to pay it to get Sylvia back."

My breath caught in my throat. "Is Miss Gruber part of this plan?"

"Oh no. I expect she's sick with worry. So give me the paper and I'll tell you where she is."

I pulled it from my notebook. "All right. Where is she?"

Mrs. Mollison frowned. "She's fine. Mr. Mollison followed her and made sure she wouldn't go nowhere . . . not until Miss Gruber agrees to erase our debt. I'll take that paper, then we'll talk!"

It had been in my hand, but Mrs. Mollison lunged forward and took hold of one end. "Let go, Hazel!"

"Tell me where Sylvia is!"

Mrs. Mollison tugged harder at the paper, her temper boiling over. Just as she snatched it from my hands, I pulled back on it. We both lost hold of it as the wind caught it, and the paper fluttered high into the air.

Mrs. Mollison pushed me aside as she jumped, trying to catch the paper before it was carried even higher in the wind. It flew over the rails, then like that, it was gone.

The only thing in the world I had to make a bargain with Mrs. Mollison was gone.

I stood there, watching it fly away. A long silence followed before Mrs. Mollison turned back to me with a smile as icy as the wind. "That ended better than I'd expected. Our negotiations are over. And don't you get ideas about telling anyone the story I just gave you. Nobody would ever believe you."

"Where is Sylvia?" I asked again. "Please, Mrs. Mollison, tell me!"

She opened her mouth to answer, then stopped as an elegant couple walked by, a man with a black top hat and tuxedo and his wife in a deep blue gown with a strand of pearls. For the smallest moment, I was caught up in watching them walk past, wishing I could ask them questions for my news story. Seconds later they were gone.

When I turned to look at Mrs. Mollison again, she was gone too.

I sank onto the deck chair, angry and heartbroken, but more than anything, I was desperately worried for Sylvia.

For Charlie as well, who was only in trouble because he was trying to help me.

I didn't know where either of them was, nor Miss Gruber nor Mrs. Abelman, the only two people on board who might possibly believe me.

I sat there for some time, trying to figure out what my next move should be. Finally, I decided that I had to at least try to report the matter to an officer on board. I'd been in this area enough to know some of their names by now, so I marched forward, toward Second Officer Lightoller.

He looked younger than Officer Murdoch and struck me as being a little more friendly. As I came closer, I saw a message in his hand, written on the same paper as the messages I'd seen Charlie with earlier.

"Think we should notify the captain?" he was asking another officer, a longer-faced man with the name "Moody" on his uniform.

Officer Moody seemed to have the kind of eyes that always looked worried, but they were especially concerned right now. "What does it say?"

Lightoller checked the message again. "Another ice warning. This time from the *Californian*, not twenty miles from our position."

Moody nodded. "If that holds true, then I'd expect we'll start to see ice around eleven tonight."

"That'll be Mr. Murdoch's shift, then," Lightoller said. "Be sure to record the ice warnings on the ship's map."

While Moody went to obey that order, Lightoller stepped away, farther than I dared to follow.

Seeing no one else who might help me, I decided to go looking for Miss Gruber instead, to ask her about Sylvia. Most likely she would be in the dining room, perhaps expecting Sylvia to join her for dinner.

However, before I took my first step onto the Grand Staircase, a steward stopped me, his arms folded and his lip curled in disapproval. "You're not first class," he said. "Get back to your area or I'll report you."

"A girl might be missing," I said.

"That's you, missing from your place belowdecks. Now go away at once. I won't have you interfering with the captain's party."

I frowned back at him, then turned to find a different set of stairs down. I made it as far as D Deck when I heard music playing and followed the sounds into the second-class saloon, where a large group had gathered. A minister was in front of them and at his cue, everyone began singing. I recognized the tune from the song "For Those in Peril on the Sea."

My heartbeat quickened. Sylvia was in peril! How could everyone be seated here so calmly?

I glanced over the group and was certain I saw Mrs. Abelman at the far end of the room. I started toward her but should have been looking all around myself, for a hand wrapped around my arm and Officer Kent's familiar voice said, "I heard you were wandering up top again."

"But—"

"But nothing, Miss Rothbury. Didn't you agree to remain in third class?"

"I did, but there's a girl missing from first class—"

"Sylvia Thorngood. Her governess has just informed us that she failed to show up for dinner. Most likely she has fallen asleep in one of the public rooms, or went below to explore. We'll find her, but we don't need your interference. Come with me."

He was taking me back up the stairs again, but this time I was pulling against his grip. "You need to speak to the Mollisons. They know where she is!"

"We spoke to Mr. Mollison only minutes ago. He told me that he has no idea where Miss Thorngood could be."

"He's lying to you!" Now I was getting angry. "How can you not see what is in front of your own eyes? That's the true refraction here."

"Refraction? That word again?"

"Sir, if you can't see the truth about the Mollisons, how could you acknowledge the iceberg warnings on this ship?"

He stopped there. "What are you talking about? What iceberg warnings?"

His stunned reply left me equally surprised. "Surely you've seen them. They've been coming in all day."

"I've heard of a few. But how would you know about them?"

Now it was my turn to stop. I'd gotten Charlie into enough trouble already and couldn't make it worse. "I just . . . know. Haven't the warnings been shared with all the officers? I thought the captain was obligated to post them."

"I'm sure that the captain has told his senior officers about the warnings."

"He hasn't! Or . . . I don't think he has. Maybe he forgot. Maybe he doesn't think the warnings are that serious."

By then, we had returned to the bridge, the very place where I had been ordered to leave only a half hour earlier.

Officer Kent reopened the very same door to the room where Charlie and I had been held yesterday, the officers' lounge. Only this time, it was empty.

I had thought when Charlie was taken away, that they'd keep him here until the captain settled the complaint against him.

But Charlie wasn't here. Where was he?

And where was Sylvia?

THIRTY-TWO

Hours Felt like Days

I stopped in the doorway of the lounge room, confused. "Where is Charlie Blight? I thought he'd be here."

"Young Mr. Blight is in serious trouble," Officer Kent explained. "Unfortunately, the *Titanic* does not have a brig, but we do have another place to hold passengers or crewmen who have become a problem. The officer on duty might order me to take you there as well. So you'd better sit still and hope Officer Lightoller is in a good mood when I report this matter to him."

I didn't care what mood anyone was in. I was angry with Officer Kent for ignoring my warnings about Sylvia, and worried about the possibility for a mist or haze to rise above the water just as we were about to be "in among the icebergs," as Mr. Ismay had said.

Besides that, I was feeling impatient. Mr. Kent had closed the door behind me, but it wasn't locked. At first, I nudged it open, hoping to hear any passing conversations. When that didn't work, I widened the door a little more, and when nobody came by several minutes later, I decided to creep outside and see how close I could get to the Marconi Room.

Its door was also open. If I sat close, I could hear the tapping out of messages being sent, but I doubted any of them were worth listening to. They'd be the telegrams purchased by guests over the last few days. They wouldn't be worth my trouble to attempt to translate.

Far more important were the messages being received from other ships in the area. I was desperate to hear them, but when I peeked inside the Marconi Room and saw the operator on duty wearing headphones, I knew I'd have no luck with hearing anything useful.

However, from somewhere nearby, I did hear Second Officer Lightoller greet Captain Smith, saying, "I am sorry to pull you away from the party, sir."

I sat up straighter. Something big had to be happening to call the captain away from his own party.

Captain Smith chuckled. "They are having such a good time, they will hardly notice their guest of honor has left." Now his tone became more serious. "I understand we have more messages."

"Yes, sir. The *Californian* reports three large icebergs in their area. We're not far behind them, and on a similar course."

"Understood. And have you noticed any sign of icebergs here?"

"No, sir," Lightoller said. "But as you can see for yourself, the water is at a flat calm. I can't recall ever seeing the water so still. That does make me nervous."

"Why is that?" Captain Smith asked.

"Ripples in the water will bump against icebergs. That makes those devils easier to spot. The water won't give up any secrets when it's this calm."

A short silence followed before Captain Smith asked, "What is our visibility tonight?"

"There's a slight mist in the air," Lightoller said. "But we should see everything for at least two miles. Very favorable conditions."

"That's good." Captain Smith nodded at his officer. "I will take a final turn around the deck, then go to my quarters for the night. Be sure to inform me at once if anything seems off."

I nearly called out right then. Of course something was off. I wanted to leap out from my hiding place and talk to them about refraction. Or more importantly, to ask why they were worried about ripples on the water when they could simply give binoculars to their lookouts.

I drew in a deep breath, ready to stand up tall and ask my question. But before I could, both men had already left, leaving me alone in the area.

Alone, and terribly cold. The tips of my fingers were already aching with numbness.

My attention shifted back to the tapping sounds in the Marconi Room. With nothing better to do, I pulled out my notebook and tried decoding the Morse code as the operator inside sent the messages.

I didn't catch most of the code. He was tapping too fast, and my cold fingers were too slow. By the time I'd decoded a single word, he'd be on to the next message.

However, finally there was a pause as the operator listened, then he muttered to himself, "Yes, we know about the icebergs! Enough already!"

I sat up straight. Another message must have just come through for the captain. I scrambled back into the officers' lounge, expecting the telegraph operator to come out to deliver this latest warning.

But he didn't.

No one left the Marconi Room, or entered it. I widened the door again, eager to see if there was a problem, but the tapping sound had resumed. He was sending messages again.

Why wasn't he reporting the warning?

I was still there listening when Officer Kent returned. He said, "I must apologize for leaving you here so long, Miss Rothbury. There were other matters that required my attention."

"Like the iceberg warnings?" I asked.

He arched a brow. "I'm sure the officer on duty has that managed."

"Has Sylvia been found?"

"Not yet. But we have begun a search for her."

Sylvia had told Miss Gruber that she intended to prove that

the Mollisons had stolen her family's money. Mr. Mollison had followed her, then locked her in somewhere. Where would Sylvia have gone?

I could think of only one possibility, a place I'd been before.

I jumped up from where I had been sitting. "Mr. Kent, if I promise to return to third class and to stay there, will you let me go?"

He rolled his eyes. "I was already coming here to release you, but I must tell you that if you leave third class again, we do have a place on board that functions as a brig."

"Where is that?" Surely that would be where Charlie was, though for now, I only wished to get down to the Orlop Deck.

He cleared his throat. "Goodbye, Miss Rothbury."

"Goodbye, and thank you!" I pushed past him and began running. The promenade was almost entirely empty now, and the few passengers who remained seemed to be retreating from the cold. I spotted a set of stairs near the front of the ship and took those down, surprised that they passed from one deck to another, lower and lower until finally I reached a sign at F Deck forbidding passengers to continue on any farther.

I tiptoed past the sign and went even lower, down to G Deck, and then finally, I was back on the Orlop Deck, the very level where I had begun my journey on the *Titanic*.

It took a minute to get my bearings, and to be sure that I was alone, but once I did, I was able to walk toward the baggage storage area.

There wasn't much down here, and I certainly understood

that this was no place for me. I turned to go back upstairs, to get a crewman to help me search this area.

Except somewhere nearby, I heard a tapping sound, a clanging against metal. I listened long enough to recognize this was a pattern: three short taps, three longer taps, and three short taps again.

SOS.

That was the newer code to call for help.

The sound was coming from behind a set of doors marked with a sign for large cargo. I banged on the door. "Sylvia? Are you in there?"

A voice called back, "Hazel? Hazel, I'm here, but I'm stuck!"

I pulled on the heavy door, calling out as I did, "Don't worry, I'll have you out soon. Are you all right?"

"I think so. But a trunk fell on my leg and it's trapped me here."

Finally, I widened the door enough to get inside. I ran into the room and found Sylvia near the center, but down on the ground with one leg trapped beneath a fallen trunk.

Immediately, a hundred things that had to be said were exchanged, faster than either of us could respond.

"How did you find me?"

"How long have you been here?"

"Does Miss Gruber know I'm gone?"

"Are you injured?"

None of the questions were answered, except for the last.

Sylvia shook her head, but pointed toward her leg. "I think I'm all right, but can you help me get out?"

I stood, grateful for my years of hard work on the farm. I'd need all my strength for this. The trunk was flush against the ship's wall, so I needed to lift it enough for Sylvia to pull her leg out.

I crouched low, wrapped my fingers around the bottom of the trunk, then with a particularly unladylike grunt, I began to lift it.

Sylvia said, "I can wiggle my leg, a little."

"Hurry!" I couldn't raise the trunk any higher than I had, and I certainly couldn't hold it for much longer.

"I'm trying!" Sylvia said.

The trunk began slipping from my fingers. "Sylvia, hurry!"

Even before I finished speaking, I lost hold of the trunk and it fell again, but I glanced over at Sylvia, who seemed to have just pulled her leg free.

I hurried over to her. "How is your leg now?"

She moved it, though her face tightened into a grimace as she did. "I think it's just a little sore. Maybe if I walk on it."

I helped her to stand and then braced her weight as we walked a circle around the cargo hold. She glanced over at me. "You know, this is exactly the reason why I need a companion."

I chuckled. "*This* is the reason? Do heavy trunks fall on you very often?"

"No, but I'm glad you figured out where to find me." She

went silent a moment, then asked, "Why didn't you accept the offer to be my companion? Was it something about me?"

"No, of course not! I just . . ." I took a deep breath, then said, "I think you need Miss Gruber a while longer, and I know that Miss Gruber needs you."

"I'm not sure about that." When Sylvia spoke again, it was barely a whisper. "Will you help me down the stairs?"

I kept my arm around her to brace her as we walked toward the lower cargo area. "Why are we going down there?"

"Because I couldn't find Miss Gruber's trunk up here." Sylvia looked over at me. "You were right. The key was in the pocket of her dress, so I had to wait until she was asleep to get it. After leaving my room, I opened our safe deposit box. It was exactly as you said. Four hundred and twenty pounds were missing. But the purser told me nobody had opened the box since we boarded the ship. That money was missing before the *Titanic* left port." Now Sylvia's eyes widened. "That means Miss Gruber had to have taken it!"

We reached the bottom of the staircase, entering the lower cargo hold level. It was darker than above, and I was grateful for the small lights posted on the walls. Sylvia began searching in one area and I started in another. Minutes later, Sylvia said, "I found it!"

I started toward her, only to pause at the sound of a deckhand in the room above, who must have been calling out to someone else. "How many times do I have to tell you all to keep this door locked?"

"Wait!" I called up to him, but with the sound of the ship's engines so near us, he obviously didn't hear. However, I did hear something, and it horrified me: The heavy door to the cargo room had just closed.

"Hurry!" Sylvia said. "Maybe you can still catch him!"

I left her there and raced back up the stairs, calling out for help. No one answered and the door did not open. When I reached it myself, I pushed as hard as I could, but it did not give way.

We were locked inside. Trapped, and not a single person on this ship knew where we were.

When I returned to Sylvia with the bad news, she said, "I don't think things could get any worse."

That question stirred a deeper worry inside me. No matter how difficult our lives at home were, Mum always reminded us to be grateful for what we had, because our problems could always get worse.

And maybe they would soon.

Because I also knew the latest warning of ice had been ignored by the telegraph operator. I knew that a mist rising from the ocean would make it more difficult to see an iceberg's location accurately. And that the lookouts did not have binoculars to help them see an iceberg if it was ahead.

The far end of the wall of this cargo room was rounded, marking it as the ship's hull. We had to be somewhere below the waterline now, with only a single metal sheet separating us from an entire ocean of water. Maybe we were sitting in one of the compartments that could be sealed off in case of an emergency. Sealed off from any chance of reaching an upper deck.

The very idea of that sent a chill through me. I was frightened and worried and felt utterly helpless.

Mrs. Abelman had talked about listening to my gut feelings. I was finally beginning to understand exactly what that meant. Despite where Sylvia and I were right now, I knew it was possible for things to turn very much for the worse.

Training for an Ocean Liner Radio Telegraphist

While on the ship, you will work in six-hour shifts, usually in rotation with a second operator. However, there are times when both operators will be needed. Your weekly salary will be $4-$12 with board and lodging.

International Morse Code is the standard code for travelers. Operators should be fluent in the code, eventually being able to receive up to 25 words per minute.

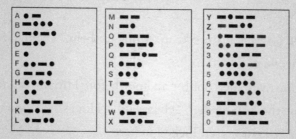

Emergency Codes

Remember that a telegraph signal will be received by every operator within range of the signal, so if an emergency signal comes in, you may be in a position to respond, or another ship may be closer. Be warned against filling the bandwidth with unnecessary communications during a time of emergency.

CQ: Requests a response from listeners
D: An urgent message
CQD: The Marconi Distress Signal
SOS: The International Distress Signal

THIRTY-THREE

But Only Minutes Later

"I should go back up and keep calling for help," I said to Sylvia. "Someone will hear us."

"I must've called out for an hour before I finally began tapping out the SOS code," Sylvia said. "Honestly, I don't even know how I got myself locked in here."

I knew, but I wasn't ready to tell her about Mr. Mollison yet and the pretend ransom. I didn't want to add to her worries.

"There's something I need to find, then we can plan our escape," Sylvia said.

She limped over to Miss Gruber's trunk, then unlatched its hinges. Together, we lifted the lid and stared down at a stack of neatly packed clothes, all of them the same shade of black.

"What are you looking for?" I asked. "Your family's money won't be in here."

"After discovering the missing money, I heard the purser give orders to a porter to bring a receipt down to Miss Gruber's trunk. Why would Miss Gruber want a receipt delivered here unless she wanted to hide it from me? So, I followed the porter." Sylvia lifted a paper. "Here it is!" She pulled it closer to her face to see the paper better. "This doesn't make any sense. It's a receipt for three pounds."

Three pounds. The price of my third-class ticket. If Miss Gruber had gone to such lengths to hide the receipt for my ticket, could I reveal her secret? I did say, "Maybe there's more to understand first. Let's find a way out of here and ask Miss Gruber ourselves."

Sylvia nodded. We closed up Miss Gruber's trunk, then together walked back up the stairs.

"I was frightened to be in here alone," Sylvia said. "I'm very sorry you're locked in with me now, but I am glad you came."

"I heard you tapping out Morse code," I said. "Miss Gruber told me that your father taught it to you."

"My father is helping to design airplanes of the future," she said. "All pilots learn the code, so he insisted that I learn it too."

"I know a few of the letters," I said, "but I'd be so slow to translate, I doubt I could ever put the code to use."

"My father would teach you." Sylvia glanced over at me. "I mean, you wouldn't have to be my companion. You could simply visit us as a friend."

I frowned back at her. "Once we reach America, I won't have time to visit. I won't have time to be anyone's friend."

"It isn't too late to say yes to my offer." Sylvia laughed a little. "I never thought I needed a companion. I'm perfectly capable of looking after myself. But the instant we met, every-thing changed. Now I don't know what I'd do without you!"

Those were kind words and lifted my heart, but they were empty words too. The truth was that I had only caused Sylvia a good deal of trouble.

"There's nothing I can offer that you don't already have," I said.

"That's not true! There's so much that you could teach me."

I shook my head. "Miss Gruber can teach you every rule of manners, and probably eight different languages and anything else there is to know."

Sylvia was silent for what felt like a very long time, then she said, "I cannot swim."

I looked over at her, confused. "What?"

She shrugged. "Can you swim?"

"Of course. We have a little pond in front of our house. We'd spend all day there in the summer, if we didn't have chores to do."

"I've never had chores," Sylvia said. "So, you can wash your own clothes, bake your own bread?"

"All of that." It seemed equally strange that Sylvia might envy me for having chores, as if they were a privilege, rather than something I was required to do.

Sylvia squeezed my hand. "We already have servants and tutors and teachers, and one Miss Gruber is enough for me. But only one person can teach me about the real world, and that is Miss Hazel Rothbury."

Maybe they weren't *entirely* empty words. I smiled. "Perhaps there are things we can teach each other."

Sylvia gestured to the door between us and freedom. "Could you teach me anything about escaping this cargo hold? Surely the girl who figured out how to sneak onto the greatest ship the world has ever seen would know a thing or two about breaking through a locked door."

I began looking around for anything that might make enough noise to call someone's attention to us, but if her clanging out the Morse code upon the metal walls didn't summon anyone, I couldn't think what else here would. The room was full of large pieces of luggage and trunks and crates, none of which I wanted to dig through in the hope of finding a noisemaker.

At the far end of the room was a very fine car, maroon with glass sides. It looked as if it had been enclosed in a crate, but the front side of it had fallen open.

"I pried it open with a stick when I first came in." Sylvia admitted this as casually as if she had merely peeked at a wrapped Christmas gift. "I was curious."

I'd seen automobiles similar to this before. One had even blasted a horn at me a month ago when I was walking in the road as it tried to pass by.

Sylvia said, "My father owns a similar automobile. I've watched his driver start it up before. Is there a key inside?"

I checked. "Yes." Then I understood why she had asked and began shaking my head. "You can't be serious."

Sylvia called out instructions for what to do with the levers on either side of the steering wheel, then said, "There's a hand crank out here. I'm going to turn it and with some luck, the automobile will start. Be ready."

"Ready for what?"

Sylvia bent low and began turning the hand crank. The engine rumbled.

"I don't know anything about driving," I said, though I climbed into the seat anyway.

Sylvia turned the hand crank again. "My foot hurts too much to use the pedals. You'll have to do it."

"I can't!" If there was one thing I was certain of, it was that I could not, and *should not*, do this.

With the next turn of the crank, the engine came to life. Sylvia darted out of the way as the Renault rolled forward. I gripped the wheel but had no idea what else to do. The automobile rolled out from its crate, then continued rolling toward the cargo doors.

"The brake!" Sylvia called. "Push down on the pedal!"

I looked down. There were two pedals, and I had no idea which was which. I closed my eyes and pushed down on one with my foot, just as the Renault bumped the cargo doors. They split apart, and the Renault stopped there.

"Keep your foot down!" Sylvia limped toward me, then opened the Renault's door and turned the key. The engine sputtered off. Sylvia pulled another lever, explaining, "That will keep the car from rolling forward any farther."

"Did we damage it?" I asked.

I got out of the automobile, and we ran around to the front. One side looked a little banged up and I cringed to see it. I couldn't begin to imagine how much trouble I'd be in now.

"At least we're free," Sylvia said, then shrugged. "My father will be furious with me. Come on!"

She wrapped an arm around my shoulder and I thought that despite everything, I saw her smile, which made me smile too.

As I helped her back upstairs, I wondered if this was how it felt to be a companion, something more than a friend, perhaps. I liked this feeling, of helping to save Sylvia. Maybe I liked this even more than writing questions in my notebook.

We had several flights of stairs to climb before we reached the purser's office, and both of us were out of breath from our hurry. Miss Gruber was there as well, nearly in a full panic as she spoke to the purser.

"There must be more that you can do!" She clutched the purser's arm and from his expression, the strength of her grip was hurting him.

Sylvia stepped forward. "Miss Gruber?"

Her governess let out a cry and rushed forward, pulling Sylvia into a close hug as tears streamed down her face. "Oh, my dear, Sylvia, where were you all this time? I've been horribly worried!"

"We were locked into the cargo hold." Sylvia nodded my way. "Without Hazel's help, I'd still be trapped down there."

"Why would you ever go down to the cargo hold?" Miss Gruber asked.

Sylvia's expression hardened. "It's about the money—"

Before she could continue, I jumped in. "Miss Gruber says that I remind her of herself when she was younger."

"What does that have to do with Sylvia's absence?" Miss Gruber asked.

I turned to Sylvia. "I have four brothers. If there was anything in the world they needed, I would help them, even if it made my life more difficult. Back in your room, I saw a drawing of Miss Gruber when she was a child. She had four brothers too, and also one sister." Now I looked at Miss Gruber. "I would guess that sisters would help each other even more. Your sister owed four hundred and twenty pounds in debt. When Mrs. Mollison begged you to help her pay it off, there was only one thing you could do."

Sylvia's eyes widened. "Mrs. Mollison is your sister?"

Miss Gruber stepped backward, staring at me. "How did you know?"

"When we had supper together in the Parisien, Mrs. Mollison said her father believed that unless she had an original thought, writing was a waste of ink. You told me nearly the same thing in your cabin earlier today. Your father was wrong about that, by the way."

Sylvia said, "That's why you and Mrs. Mollison have acted like such close friends." Her voice remained as accusing as before. "But you never should have given her my family's money."

"It was a loan, not a gift." Miss Gruber seemed to have crumpled with shame. "I didn't want to do it, but Letha told me they were threatening to put her in prison for failing to repay her debts. What else could I do?"

"You should have told me," Sylvia said. "Or wired a message to my father first. You know he would have given his permission."

Miss Gruber frowned. "Letha claimed they had a plan to pay it all back before we reached New York. No one would have to know. Until the card game last night, I didn't know their plan was to get Mrs. Abelman's stock certificates."

"You should have known the kind of people they are," Sylvia said. "You stood right beside Mrs. Mollison as she held Hazel's stolen shoulder bag."

Miss Gruber's shoulders sank even further. "They didn't steal the notebook. I did that."

My heart skipped a beat. "Why?"

"You said you wanted to write about the secrets of the *Titanic*. What greater secret could there be on this ship than what I had done?"

At least a dozen greater secrets, I thought, but I only said, "You thought I'd write about you? That's why you asked the Mollisons to stop me."

"You must understand, I love Miss Thorngood, almost as much as a mother would. I thought something in the notebook would prove how unfit you would be as her companion. Instead, I read the words of a young lady who was intelligent and curious and who was trying very hard to reach her dream. I knew I had to make everything right again. I hope you can forgive me."

"You did make it right." I turned to Sylvia. "The receipt you found in the cargo hold was for my ticket on this ship. Miss Gruber paid for it."

"With my own funds," Miss Gruber said. "I put the receipt in my trunk, hoping no one would find out."

Sylvia smiled from me over to Miss Gruber. "I wish you had told me from the beginning, but I'm glad to know the truth."

Miss Gruber folded her arms around Sylvia again, then said, "I will repay the Thorngoods from my own funds. I will not accept any money that comes from Mrs. Abelman's stock certificates."

The purser had become distracted with the needs of other passengers, but now he looked down at Sylvia. "Miss Thorngood, we were all quite worried for you."

"She seems to be well enough," Miss Gruber said, "but I would like to get her back to her room."

"Where was she?"

Sylvia looked to me to answer. I said, "The cargo area, down on the Orlop Deck. But someone locked the door while we were in there."

"And how did you escape?"

I winced, dreading to have to explain this. "There is an automobile . . ."

"The Renault?" His face paled. "Tell me you did nothing to the Renault!" He turned to Miss Gruber. "If you'll excuse me, I must know what damage was done down there."

"I'd better come too," Miss Gruber said. "I will need to see it for myself so that I can report it to her parents."

"No passengers are allowed there," the purser said.

Miss Gruber straightened up. "When Edgar Thorngood asks for an explanation of what happened to his daughter today, would you like me to tell him, or shall I send him to you?"

The purser swallowed hard. "Very well." He then turned to me. "You and Miss Thorngood will go up to the boat deck, where I know you will be safe. Tell the officer on deck that I sent you there."

"Sir," I said, "they have seen far too much of me already. Is there somewhere else—"

"The boat deck. Now!" Miss Gruber ordered.

I walked back to Sylvia. "They'll be happy that you were found," I said. "But they've surely had their fill of seeing me."

THIRTY-FOUR

Time Stopped

As I had predicted, Sylvia was warmly greeted by Officer Kent, who claimed it was an "utter miracle" that she had been found. I didn't see it that way. She'd been found because I figured out where she must be. That was good sense, not a miracle. When I tried pointing this out, I received a glare and the comment that "until Miss Thorngood's governess returns, I assume you'll want your usual room up here."

"I'd rather remain out here on the bridge," I said. "I'm writing a news story and watching everyone at work—"

"No, Miss Rothbury." He opened the door to the officers' lounge and we both entered. "White Star has no interest in the thoughts of a twelve-year-old passenger from third class. While you wait, since Miss Thorngood has had such a difficult time, I'll have some tea sent in for her."

Sylvia called after him as he left, "Hazel had a difficult time too!"

If he heard us, he said nothing and only continued to walk away. Meanwhile, Sylvia lay back in one of the chairs, resting her head on her hands. "How can you be so alert, Hazel? I'm exhausted."

A clock was set inside the room. I should have been more tired, that was true. By now it was just after eleven o'clock.

"It's terribly cold out there," Sylvia said. "I hope Miss Gruber will hurry so that we can all return to our rooms and go to bed."

I wanted that too, but I was curious about the Marconi Room once again. As it was before, the door was slightly ajar, and the operator's back was turned to it. When I pushed open the door to the lounge, if I listened carefully, I could hear him tapping out messages once again.

"Sylvia," I whispered. "You know Morse code, right?"

"Yes, Hazel." Her eyes were closed now. "But can we talk about this in the morning?"

I walked over and shook her arm. "Just translate one code for me. I want to know what kind of messages he's sending."

"Those messages are private."

"One message, please. Then I'll let you sleep."

Sylvia groaned, then pulled herself back to her feet and trudged out the door behind me. We crept to the door of the Marconi Room and began listening to the transmissions.

For the first minute or two, it was the same pattern as before, tapping out the code, then the scratching of the operator's pen as he recorded the messages coming in. I had my notebook out but wasn't bothering to write the codes down anymore. I was simply trying to listen, with my eye on the Morse code in front of me, trying to figure out any of the letters as they were tapped out.

"This message is just a passenger's simple hello from the *Titanic*," Sylvia whispered. "Nothing worth—"

That was as far as she got before we heard an angry shout from the operator, then he slammed his headphones down on the desk. "You'll make me lose my hearing!" he shouted. He was in the room alone, so the message he had just received must have come through very loud.

The operator grunted, then began tapping out a reply, this one so forceful that I was able to distinctly record the dots and dashes into my notebook.

Sylvia watched as I wrote them down, her eyes widening as she mouthed the different letters. By the time I finished, she motioned for me to follow her back into the officers' lounge.

When she closed the door, her eyes were wide. "I can't believe it," she said. "How much of that did you understand?"

I stared down at the code. "Only a few of the letters."

She held out her hand for the notebook and began writing. "I hardly dare to speak the words that he just sent to that other ship."

When she returned the notebook to me, I read aloud, "Shut up! Shut up! I'm working Cape Race!" Then I looked up, my eyes wide. "Is that really what he wrote back? That's terribly rude."

"That's what he wrote, I'm sure of it," Sylvia said firmly.

"What's Cape Race?" I asked.

"That's in Canada. It'll be the nearest receiving station to us," Sylvia said. "After I found the missing money, I asked the purser about sending my parents a telegraph. He told me it would be sent to Cape Race tonight, if it could be sent before the *Titanic* went out of range again. He explained that the operator has to hurry with these messages when he has the chance, because within two or three hours, we'll lose the signal again, and I'm sure he has a lot of messages to send."

"Then who is he telling to shut up?"

Sylvia pressed her lips together. "I know that when my father receives transmissions from test pilots, if they are far away, the signal is faint and difficult to hear. When the signal grows louder, then the sender is closer."

"So, you think the message he received was from a ship that's close to us?" I asked.

Sylvia nodded. "Cape Race is very far away, so the operator won't hear the signal unless the volume of his headphones is as high as it can be. Now, if a new message came in from someone only twenty or thirty miles from us, that message would come through loud enough to—"

"Make him lose his hearing," I said. "That's what he said when he tore off his headphones. That's why he was angry."

"Then he sent a reply, telling the sender in the rudest possible way not to transmit to us again." Sylvia looked up. "What message do you suppose he received?"

I shrugged. It could have been anything at all, but if it was in keeping with so many other messages the *Titanic* had received today, it was an iceberg warning.

If that was true, and if it was coming from a ship near ours, then it meant we were not far from seeing icebergs ourselves.

Hearing some conversation outside, I snuck out of the room once more, seeing First Officer Murdoch dismiss one crewman, then walk to the helm of the ship, binoculars in hand. Everything on deck seemed perfectly still.

Almost without thinking, I walked out onto the bridge deck and leaned over the side rails. Using the light from the ship, I saw a thick mist hovering over the ocean waters. The moon had still not risen, making the stars seem even brighter in their sphere. Aside from the ship's engine propelling us forward, the night was almost entirely silent.

Sylvia came to stand beside me and gazed out over the water.

"What are you looking at?" she said.

"Nothing at all," I whispered. "But it's so much nothing ahead that worries me."

"What do you mean?"

For the next several minutes, I tried explaining refraction to Sylvia, how light would bend once it hit the water, throwing everything behind it at a different angle. She nodded, but still said, "I don't see how it matters for us. Even if the angle is slightly off, surely a little mist can't hide an entire iceberg."

Maybe it could, if it was a blue iceberg, or a dark one. My stomach seemed to roll within me. I trusted my gut now, and it was telling me to stay alert. Even if I were one of the lookouts right now sitting ninety feet over the deck, I could not have been searching the horizon any more carefully.

I turned around and stared up at the crow's nest. Sure enough, the two men up there were as alert as any lookouts ought to be. They were serious in their work, which made me feel better. Even if one lookout failed to spot something, surely the other one would.

Beyond that, if today's iceberg warnings were truly of any concern, the telegraph operators would have reported it, the captain would have posted the notes, and the officers would have shared their information with one another.

And the crew would have prepared themselves at all times for any emergencies.

Wouldn't they?

Once again I felt a prickling, right to my very center, reminding me to listen to my own instincts, to trust when something did not feel right.

And at the moment, nothing felt right.

Charlie had said the captain was required to post the warning messages. He had not done so.

The crew was supposed to hold a lifeboat drill earlier today. It had been canceled.

Nor were there enough lifeboats for everyone on the ship.

Sylvia touched my arm. "You look so worried, Hazel. Why?"

One of the lookouts above provided my answer. Before I could even open my mouth, the bell up in the crow's nest rang out with three distinct alarms. I heard one of the men call down, "Iceberg, right ahead!"

My eyes shifted toward the front of the ship. I opened my mouth to scream, but not a single sound came out.

I'd read about icebergs. Discussed them. Sketched them. Imagined them for days, every time I'd closed my eyes.

Nothing that I'd imagined compared to what I was seeing now.

The *Titanic* was headed directly for a large iceberg. It was tall and jagged and grew more terrible as we continued straight on toward it. Until seconds ago, it had been completely invisible.

Just as a dark iceberg would be.

THIRTY-FIVE

11:40 p.m.

Over the next two hours, I would learn something about time. Something devastating.

There are moments in life when time moves with its own will, not bound by any timekeeper's measure.

It may speed up, passing so fast that life itself becomes a blur, a memory before it is a moment.

On a different occasion, time may slow to a crawl, each second becoming an hour, a day, or a lifetime.

Which means that time cannot be trusted.

I began to understand that the instant I saw the iceberg looming in the distance, when the next thirty seconds passed so slowly that for all I knew, time itself had stopped completely. When everything stopped except for the *Titanic* itself, steadily moving forward.

Tick. Tick. Tick.

All eyes on the bridge turned to First Officer Murdoch, the man now in command. As slow as time moved for me, I thought that for him, every possible scenario must have flashed through his mind in only a fraction of a second.

Do nothing, and we would face a direct collision.

Turn to starboard, and we would career sideways into the iceberg.

There was only one chance for us, and from my view, it didn't look like much of a chance.

"Port your helm!" Murdoch shouted.

"They're going to turn the ship," Sylvia whispered.

The bridge erupted into an organized chaos. Each man flew into action to perform his duty, bells rang, and orders were shouted on all sides.

Despite all of that, the ship was still on a direct course toward the iceberg.

The nearer we came, the higher it rose above the deck, beautiful, yet still a frozen monster upon the water. As with all monsters, the most frightening of all was not what could be seen, but what was not seen. Its claws lay hidden below us.

If the seconds had crawled along before, that was nothing compared to how I felt now. Over the next thirty seconds, time sped up for me. The *Titanic* seemed to be racing forward, indifferent to the will of the crewmen trying desperately to shift its course.

Five seconds passed, and nothing had changed.

Ten seconds. The iceberg still lay directly ahead.

Then the engines stopped, and the ever-present humming

of the ship fell silent. Yet still we were drifting forward, as if pulled along by an unseen magnetic force.

"What happened to the engines?" I whispered to Sylvia, but she did not move. She did not breathe out a single word.

Fifteen seconds. The engines started again, and this time the *Titanic* angled sharply to the left, exposing the right side of the ship to the danger.

"We're going to make it." Sylvia's eyes were locked on the iceberg, as were mine. She clutched my hand. "Hazel, are we going to make it?"

Even before she finished speaking, a shudder ran through the ship. Something creaked below us. The entire ship seemed to bump ever so slightly. If I'd been asleep, I would never have noticed.

But here, standing on the deck and wide awake, I felt all of it, heard all of it. And I knew what this meant.

"Hazel?"

I heard Sylvia's voice, but once again, time was moving so slowly, the thought had not yet come that I should answer her.

The *Titanic* continued onward, sliding alongside the iceberg. The rails sheared off ice in chunks that fell onto the deck, only meters from where we stood. And still below us, muffled beneath the waterline, was the blunt sound of scraping, then tearing.

Then silence.

Once again, time stood still for me, the spell broken only when Sylvia touched my arm. "What has happened? Did we escape the worst of it?"

Did we?

I closed my eyes as every question I'd asked since boarding the ship ran through my mind. What would the lookouts do if they saw an iceberg? How long would it take the ship to stop if an obstacle was in the way? Did the lookouts have binoculars?

None of those questions mattered anymore. None of their answers mattered anymore.

Except for one answer only: The *Titanic* had a double hull on the bottom, but a single hull on the side.

If the iceberg had struck us on the bottom of the ship, we had a chance to survive.

But if it had struck us on the side . . .

I drew in a slow breath, trying to hold my thoughts together. Because I already knew the answer to that question, and it was devastating.

In that moment, once again, time could not be trusted.

Time.

Stood.

Still.

CHAPTER

THIRTY-SIX

11:50 p.m.

Within minutes, Captain Smith strode onto the bridge. This time, he did not pause to greet anyone nearby, not even to offer his customary smile. He stared at the iceberg, now at a slight distance from us, then gave his first order in four terse words: "Close the emergency doors."

"The doors are already closed," Officer Murdoch immediately replied.

From there, the other officers on board hurried over to speak to their captain, and he sent them out with new orders almost as quickly as they came in.

Yet my thoughts remained with the emergency doors. Mr. Waddington had told me that the bulkheads weren't completely sealed off because the firemen had to be able to move from one area to another, so they were fitted with watertight doors that could be closed from below or at the push of a button on the bridge.

Those doors had already been closed, which meant the firemen below were now bound to their fate. Unless they had escaped, they were trapped until the doors opened again.

If they opened again.

The *Titanic* had fifteen bulkheads, creating sixteen watertight compartments. If two flooded, we would remain afloat. Even if three or four compartments flooded, we still had a chance.

"Keep hoping," I told Sylvia. "I think it's likely that the iceberg cut only one small part of the ship."

She nodded, but her eyes remained as wide as saucers and her voice trembled as she said, "I hope you're right." She pointed to several passengers who had emerged onto the promenade, still in their evening clothes. "Nobody else seems worried."

Perhaps at first, their expressions had seemed cautious, but once they saw the scattered chunks of ice on the deck, laughter broke out among them.

"Look at this, my dear," one man said to his wife. "It must have rained ice!"

He picked up a small piece of ice and carried it over to show her. Other passengers gathered around them, asking each other what had happened to put ice on the deck.

"Does the ice pose any danger to us?" another man called to a crewman standing near the rails.

He smiled over at them, looking as if he didn't have a care in the world. "Oh no, it was nothing at all. We just hit an iceberg."

"You heard the way he spoke," Sylvia said. "He wouldn't sound so cheerful if there were any problems. We must have turned enough to avoid the worst of it."

But they had spoken cheerfully even when the ship was on fire. Those were their standing orders, to never alarm the passengers.

And more worrying still, as soon as the passengers on the deck turned away, the crewman leaned over the side of the rails, possibly trying to see if there had been any damage. After a minute, he straightened up and looked over at Captain Smith, shaking his head with an expression so grim, I could see it in the dim light from the deck.

"How could ice do any real damage to a ship with a steel hull?" Sylvia asked. "Surely the metal is stronger than ice."

Stronger than a growler, perhaps, or white ice, the newer, younger ice. But could that have been a blue iceberg, or a dark one?

From my left, I saw Mr. Ismay march onto the deck. At first, he had seemed angry, perhaps that the ship he had bragged would speed through iceberg territory was now at a complete stop. But within seconds of speaking to the captain, I watched his body begin to crumple. He looked around, then slowly walked to the very bow of the ship. One step followed another, then another, until he gripped the rails and stared forward. Never in my life had I seen anyone look so defeated.

Behind him, Captain Smith gave another order to one of his officers, who left in the direction of the Marconi Room.

"They're going to send a message to the other ships in the area," Sylvia whispered. "They're going to ask for help."

"How do you know that?" I asked.

Sylvia pointed to one of the round chunks of ice ahead of us on the deck. Very slowly, it was rolling forward.

"I don't know how much water there is," she said, "but the front of the ship must be taking on water already."

My eyes widened. "Charlie! We've got to find Charlie!"

"And Miss Gruber." Sylvia clutched my hands. "She was going down to the Orlop Deck to look at the cargo hold. If we are taking on water—"

"Then she's in the middle of it," I said. Sylvia pulled at me, wanting me to run with her, but I shook my head. "I don't know where Charlie is. He could be down there too!"

Sylvia grabbed the arm of a passing crewman. "Sir, can you tell me where the—"

"Sorry, there's no time," he replied, and hurried away.

I ran to another crewman. "Sir, we're looking for—"

"The two of you should grab life belts and put them on," he said. "It's only a precaution, but tell the others."

As he moved on, Sylvia and I turned to each other. "Even Charlie would want us to find Miss Gruber first," she said.

I agreed, but that wasn't the reason I felt frozen in place. I was already terrified to think about what might be happening below. Now Sylvia wanted us to go down there, and see it for ourselves?

"Please, Hazel. Miss Gruber needs us!"

I turned to her, feeling almost numb. Her eyes were so desperate, so fearful, it snapped me back to reality. And nothing in my life had ever felt so real as this very moment.

I nodded. "Let's go."

I followed Sylvia to the stairs. We ran down them as fast as we could, lower and lower into the ship. On our way, we passed several passengers who were beginning to enter the stairways, all of them asking one another what the commotion was.

"I felt a vibration near my cabin wall," one woman remarked.

"Perhaps it was only the shudder of the engines," a man next to her said. "I heard them shut down, just for a few seconds."

"They are ordering life belts for everyone," Sylvia announced as we passed.

"Why on earth would they do that?" someone responded, but by then we were already hurrying farther down the stairs.

At C Deck, we encountered the first waist-high gate. Third-class passengers had gathered there, hoping to continue moving higher on the ship, but so far, they didn't seem to have passed by.

I swung the gate open and pointed up the stairs, shouting, "That way!" Yet the group up front only stared at me, not understanding my English. I pointed again, then grabbed the arm of one woman, pulling her forward. Now they understood and began walking forward, though they seemed uncomfortable, and a few even turned back. Could they not dare to break the rule about entering first class, even now?

Charlie's words from my first day on board returned to me, almost as clear as if he were saying them now: "If there ever is a problem, do not wait to find out. You get to your feet, and you move toward safety."

"Move!" I shouted at the passengers. "Please just move!"

There was no time to see what happened next. Sylvia and I continued on down the stairs, surprised at how quickly the crowd of people thinned out. As we passed E Deck, where my own cabin was, I saw several cabin doors open as the passengers talked with one another about the vibrations they had felt. Some were at the far end of their cabins, opening their portholes in hopes of seeing for themselves whether anything was wrong.

"This way!" I grabbed Sylvia's hand, pulling her along with me toward the stairs that would take us to F Deck. There we were stopped by a barred gate rising from floor to ceiling. I grabbed the bars and shook it, hoping to move it aside, but it would not budge.

"It's locked," a crewman said, walking up the stairs from the other side. "You don't want to come down here, miss."

He looked a little like I imagined my father looked in his younger years, and the expression in his eyes seemed as haunted as Papa's must have been before he was lost as sea.

This crewman knew he was already lost at sea as well.

I said to him, "Please, sir, is there any way past this gate?"

"My governess went down to the Orlop Deck with the ship's purser," Sylvia added.

He slowly shook his head. "With my apologies, miss, the Orlop Deck flooded in the first ten minutes after we were struck. If they weren't already out, they probably never got out."

"Oh." Sylvia clutched my hand, her nails digging into my skin. Her shoulders folded inward, and tears welled in her eyes, but she pressed her lips together. "Miss Gruber had her faults, but she was a good woman."

The crewman said, "I was the last man out from my area. Heard the alarm bells ringing so I knew it was only a matter of seconds before the emergency doors closed for good." He sighed. "A lot of good men were left behind. They'll continue on as long as possible down there."

"What about you?" I asked. The legs of his trousers were wet almost to the knees, and behind him, water was seeping onto the deck.

He smiled through the sadness in his eyes. "There is still a lot I can do. Now run along, both of you. Get up to the boat deck while you can."

"We have a friend," I said, "a porter—"

"It'll be women and children only," he said. "Now, I'm sorry, but I'm needed elsewhere."

Before I could say anything more, he ran on. I turned to Sylvia and saw tears on her cheeks. "It's my fault," she said. "Miss Gruber went down there because I had been down there."

"You did nothing wrong," I said. "Besides, ten minutes is enough time for Miss Gruber to get out. She might be up on the boat deck waiting for you right now."

Sylvia sniffed. "Do you really believe that?"

No, I didn't. The water must have begun entering the Orlop Deck as soon as the iceberg cut through the ship's hull. Miss Gruber wouldn't have had ten minutes to get out. She'd likely had less than one minute.

One minute. When Papa's death was reported to us, his crewmates said he'd promised to return in one minute if he couldn't help the other sailors get out. None of them returned.

I tried to smile, pretending that I wasn't collapsing too. I remembered the lesson from the other crewmen and spoke as confidently as I could. "I'm sure Miss Gruber is fine. You need to get up top and find her, or else she'll come back down to find you."

"What about you?"

"I have to find Charlie."

"But you don't know where to even begin!"

"I'll figure it out. But he may have only a few minutes left. I need to find him."

Sylvia brushed away her tears. "Miss Gruber will have to wait a little while longer. I'll help you find Charlie. Then we'll all go up top together. Where do we start?"

I looked around. Near me was a sign noting that all cabins beyond this point were for the crew only. Charlie had told me that his room was on E Deck, same as mine. If he had been locked in his room, then he wouldn't be far away.

"You take the rooms at port, I'll go aft," I said. "Knock on every door and then pray we don't hear Charlie's voice in answer."

Because if we did, I had no idea how we'd break the lock into his room. And water was already spilling into the passageways only one deck below where we now stood.

Our search had not yet begun, and we were already nearly out of time.

THIRTY-SEVEN

12:20 a.m.

"Charlie!"

I shouted his name as I ran through the passageway, which was now crowded with crewmen. Some were hurrying toward the stairs, while a few others shouted at the younger crewmen to return to their quarters and remain there.

I followed the younger boys. Charlie probably shared a room with them.

I caught up to one boy as he walked toward his open door and touched his arm to get his attention. "Charlie Blight," I said, almost breathless. "Do you know Charlie Blight?"

The boy nodded. "Aye, miss. Where is he?"

My brow furrowed. "You haven't seen him?"

"Not since this mornin'. Someone heard Charlie got himself into some trouble up in first class."

"He did," I said. "Where would they have taken him?"

The boy shrugged. "Couldn't say."

I thanked him and started to leave, but the boy called after me. "Oi, miss!"

"Yes?"

"Is it true? We've hit an iceberg?"

I nodded, but could find no words to add to that.

He frowned, as if he already knew what that meant for him. With the saddest possible voice, he said, "I'm only fourteen."

I stepped toward him again. "They say it's women and children for the lifeboats. Surely that includes you too."

"It's women and children," he said. "I'm crew."

So was Charlie.

He shifted his weight from one foot to the other. "If you survive this, tell my family that I loved 'em. My last name is Glendow."

I wanted to offer him comfort, to tell him that there was still hope, but it would have been a lie, and we both knew it. When we had received the news about Papa, I'd had to be the one to comfort my mum. I'd learned then how to stay strong, but it was even harder this time.

With tears at the creases of my eyes, I nodded back at him. "Glendow. I'll tell them."

The boy tipped his hat to me, then hurried along in the direction the other boys had gone. I heard a door close, though water would soon be seeping beneath it. It was only a matter of time.

Time. We were running out of time.

The sharp feelings of panic returned to me again. Were the decks below us already flooded? Was the crewman we had spoken to only minutes ago . . . gone?

If so, then I also knew what that meant for all the boys who'd just been ordered back into their rooms. My broken heart shattered even more. They hadn't been given a chance to save themselves.

Nor would Charlie, if we could not find him.

"Hazel!" Sylvia rounded a corner, then I hurried over to her. The fear in her eyes was so fierce, I worried she might begin to lose her reasoning. "I couldn't find him," she said. "I knocked on every door, called his name—"

"Me too, but I don't think he's down here."

"I'm not sure that it matters," Sylvia said. "Maybe he's already—"

"Of course it matters!" I nearly shouted those words at her. "Charlie is my friend!"

"I know that!" Sylvia grabbed my shoulders, forcing me to look at her. "But I heard what that boy said to you. Charlie won't get on the lifeboats, even if he was up on the deck. He's part of the crew."

I shook my head. "You don't know that."

"I do. I heard it myself!"

"No, you don't *know* that, Sylvia. We've got to find Charlie, to at least give him the chance."

Yet even as I spoke, I knew that Sylvia was right. What if we rescued Charlie now, only to abandon him on the deck anyway?

"Now what?" Sylvia's eyes traveled downward at the sound of water splashing against the stairways near us. This time when she spoke, I heard the fear in her voice. "What I told you before is true. I can't swim."

"Then you need to get up top," I said. "How's your ankle?"

"It's sore, but I can stay a little while longer. I can help you."

I shook my head. "The ship is sinking! We only have a few minutes until the water is on this deck too!"

"Then we don't have much time. How can I help?"

An idea came to me, one that could be vital. "Close the portholes," I said. "The ship is getting lower in the water. When this deck is at the waterline, water will spill into the ship through those portholes."

Now Sylvia nodded. "I'll get them closed. Please don't stay here for one minute longer than you must."

"There're only a few more places that I can look, then I'll find you, I promise."

Sylvia ran one way as I continued racing along the deck, though I was now in the area for third-class cabins. The passageway was filling with people, but many doors remained closed. Surely the guests couldn't sleep through all of this commotion! What were they waiting for? Didn't they know how serious this situation was?

"Charlie!" I called. "Charlie!"

A man in a fine wool suit passed by me. "You must not be down here, miss. Go upstairs!"

He couldn't have been third class, and likely not even second class, based on the way he was dressed. I asked, "Sir, are you part of the crew?"

"I designed this ship," he said. "Pray that I will be forgiven for any mistakes I made, and that White Star will be cursed for refusing to listen to my warnings."

"Is there any chance of saving the ship?" I asked.

He stared directly at me. "The *Titanic* will be underwater sooner than any of us want to believe. Wherever your friend is—Charlie—if he is down here, then he is already lost to the sea. You must save yourself."

"There's still time—"

"No, there isn't! I have enough guilt as it is. Please go up the stairs!"

"Sir, where is the—"

I'd wanted to ask him where Charlie could be, but he was gone too fast. If E Deck was beginning to flood, I needed to find Sylvia again, as I'd promised. So, I turned to run in the direction she'd gone, but stopped one last time to look back, hoping Charlie would be there following me.

He wasn't.

When I turned forward again, I knew I was leaving him behind.

That single thought devastated me. Had I just abandoned him? Was he in one of the cabins I'd missed, pounding at a locked door, certain that someone would come for him?

My fear of that became so real that I turned to go back for one more look when Sylvia called my name.

"Hazel, I need your help! Over here!"

My feet squished within my boots, and I realized water had begun flowing across E Deck. I wasn't sure how long it would take to rise, but one glance toward the stairs told me it would come faster than I believed possible.

I ran toward Sylvia, who was desperately motioning me forward, but my only thought now was that the bulkheads ended here, at E Deck. If water was on this deck now, the entire hull was about to flood.

And when it did, the weight of the flooded bulkheads would pull this entire ship down to the ocean floor.

By then, I had reached Sylvia, but my eyes went to a cabin door on the right, already opened a crack. A walking stick was poking out through the gap with a carved eagle's head at the top.

I knew that walking stick.

Mrs. Abelman's room was supposed to be on D Deck, one level above us. What was she doing here?

That wasn't the question that mattered, of course. What mattered most was that Mrs. Abelman seemed to be trapped.

THE CALIFORNIAN

7:20 PM
The Titanic intercepts three messages from the Californian, only fifty miles ahead, warning of three large icebergs in the area.

Captain Smith gives no orders to change course or to slow down.

Captain Stanley Lord orders his ship, the Californian, to stop for the night, believing the area was too dangerous. Before going off duty, he notices the Titanic's lights in the distance, about five miles away.

11:07 PM
The Californian sends a message directly to the Titanic, warning of ice.

The Titanic's wireless operator, Jack Phillips, radios back, "Shut up! Shut up! I am working Cape Race!"

11:30 PM
The Californian's wireless operator goes to bed for the night, ten minutes before the Titanic strikes the iceberg.

12:05 PM
The Titanic spots the Californian in the distance and fires distress rockets. Officers on board the Californian ask Captain Lord about the rockets. He is in bed and suggests they contact the Titanic with a Morse Lamp, but the Titanic never responds. Their wireless operator is never awakened.

2:00 AM
Seeing the fading lights in the distance, the Californian believes the Titanic is leaving the area. Twenty minutes later, the Titanic sinks.

3:00 AM
The Californian sees rockets coming from the south. These are from the Carpathia, coming to rescue any survivors.

4:16 AM
Back on duty, the Californian's wireless operator hears the chatter about the Titanic and notifies the Captain.

5:30 AM
Captain Lord orders the Californian to the coordinates from the Titanic's last message. It will clean some of the wreckage after the Carpathia has rescued the survivors.

THIRTY-EIGHT

12:40 a.m.

"Mrs. Abelman, I'm here!" I cried as I rushed to Sylvia's side. Together we shoved our weight against the door, but it wouldn't give. "What's blocking the door?"

"She came down here to help me close the portholes," Sylvia explained.

Mrs. Abelman added, "The one in here was wide open. I closed it but the water spilling into this room lifted a trunk, and now it's lodged against the door. I can't move it on my own."

I looked down. Sure enough, water was seeping out from beneath her door.

"Let's try again," Sylvia said. "One-two-three!"

Our second attempt at pushing on the door may have widened it by another centimeter, but that wasn't nearly enough.

"What now?" Sylvia asked. "This won't work!"

"I'll begin pulling everything out of the trunk," Mrs.

Abelman said. "That should lighten its weight. Give me a minute to do that."

Sylvia leaned against the wall to catch her breath. As she did, I saw the tears in her eyes. "We're not going to survive this, are we." It was a sentence, not a question.

"You will," I said. "I can get Mrs. Abelman out of her room. You should go up to the boat deck."

"No, we'll get her out together." Sylvia stood again and called through the gap. "We're going to try again, Mrs. Abelman!"

We lined up beside each other, and once again rammed our shoulders into the door, but it had already given up its few centimeters. It would open no farther for us.

"Hazel!" Sylvia looked down at the water, already up to her ankles.

This was happening too fast. How could this all be happening so fast?

Mrs. Abelman must have seen the water too. Through the door, she said, "Girls, I want you both to go up top now."

"No!" I cried. "Keep unloading that trunk! We'll try again."

"The trunk is empty, Hazel. It's still too heavy. Go up top now."

I turned to Sylvia, hoping she had better ideas than me. "What can we do? What else?"

Sylvia's eyes moistened again, but she began looking around. "We can break down the door. Look for an ax or a hatchet."

I liked the idea, but we weren't going to find tools like that anywhere near the passenger rooms.

"Knock on the other room doors," I said. "A lot of passengers are still down here. We can warn them, and maybe find someone to help us."

"I think help is here," Sylvia said, her voice cracking with emotion. "But it doesn't seem possible."

I turned to see who she was looking at, and there stood a very wet Miss Gruber, her tidy bun now hanging crookedly from her head, her stiff black clothes clinging to her.

Miss Gruber saw Sylvia and let out a cry of deep emotion. She ran forward, her heels kicking up the water already on the deck. She pulled Sylvia into a tight hug, openly weeping now. "What are you doing down here? Why aren't you on the boat deck?"

"We came looking for you!"

"The purser and I were on our way upstairs when the boat struck the iceberg," she said. "Another minute and we'd have been trapped in there. The water came in so fast."

"Miss Gruber," I said, pointing to Mrs. Abelman's door, where the walking stick was still poking through. "We need help."

She immediately stood tall and called through the door. "Please stand back. We're going to get you out of there." Then she turned to me and Sylvia. "When I pull on this walking stick, I want you to push on the door as well. Go!"

We pushed, and she pulled until she was grunting with the effort, but this time, the door was finally giving way. We heard a scraping sound, the trunk sliding across Mrs. Abelman's floor, and the door swung open.

I rushed in, expecting to find Mrs. Abelman ready to leave with us, or at least preparing to leave. Instead, she was at her writing desk holding a fountain pen in her hand. Scattered papers and a woman's hat were floating on the water around her.

"We need to go!" I said.

But Mrs. Abelman shook her head. "Some of the passengers down here don't speak English; they won't understand the orders that are being given. They haven't been to the upper decks before, so they won't know how to get to the lifeboats. But I do."

I didn't understand at first, not until Miss Gruber stepped into the room as well and said, "This might be our last chance." Mrs. Abelman only stared back at her. As if she could understand words that had not been spoken, Miss Gruber quietly added, "It's an honor to meet you, Mrs. Abelman. You are a better woman than I am—I can admit that."

"This is no time for either comparisons or compliments," Mrs. Abelman said. "I will be where I am needed most, and you must go where you are needed most."

I knew what those words meant, but I could not—I *would not*—accept it.

I took her hand, hoping to pull her along with me. "Please, Mrs. Abelman, you must come with us."

She wrapped her hand around mine. "When we first met, you promised that you were smart enough to get out of a difficult situation. Can you do that now?"

"Yes, but you must come with me."

"Do you know what Mr. Mollison whispered to me after the game last night?"

I didn't know, nor did I care. "Please, Mrs. Abelman. I'll help you."

"He asked what my wealth was for, if not to help people in need. Since then, I have thought about a phrase we have in Judaism, *tikkun olam*. It means to repair the world. If I can see the help that is needed and know how to give that help, then I have found the piece of the world that was meant for me to repair."

I shook my head. "You can't fix this. No one can."

She smiled at me and brushed a hand over my wet hair. "I was wrong before. I do still have a purpose for my life. That is to help the people down here."

The water was past my ankles now. Miss Gruber was already back in the passageway with Sylvia, knocking on doors and telling people to go upstairs.

Mrs. Abelman pointed to the satchel slung over my shoulder. "Is your notebook still in there?"

"Yes, but that doesn't matter either."

"Everything that we learn matters. Give me the notebook." When I did, she began stuffing it into the same metal box that Mr. Waddington had showed to me only two nights ago. Mrs. Abelman smiled. "I borrowed it for study and now I am giving it to you."

The box was only large enough to hold my notebook and pen, and they barely fit alongside other papers already inside, probably those belonging to Mr. Waddington. She closed the box up tight, then gave it to me. "This should protect your notebook from the water. Put this in your shoulder bag and keep it safe."

I did as she asked, but held out my hand to her. "You can't repair the world from down here."

"My world is this deck and the people on it. When everyone here is safe, I will come up too. Is that good enough?"

I nodded. It had to be good enough.

"Now protect those notes. The outside world needs to know what has happened here tonight." She squeezed my hand and smiled. "Hazel, it's time to go. Get on a lifeboat while you still can."

Tears began to fall as I left, though I was so wet now that no one would notice. My heart ached too much to look back at Mrs. Abelman one last time, but as I entered the corridor, I heard her sing, "You take the high road, and I'll take the low road, and I'll be in Scotland afore ye."

"Hazel, come see!" Sylvia called, gesturing me to the neighboring room. She and Miss Gruber were staring out the porthole window as colors lit up the dark night, accompanied by a popping sound like fireworks.

"Those are distress rockets," Miss Gruber said. "They are calling for help."

"Why aren't they sending out messages by Morse code?" I asked. "Then the other ships can answer the call."

"That's just it," Sylvia said. "If anyone had received the messages, they wouldn't need to fire those rockets. Nobody has answered our calls for help."

How was that possible? We had been receiving messages from other ships all day, warning of icebergs. Those ships couldn't be that far from us now, and I had thought that some were quite close.

But Sylvia had to be right. Nobody was receiving our messages. Nobody was coming.

"Let's go, Sylvia," Miss Gruber said, pulling her back along the passageway. "They are loading the lifeboats. We must get on while we still can."

"Hazel, are you coming?" Sylvia asked.

Mrs. Abelman entered the passageway. "Go with them, Hazel," she said, her voice as commanding as any ship's officer. "Now."

I turned to her again. "Earlier today, Charlie got into trouble and was removed from the deck by a ship's officer. Any idea where they might've taken him?"

The answer came immediately. "He'll be in the ship's hospital."

"Are you sure?"

"I have been on several tours of this ship. On one of them, I learned that the hospital has a padded room that can be locked from the outside. When necessary, that room can function as a brig."

Charlie had been locked all day inside a padded room? I couldn't imagine what that must have been like for him. What it must be like for him now.

"Where is the room?" I asked.

"Almost directly above us here," she said. "Go to D Deck and follow the signs."

"Thank you, I will!" Then I paused. "Remember, you promised to get to the lifeboats."

"I promised to try," she said. "Now hurry, Hazel, hurry. We are all running out of time."

THIRTY-NINE

1:05 a.m.

I was expecting to fight the crowds on D Deck, throngs of people trying to push their way onto the lifeboats.

Truthfully, I was expecting anything but what I saw.

"Hazel?" Sylvia and I looked at each other in total disbelief. She asked, "Have we crossed onto a different ship?"

"I think we have." A clock posted on the wall read just past one in the morning. More than an hour had passed since we'd struck the iceberg. Half of this ship was already flooded or was taking on water.

And the passengers here were acting as if they were attending an overnight party. Their life belts were on, which they seemed to find inconvenient while holding their drinks or wearing their wraps and furs. Some were gathering in groups to speak with one another about what they should do, while others stared out the windows. Surely, they could see that the ship was much lower in the water now.

Yet a waiter passed through with a tray of food, conducting himself as if this were an afternoon dinner party rather than a serious emergency. In the corner, a man played ragtime music at the piano. Dance music.

"I don't understand any of this," Sylvia whispered to me.

Nor did I. Didn't they care that the ship was going down? Or did they not know?

"This is a most inconvenient time for a lifeboat drill," one man was saying to a group around him. "I think I might go back to bed and speak with Captain Smith about this in the morning."

He yawned and left the room, but Miss Gruber said to those who remained, "This isn't a drill. Go upstairs and get on the lifeboats."

She walked on, intending for me and Sylvia to follow her, but I stood back, listening to one woman wave away Miss Gruber's words with a laugh. "The *Titanic* is unsinkable." She laid her handbag on the table, adding, "Whatever is happening, there is no danger."

Hearing a thump, she turned to see her handbag sliding sideways onto the floor.

Her husband took her arm. "My dear, we must get you upstairs at once."

"My handbag," she cried, but he continued to pull her forward.

"Stay close to me, girls," Miss Gruber said.

"I can't," I told her. "Not yet."

She turned. "This is no time to be stubborn."

"I have to find Charlie."

Miss Gruber shook her head. "We must stay together."

"He's locked in that room because of me!" I said. "I asked for his help, so I have to help him now."

Miss Gruber nodded at me with something that looked like respect. "You are not the young lady I first judged you to be. But you must come—"

"I'll help Miss Rothbury." We turned, seeing Mr. Waddington step forward from the crowd. His brows were pressed low, and deep lines crossed his forehead. I hadn't noticed him earlier, but here he was now.

"Promise me that she will get on a lifeboat," Miss Gruber said.

"We only have to find her friend, then I will put her in a lifeboat myself."

Miss Gruber nodded, then took Sylvia by the hand, and they hurried upstairs.

"Come with me," Mr. Waddington said.

I followed at his side, but asked, "How did you know about Charlie?"

"I just saw Mrs. Abelman below. I understand that she gave you my metal box."

"Yes, sir." I noticed then that Mr. Waddington's trousers were wet up to his knees and he wore no life belt. That concerned me.

"Will you take care of yourself, sir?" I asked.

He smiled, rather sadly. "I will care for those who need to

get on the lifeboats, which includes you. If the water reaches your knees, I will insist you go up top while I finish finding Charlie on my own. Agreed?"

I didn't know how long we would have until this deck began to flood too, but surely we had enough time to find Charlie. Besides, Mrs. Abelman still hadn't come up from below.

"Has there been a reply from any rescue ships?" I asked Mr. Waddington. "Is anyone coming to help us?"

"I don't know. We must pray for as much time as possible."

There it was again, the question of time. Every minute mattered now, yet holding on to those minutes felt like holding smoke in my hands.

"I saw the distress rockets," I said. "Isn't the *Californian* close by? Surely they saw the rockets."

"I've been told the *Californian* is only twenty miles away," Mr. Waddington said. "I find it impossible to believe their lookouts didn't see the flares, but I've heard no word that anyone is coming."

I stopped to stare at him. "What about calls from the Marconi Room?"

"I asked the same question. There was no response from the *Californian*. They heard from the *Frankfurt*, but the operator questioned whether our problem was as serious as we claimed. Our next hope is that the *Carpathia* will answer. They are nearly sixty miles away, but perhaps they have responded already and are on their way."

Sixty miles? Even if the *Carpathia* did answer, sixty miles was a long distance. Too long.

Tick. Tick. Tick.

They'd never get here in time.

By then, we had reached a lower entrance for the ship's hospital. Mr. Waddington opened the door and led me through a small corridor lined with cabinets detailing every sort of medical equipment a physician might need while on the ship.

A nurse passed by, her arms supporting the weight of a man with one leg in bandages, trying to help him up the stairs. "What are you doing in here?" She motioned us to come along with her. "There is nothing we can do for you here. We must get up to the boat deck."

"Charlie Blight, the porter. Is he locked in a room somewhere here?" I asked.

The nurse's eyes widened. "Oh my goodness. He's been so quiet in there, I must have forgotten about him!"

"Are there keys to his room?"

"Yes, but the physician has them, and I don't know where he is! I'm sorry I can't help more. I need to get these patients upstairs!" She left with the injured passenger, and I looked to Mr. Waddington for answers. What were we supposed to do now?

"We can manage this," he said, walking into a room marked for patient recovery. There at the end of the room was a sturdy wooden door. On the other side of it, I suspected, was a padded room.

But the door was so big, and so thick, we'd have no chance of breaking it down.

"It's a good thing I'm an engineer." Mr. Waddington stopped beside a desk with a surgical tray on the counter. He rummaged through the various tools and when he couldn't find what he was looking for, he opened the desk drawers. "There it is!" He lifted a tool that looked similar to a screwdriver, but with a flattened end, adding, "I don't want to know how this is used in surgery."

Nor did I, but I also wasn't sure how he thought it could help Charlie. The end was much too large to fit in the lock and I doubted it was strong enough to pry open that thick door.

I ran ahead of Mr. Waddington, banging on the door and shouting out Charlie's name. Immediately, I heard his answer.

His voice was groggy and dull, as if he'd been sleeping. "Hazel? What are you doing here?"

"We're rescuing you."

"Rescuing me from what?" He was quiet a moment, then said, "I'm in enough trouble as it is. You'll only make it worse if you open this door."

Mr. Waddington lifted the tool to begin prying a pin up from one of the door hinges. As he worked, he said, "Charlie, the ship has hit an iceberg."

Now I felt the silent tension coming from the other side of this door. When he spoke, Charlie's voice was low and as serious as I'd ever heard him. "Get me out of this room. Please."

Mr. Waddington popped out the first pin, then began working on the other. As he did, I said, "Didn't you feel it happen?"

"I was asleep. I felt the ship vibrate and I heard the engines stop. I thought we must have finally come into an area of icebergs and stopped for the night. How bad is it?"

By now, Mr. Waddington was on the final pin and the door was beginning to widen. I waited to answer until he had finished and slid the door aside.

Charlie was standing in a room that was made entirely of fabric padding. Water from this deck began seeping into the fabric walls, climbing upward.

"The ship is going to sink," I told him. "If we hurry, we might still get a seat on the lifeboats."

For the rest of my life, I would never forget the way Charlie stared back at me, his eyes sad, but with a firm resolve. He said, "*You* must get a seat there, Hazel. You must survive to tell our story."

"Take her up to the boat deck and see that she gets a seat," Mr. Waddington said. "I will stay and help anyone else still down here."

I followed Charlie up the stairs, the same way the nurse had gone. Yet my thoughts had become numb, and I barely could make myself look at him.

Charlie was not planning to get on a lifeboat.

Like the other crewmen on board, he intended to go down with the ship.

CHAPTER
FORTY

1:20 a.m.

My heart felt hollow as I climbed the stairs with Charlie at my side. We should have had so much to talk about. I had expected to tell him everything about this past day, how his courage to find the paper in the Mollisons' room might have saved Sylvia's life. I even wanted to tell him about seeing the iceberg, and about the crewman on F Deck who knew he'd never get out, and about Mrs. Abelman, who might not get out either.

But none of that mattered now. I only wanted to tell Charlie that he *had* to get out.

"Have you written your story yet for the newspaper?" Charlie asked.

I nearly choked on my reply. "Why does that matter?"

It didn't matter. How could he ask me to care about some silly dream of a future writing for a newspaper? I might not have any future at all.

And Charlie already knew he didn't.

"It's all right," he said, answering the question I still refused to ask. "You're going to be all right."

Did he really think that was all I cared about? What about him?

For that matter, what about Mrs. Abelman and Mr. Waddington, both of them still below, on decks that were already filling with water?

"Mrs. Abelman won't be able to climb the stairs with so much water," I said. "We should go back—"

"No, Hazel," Charlie said.

"But—"

"No, Hazel. Listen to me." Charlie gestured with his hand. "*I* will go back. *I* will help Mrs. Abelman up the stairs. But I can't help her until I know you are safe in a lifeboat. So please, come with me."

I followed him, though the passengers on these decks seemed as calm as the others I'd seen on D Deck. Crewmen were knocking on each door as they moved through the passageway, calling out, "On the orders of Captain Smith, please make your way to the boat deck promenade at once."

"It's a terribly cold night," one woman said as she followed us up the stairs. "What on earth could this be about?"

"I told you I felt something scrape along the side of the ship," her husband replied. "We'll be fine, of course, but this must be a precaution."

"You don't think it's anything more serious than that?" the wife replied.

"Not at all," came the answer. "If it was, you'd see a great deal more panic among the crew."

It was true that the crewmen were behaving with extraordinary calm, their voices firm but perfectly in control as they motioned passengers upstairs, handing out life belts to any women and children who did not have one.

Charlie grabbed one from a crewman and passed it over to me. "Do you know how to put this on?"

I put the vest on, locking my shoulder bag against my body, but I couldn't figure out the straps in front. At the next landing, Charlie pulled me aside and began tying the straps tight.

As he worked, he said, "I need to ask a favor of you. It's about my family."

Tears filled my eyes as I anticipated his question. "Please don't ask this, Charlie."

"I have to. My family lives in the States, in Connecticut. I need you to find my mother, tell her and all my family how much I love them, and that all I ever wanted was a way to take care of them. And please"—he swallowed hard—"please don't tell them that I was fired from my job. They shouldn't need to know that."

With the life belt on me now, I said, "They're saying the lifeboats are for women and children. If you *were* fired, you're not a crewman. You can claim a place on the boats."

"There aren't enough seats for everyone," he said. "I'd be ashamed to save myself if it meant that seat could not be claimed by Mrs. Abelman or you, or anyone else who'd deserve it more." He stared at me a moment, almost as if he wished to tell me something, then gestured toward the stairs. "Let's go. We can't have much time."

We climbed another set of stairs, then finally emerged onto the boat deck. The first thing I noticed was the music, cheery dance tunes similar to what had been playing down below. I looked for the musicians and found seven of them in a semi-circle near the lifeboats with their conductor leading them on. Strange as that was, I wondered if the music was helping to keep the passengers calm. After all, how bad could everything be if the band was playing such happy music?

Charlie led me across the deck, far more crowded now than I'd ever seen it before, with passengers lined up facing the lifeboats. Each boat was built of wood and seemed to be about nine meters long, with four rows in the middle to sit on and a seat at either end for two oarsmen.

A long rope was attached to each end of the lifeboat, which the crewmen were using to slowly lower the boat into the water. Officer Lightoller stood beside them, giving directions.

"Keep both ends even," Lightoller shouted above the sounds of the music. "Be careful, mates."

"None of them know what they're doing," Charlie muttered. "Not like we would if we'd had that lifeboat drill anyway."

I looked down at the boat. It wasn't even half-full.

"Charlie!" I waved him over beside me. "Couldn't they fit more people onto the boats?"

He shrugged. "There's always the fear of capsizing once that boat hits the water. More people means more weight that has to be balanced." Now he glanced up at me. "But if I was giving the orders, I'd fill each boat and then some."

I had been looking around the deck, but I didn't see Sylvia or Miss Gruber anywhere. "Maybe they've already gotten onto a lifeboat."

"I'm sure they have," Charlie said. "They just lowered the third lifeboat here, and they'll be lowering some on the starboard side of the ship as well."

When that lifeboat was safely lowered, the crewmen moved on to the next boat. The crowd followed them, some pushing to the front.

"Women and children only," Officer Lightoller shouted. "Gentlemen, you will stand back."

Women began stepping forward, some of them with children in their arms or close at their sides. I saw the fear in their eyes, the shaking of their hands and legs as they watched others boarding the lifeboats. I understood that perfectly. Somehow, even a sinking ship felt safer than those small boats, about to be set adrift on a vast ocean in total darkness.

To my surprise, even up here, there was no pushing or shoving, no need to issue threats or warnings. We did see one woman clinging to her husband, crying out, "If you cannot go, I will not go."

"This is only a temporary separation," he answered. "They'll load the men later on, after all of you are safe. The sooner you are on the boat, the sooner I can get on the next boat."

I watched them embrace, then saw the expression in the eyes of the husband as he helped his wife onto the lifeboat.

"He knows," I whispered to Charlie. "He knows there will be no boat for him."

"All of the men know," Charlie said. "But there are times in life when we each must live for something greater than ourselves."

"The high road," I mumbled. "This is the high road."

For the first time, I understood the decision my father had made. He could have saved himself, but he chose the high road. He chose the lives of others over his own. My father had been a hero.

Charlie held out his hand, offering to help me into the lifeboat as well. "I'm glad we were friends, Hazel. When you finish your story, I hope you'll include me in it."

I climbed inside the lifeboat, taking a seat near the end. But I stood again to look for him, hoping for one last memory of him. To my dismay, he was already fading into the background, allowing other passengers forward. The tears that had been so close for an hour now spilled onto my cheeks. He gave one final glance back, waved goodbye, and after that, I could no longer see him.

Then a familiar face pushed through the others. "Make way!" Mrs. Mollison said. "We are first-class passengers."

"We are loading all classes," the officer replied. "Women and children only."

"It's just me and my sister." Mrs. Mollison pulled forward another figure in a dress and with a hat low over their face. "In you go, Mary."

"Mary" entered first, sliding to the far end of the row,

directly across from me, then Mrs. Mollison slid in next. Mrs. Mollison did have a sister, but this was not her.

Perhaps they felt the heat of my glare, because Mr. Mollison peeked up at me from beneath the hat. I started to open my mouth, ready to report them.

Mrs. Mollison leaned forward, hissing, "Keep this quiet, dearie, and a share of the stock certificates is yours."

I stared back at her. How could she possibly care about anything so meaningless in this moment? I opened my mouth to call to the crewman.

"No, wait!" Mrs. Mollison pulled out an envelope and began to tear it open. "The certificates are right here."

"What do they matter now?" I said. "Look around you, at what's happening!"

"Let the ship sink, what do I care?" Mrs. Mollison had unfolded the papers and was slowly shaking her head. "No, no, no," she mumbled. Then she glared up at me. "First chance I get, I'll dump you into the ocean myself. This is all your fault!"

LIFEBOATS

64 The number of lifeboats the Titanic could have carried.

20 The number of lifeboats the Titanic did carry on board.

18 The number of lifeboats that launched with passengers.

472 The total number of empty seats on the launched lifeboats.

30 The number of people who survived by sitting on the overturned Collapsible Lifeboat B.

9 The number of people pulled from the water after the Titanic sank.

1 The number of lifeboats that went back to save survivors in the water.

Uncaptioned photograph of Titanic survivors in a lifeboat after the sinking; 4/15/12; In the Matter of the Petition of the Oceanic Steam Navigation Company, Limited, for Limitation of Its Liability as owner of the steamship TITANIC, Admiralty Case Files, 1790 - 1966; Records of the United States, Record Group 21; National Archives at New York, NY.

FORTY-ONE

1:30 a.m.

I stood in the lifeboat, not sure exactly what had caused Mrs. Mollison's sudden anger, but that quickly became clear.

"Blank pages! They're blank!" she cried, then turned her venom toward me. "This is your fault!"

Her face twisted in anger as she clutched at my arm, but I squirmed free and darted out of the lifeboat, landing on the promenade. Somehow the *Titanic* seemed safer than anywhere with her.

Still in the lifeboat, Mr. Mollison grabbed the papers from his wife. "We were cheated!" he snarled, tossing the papers overboard.

"Sir!" Officer Lightoller raised a gun that had been at his side, aiming it directly at Mr. Mollison. "Leave that lifeboat at once!"

"No!" With a cry, Mrs. Mollison reached for her husband, but he was already leaving the lifeboat, his head hung in shame. Once on deck, he turned to her and said, "Don't worry for me. I'll be fine, my dear." Then he left, pausing briefly to stare blankly at me before slinking away.

Almost instantly, other passengers pressed forward around me, trying to take his place. One woman jostled me with her arm, knocking me to the deck. Worried that I might be trampled, I hurried to my feet, but it felt like I was standing up on a hill. The ship's angle must have changed. I wasn't the only one to notice. Officer Lightoller looked around, then said, "The ship is listing to port." He ordered the crewmen, "Get the passengers to the other side of the ship!"

Obeying the shouted orders, I left the port side of the ship and hurried over to the starboard side, hoping to find Charlie there, but with so many passengers now filling this area, it was impossible to see anyone beyond those already around me.

I pushed through the crowds lining up for the next lifeboat, looking for anyone I recognized, but I saw no one familiar, not even Charlie.

Behind me, a woman on the deck screamed. I turned in time to see a man cross to the outside of the rails, desperation in his eyes. A lifeboat had just been lowered beneath him.

Officer Murdoch, commanding this side of the ship, raised his gun. "Sir, get back onto the ship!" he shouted.

But the man only shook his head, then turned to jump.

Officer Murdoch fired his weapon, and I nearly leapt from my skin. Women around me screamed, but Officer Murdoch turned to face the crowd, his pistol now aimed into the air. "Gentlemen, step back!" he ordered.

A large man dressed in an army uniform crossed beside

Officer Murdoch and shouted, "Women will be attended first. If any men attempt that again, I'll break every bone in your body."

More calmly now, Officer Murdoch said, "Let's try this again. Women and children first."

"If we survive this, we'll have Mrs. Abelman to thank," a woman said to me. A knitted shawl was wrapped around her shoulders and two children clung to her skirts. The dress she wore was as simple as my dress when I'd come on board. "I saw you with her yesterday. Was she your friend too?"

I turned to her. "You saw Mrs. Abelman? Where is she?"

The woman shook her head. "Still down below, I reckon."

My heart sank. Why hadn't she come up yet?

Once again, I raced toward the stairs. I had last seen Mrs. Abelman on E Deck. Charlie had said he would go down and help her back up, but at the angle this ship was listing, he might not be able to help her on his own.

The thought of going below again terrified me, but I thought of Papa, of the people he had saved. He must have been afraid too, and he still went.

I had to do this. I had to at least try.

Other passengers were coming up the stairs, as many from third class as there were wealthier ones. But no Mrs. Abelman.

Because of the ship's tilted angle, the stairs were wet and had become slippery, and I was having trouble with my own balance. What if the ship tipped over on its side? Surely everyone on board would be lost. And what of those in the lifeboats, believing they were safe? They'd be overtaken by waves of icy ocean water. No one would survive.

I made it to D Deck, where I'd first encountered water. Before, it had only been a few centimeters deep, but now when I plunged in, icy water rose to my knees.

I inhaled sharply. The water felt so much colder now than what I remembered, and my teeth began chattering.

If the water was this deep here, then what of E Deck? I sloshed down the next flight of stairs, the water rising with each step, and finally I stopped.

I couldn't do this, couldn't go any farther. My muscles were tightening, freezing up, and my mind seemed equally numb.

From where I stood, I shouted, "Charlie! Mrs. Abelman!" No answer came, so I tried again, continuing to shout until my voice became hoarse.

Finally, I heard a faint response, Charlie's voice, I thought. But where was he?

"You must do this, Hazel," I told myself. "Find him!"

Still, my breath locked in my throat as I took the final step onto E Deck, where the water rose to my hips. I waded along Scotland Road, calling for Charlie until he ducked his head into the passageway.

His eyes narrowed when he saw me. "What are you doing here, Hazel? You're supposed to be in a lifeboat!"

"So are you. So is Mrs. Abelman!"

I peered into Charlie's cabin. There was Mrs. Abelman, wrapping a blanket around a toddler in her arms.

"I'm looking for the child's mother," Mrs. Abelman said. "Charlie is helping me."

"Come with me," I said. "We can all go upstairs together."

Mrs. Abelman followed me into the passageway. I asked her, "Did you know the papers in your safe deposit box were blank?"

She said nothing, but when I looked back at her, I thought I detected a hint of a smile. "So the Mollisons finally noticed," she said. "I thought—"

"Help us!" a woman cried out from farther down the passageway.

Before I had time to react, Mrs. Abelman thrust the toddler into my arms. She said to me, "Get that baby into a lifeboat. Charlie, come with me."

There was no time to argue. Holding the child tightly, I started toward the same stairs I had just come down, but the water was too deep by now. I lifted the toddler higher in my arms and turned toward another stairway. A crowd was gathered there when I arrived, shouting up the stairs or at each other, but nobody was leaving.

"Why have we stopped?" I cried. "There isn't much time."

A man turned to me and said something in another language, then pointed ahead. I'd expected to see a waist-high gate again, but it wasn't that. Instead, we were trapped behind a locked gate that stretched from floor to ceiling. A Bostwick gate.

Someone ahead of me was rattling the gates and shouting for help, but nobody was coming to unlock this gate. Nobody would come. The officers who had the keys were all up on the boat deck.

"Elena!"

Hearing her mother's voice, the toddler's head swung around. "Mama! Mama!" she cried, reaching out with both arms.

"Hvala puno!" the mother said to me as tears streamed down her cheeks.

I began to cry too and managed only to mumble, "You're welcome" before I turned to leave.

I could not remain here any longer. The water was continuing to rise, and our options for getting off this deck were literally sinking away.

I returned to find Charlie and Mrs. Abelman in the passageway. Mrs. Abelman was speaking to another woman and pointing her toward the stairway where I'd just been.

"The gate is closed," I said. "And the other stairway is already half underwater. I don't know what to do."

"Of course you know," Mrs. Abelman said. "What is it you do better than anything else?"

I shook my head at her until the answer came. But it was so simple, so basic, that I knew I had to be wrong. "Ask questions?"

"Ask your questions, Hazel."

My teeth were chattering and my mind seemed to have already gone numb. So much that every question faded into nothingness. Every question but one.

"Is the stairway open at the far end of the ship?"

She nodded, then added, "That stairway will only take you to the third-class promenade. You will not be able to reach the boat deck from there."

"I know a way," Charlie said. "But . . ." His voice trailed off as he stared at Mrs. Abelman.

I understood the look of sadness in his eyes. Maybe Charlie

and I had a chance to climb onto the boat deck. Mrs. Abelman wasn't strong enough.

She looked at me and even smiled. "I have lived a wonderful life, and I am at peace. The people down here need me, and it feels good to be needed again. I am where I want to be."

"No!" I shook my head. "We can help you."

"Then you would rob me of the greatest opportunity I could ever have. Would you have me die, one breath at a time, fading away with the sunset itself, useless to everyone around me? Or would you allow me to use my final moments to save what lives I can?"

Once again, tears rolled down my cheeks. "You must come with us. You're my friend, Mrs. Abelman."

"I am also your teacher, and tonight I will teach you the meaning of love." She tapped the shoulder bag beneath my life belt. "You still have that box I gave you?"

"Yes, but—"

"Go now. Hurry, Hazel. Stay close to Charlie. He'll get you onto the boat deck."

I started to follow him, then let out a sob and ran back for one last hug. Mrs. Abelman wrapped her arms around me, then gently pushed me away and whispered, "Run!"

Charlie led me toward the rear of the ship. "It feels like we're going uphill!" I said.

He glanced back. "We are. The bow must be sinking first! Why did you get out of the other lifeboat?"

"The Mollisons were in there with me."

"Both of them?" Charlie scowled. "That man is a coward."

"Mr. Mollison was found out. He's somewhere on this ship and he'll be angry with me. We need to be careful."

Yet it quickly became clear that Mr. Mollison was not our problem. We reached the final stairway, but water was cascading down from D Deck. I reached for the railing, but immediately lost my footing and fell into the water.

As cold as I'd been already, that was nothing compared to what I felt now. My lungs emptied and I became confused as to which way to move for air.

Then a hand wrapped around my wrist and pulled me out. I gasped for air as I wiped my faced, then mumbled, "Thank you, Charlie."

He only frowned back. "You're not out of danger yet. Stay close to me now."

Charlie kept hold of my arm until we were on D Deck, but even then, we had to fight to get up the next stairway onto the poop deck. Dozens of passengers had already crowded together, though nothing here could save them. We needed to get to the boat deck . . . somehow.

"We're trapped," I said.

Charlie didn't seem to have heard me. His eyes were on the boat deck. "Do you trust me?" he asked.

I nodded and he led me toward the end of the poop deck, through a gate that brought us directly beneath the first-class promenade. A bench was here, bolted to the floor. Charlie climbed as high as he could on it, then locked his fingers together, flattening his palms.

"Now you," he said.

I climbed up beside him, braced myself with one hand on his shoulder, and put one foot in his hands. He grunted as he lifted me high enough to grasp the lower rail. From there, I began climbing the rails until I could lift myself up to the deck. But I refused to leave Charlie stranded below. Nearby, a woman had dropped a long mink stole. I wrapped it once around the lower rail, then lowered it to him.

"There's no point in this," he called up.

"You promised to get me on a lifeboat," I said. "Keep your promise, Charlie."

"This is a waste of precious time." He frowned but took hold of the stole. I braced my feet against the rails as he climbed, then pulled himself up to the first-class deck with me.

"Let's get you to a lifeboat *again*," he said.

I held out the stole to him. "Use this to get into a boat, the same as Mr. Mollison. No one will blame you."

He frowned. "I won't do that."

I wasn't giving up on him that easily. He had to listen to reason. "Your mother needs you, Charlie. Your family needs you to stay alive."

"But not like that!" he nearly shouted. "Look at how many people are still on this ship! I will not save myself at their expense. But I will save you. Follow me!"

I did, almost immediately colliding with other passengers entering the promenade, including the mother who had retrieved her toddler from me.

"They must have opened the gate!" I said.

"Or the people tore it down," Charlie said. "I'm glad they're here."

I was too, though it also meant the crowd size had swollen. There were now even more people waiting for fewer places on the lifeboats. Most of them could not be saved.

As before, the musicians were still playing. I recognized the somber tune as a hymn I'd heard earlier during Sunday services, "Nearer, My God, to Thee." Everyone on this deck knew by now how terrible our situation was, but the music filled my heart.

Standing there, I felt calmer than I ever had before. I knew what I had to do.

So many people were lined up for the lifeboats. They all deserved to live.

And of course I wanted to live as well, not only for my own dreams, but for my family. They needed me.

But those still on this deck had families too. They had people out there who needed them.

Once again, I thought of my father, of the hero he had been. I hoped he would be proud of me tonight. I hoped my mother would understand.

Though the idea that entered my head was terrifying, it was time for me to take the high road. I wanted to save lives where I could.

I turned to Charlie. "I'm going to stay. I'll go down with the ship too."

FORTY-TWO

1:55 a.m.

I knew Charlie would disapprove of my decision to stay on the *Titanic*, but disapproval did not begin to describe his reaction. Charlie's eyes narrowed and a blaze seemed to flicker in them.

"That's a barmy decision, Hazel. Why would you say such a thing?"

"Look at all these people!" I said. "Should I take the place of a mother holding her child? Or of another child with a real chance for a future? If I survive this, it will only be to work in a factory for the rest of my life."

He took my hand and gave it a squeeze. "And what if you do? That is honest work to help your family. They need you. Besides that, you have a good mind and a thousand questions still to ask. You have a future of your own." Charlie began pulling me forward. "Enough with this nonsense. You are getting on a boat."

We were nearly to one boat when a woman near the back of the crowd shouted, "There aren't enough seats! There's only two more lifeboats!"

Charlie and I locked eyes. We were too late. With the number of people ahead of us, I wouldn't get on those lifeboats.

"This way." Charlie motioned for me to follow him yet again, this time toward the bow of the ship. "The ship has four collapsible lifeboats. We just need time to assemble them." He pointed ahead. "There's one now."

"And a line of people waiting for it."

Charlie nodded. "Wait here. I'll find out where the others are and bring one to you."

"You won't be able to lift it alone," I said.

"I can do it," he said. "I can always take—"

"A little bit more." I stood up straighter. "So can I."

But I wasn't sure if that was true. Below us, the ship was groaning and creaking. The *Titanic*'s final gasps of life.

Charlie ran back through the crowd, only to reappear minutes later up on the bridge, along with several other men. They were speaking to one another, then pointing and shaking their heads. Charlie found me staring at him from below and frowned. Something must be wrong with the collapsible lifeboats. Terribly wrong.

To my right, Officer Murdoch stood on a wooden crate where he could be better seen. He waved his arms for attention and then with a grim voice said, "The captain has given new orders. It is now every man for himself."

My shoulders fell. All hope was lost; any possibility of

survival had just been abandoned. It was now left to each of us to stay alive any way we could, for as long as we could.

Did the rule to put women and children on lifeboats first no longer apply? Did that mean that Charlie could get on a lifeboat now?

I didn't know. Nor, apparently, did many of the people on the deck. Some of them stepped back, the same as I had done. They stared out over the dark ocean, rising ever nearer, silently making peace with their lives.

Most of those standing near me were men, though some were with wives who had refused to leave, so they sat holding each other now, taking comfort that at least their final moments would be spent together.

But others began rushing forward, hoping for any remaining seat. Only one lifeboat was left now, the collapsible model we had seen being assembled minutes ago. It was now being lowered over the side of the ship. The last lifeboat.

I walked to the rails and watched it descend. The faces inside looked up, bidding a silent farewell to the rest of us.

Two arms suddenly wrapped around me. I tried to squirm free, but then I heard Mr. Mollison say, "Hazel, you've got to have more sense than this."

Before I could get loose, he picked me up in his arms. "Let me go!" I cried.

"Give me the chance to do one good thing before my time is over."

He carried me to the edge of the rails. I glanced down but saw nothing except the dark ocean below.

I clutched at Mr. Mollison's shoulders. "No, please, sir, don't drop me."

His grip remained firm and his voice was steady. "Tell your story, Hazel. Tell all our stories."

"No, don't do this!"

He called below him, "There's a child coming down."

My final panicked cry turned into a scream as Mr. Mollison let go of me and I fell over the rails. Wind rushed through my hair and my arms and legs flailed out.

Within seconds, I landed in another man's arms. "You're safe," the man said calmly. "You made it."

He set me on a seat near him, but I was shaking violently, from fear or the cold or the horror of having left Charlie behind. The man glanced up as the lifeboat continued to be lowered into the water, then turned to me. "Consider yourself lucky, miss."

It hadn't been luck. For reasons I couldn't fully understand, Mr. Mollison had just gotten me off the ship. He had just saved my life.

When I looked up, he was still there and gave me a sad wave goodbye. The music had stopped. I noticed that too. The musicians had played their final notes, ever.

The man who'd caught me asked, "Did you see any other women or children up there?"

I didn't know. Everything had happened so fast, I couldn't separate one face up there from another. I shook my head. That was the most I could do.

Our lifeboat appeared to be nearly full, perhaps with

around fifty occupants. Half were women and children, but the other half were male passengers or crewmen. The Irish woman sat ahead of me, softly crying. Now I knew why she'd had the bad feeling about boarding this ship. Her husband was not here.

The man who had caught me looked familiar, though I couldn't recall his name until a woman beside me said to him, "I know who you are, sir. My name is Miss Hellström. You are Mr. Ismay, of the White Star Line?"

He nodded at her but said to all of us in the boat, "Listen carefully, everyone. The *Titanic* may break apart at any minute, perhaps even before we reach the water. If it does, we are lost, but if it holds together, there will be work for us to do." He lifted an oar. "I'll take one."

"I have the other." The man who spoke was already at the rear of the boat. He wore a blue suit and added, "Ladies and gentlemen, my name is George Rowe. I'm a quartermaster for the *Titanic*, and I'll be in command of this boat." He eyed Mr. Ismay. "I will be the *only* one in command here."

We were nearly to the water when the edge of our lifeboat snagged on a rivet of the ship. It tilted sideways, threatening to dump us all out of the boat and into the water. Mr. Ismay took hold of me and I grabbed Miss Hellström.

"What is happening?" one of the younger boys cried. "Mama?"

"We've got to push ourselves free of that rivet," Officer Rowe said. "Mr. Ismay, can you help?"

"I'll try." Mr. Ismay placed his oar against the hull, attempting to pry us free.

"Not too hard, sir," Officer Rowe called. "You'll snap the oar and we'll be as good as dead then."

Since I was already close to the ship's hull, I tried pushing us away, but my cold fingers couldn't pry the canvas fabric of the lifeboat out from between the rivets. If we didn't do it, very soon we'd be dumped out into the ocean.

"Hurry!" Mr. Ismay called. "Hurry, please!"

Finally, another passenger near me tore at the canvas to set us free. Our lifeboat straightened out and we were lowered the rest of the way into the water. We came down unevenly, and cold water splashed on me and the canvas sides folded inward, threatening to sink us yet again. Quickly, the men on board unhooked our lifeboat from the ropes that had lowered us. For better or worse, we were now on our own.

The instant we were, Mr. Ismay and Officer Rowe picked up the oars and began digging them into the water, putting distance between us and the *Titanic*.

The ocean remained eerily calm, yet the water wanted to pull us back toward the *Titanic*.

"Row faster," Officer Rowe urged. "When the *Titanic* goes under, we shall be in danger of being pulled down with it."

Mr. Ismay did row harder, but I noticed something else as well. He was the only one in our boat facing away from the *Titanic*, the only one who refused to look back.

Maybe he couldn't bear to see the fate of his unsinkable

ship, or to watch those we had left behind. So many people were still there. Maybe if Mr. Ismay never looked at them, he would not have to remember them.

I could not tear my eyes away from the sight of it all.

The bow was rising from the water, so high that I saw the entire hull, down to its rudder, lifting from the ocean. The poop deck, where I had spent so many lovely hours, had already vanished, along with most of the stern. The bow now became the last refuge for those left on the ship. I searched the people there until I found Charlie. He was standing against the rails, looking in all directions and clearly trying to decide what he should do.

In utter desperation, some of the men crossed to the outer side of the rails and jumped the remaining nine or ten meters into the water. Even from here, I heard their splashes, followed immediately by their cries as they hit the icy water.

"We must go back for them!" I shouted. "We're not so far away."

"And what happens when someone grabs on to the canvas to pull themselves in?" a woman near Mr. Ismay snapped. "He'll let water in and collapse our lifeboat."

"I'm sorry," Quartermaster Rowe said. "But she's right. We must keep rowing."

"Mama!" one of the children in back cried. "Look!"

All attention went to the child, who was pointing at four Chinese men. They must have been hiding on the floor of the lifeboat all this time. Their heads were bowed low as they sat up, but I could hardly blame them. Mr. Ismay and

Quartermaster Rowe were here in the boat. These other men deserved the same chance to live.

"We now have more passengers than seats," Mr. Ismay grumbled, as if that was a problem. I wished all the lifeboats could have said the same thing.

The *Titanic* was listing to port even more dramatically now. I heard some shouts from back on the ship and the motion of passengers coming to the starboard side, the same side of the ship from which we had launched.

"They're hoping to balance the ship in the water," said Miss Hellström at my side. "It's not likely to work, but they've got to try, haven't they?"

I didn't answer. So many people were on this side of the ship now, I couldn't see Charlie anymore. I couldn't bear to imagine what was still happening on the *Titanic*, the terror the remaining passengers must have felt.

One more collapsible lifeboat was being lowered after ours. I tried standing, hoping to see who was on board, praying to see Charlie, or Mrs. Abelman, or Mr. Waddington. I didn't see much, only that once again, nearly half the seats appeared to be empty. But Miss Hellström pulled me down again. "Don't," she said firmly. "You'll fall in."

The ship's lights that I had come to rely on began flickering now, becoming dimmer with each burst. The bow of the ship was rising higher, and those without a firm hold on the rails slid along the deck, splashing into the water.

That's when I heard it, the explosion on the ship, like

thunder echoing throughout all the skies above. It was so loud that I jumped again from my seat.

"Charlie!" I cried.

"It's no use!" Miss Hellström pulled me down again. "It's no use, girl. They're all lost to the sea now."

"There were four collapsible lifeboats!" I said. "He'll find a way onto one of them."

Yet I already knew he wouldn't. Charlie would give up his place for someone else.

Seconds later, a tremendous sound tore through the night, different from the explosion and ending in a terrible splash. The first of the four enormous smokestacks had collapsed at its base and fallen into the water.

That's when I saw Charlie again. He had crossed to the outside of the rails, but within seconds, every light on the ship went out and I lost sight of him.

"Don't jump," I whispered. "Oh, Charlie, please don't jump."

The ocean water was so cold, so unforgiving. But what other choice did he have? If he jumped now, he had some chance to swim away from the *Titanic* before the pull of the ship carried him underwater.

If he didn't jump, he had no chance at all. He would simply go down with the ship.

Tears filled my eyes. Maybe Miss Hellström was right, and nothing he did could save him now.

The second smokestack collapsed, which I saw only because its large outline shielded the stars, and because of the terrible sound of its fall.

That was followed by a second explosion, one so fierce that at nearly the same time, the ship itself split in half. The bow, already high in the water, sank entirely underwater, rapidly disappearing. The stern seemed to fall sideways, now with only a single smokestack visible.

I looked for any sign of Charlie, but it was too dark to see faces now. Some people were grasping the rails, one by one greeting the water as the lower rail went under.

The stern itself rose up one more time as what had once been the center of the ship sank beneath the water. It seemed to angle upward, nearly straight to the sky, and then it too was swallowed up in the sea.

For the smallest moment, everything was silent. But even that could not last.

FORTY-THREE

2:22 a.m.

Somewhere beyond our lifeboat, cutting through the silent chill of the night, came the cries of the survivors. There were pleas for help, and calls for mercy, some voices so clear that even if I should live to be a hundred years old, I never would forget them. Never could.

Mr. Ismay dipped his oar in the water and in a solemn voice said, "It will do us no good to look back. We still have the work ahead of saving ourselves."

"Turn around," said Miss Hellström to me. "It's better that way."

But I couldn't make myself do that either. Instead, I stared out at the eternal ocean, only water in every direction. Could there really have been a great ship floating on top of it all, in near perfect condition, only three hours ago?

Unsinkable.

There was no moon, yet the stars were clear like diamonds.

I found the Big Dipper, and from there the North Star. The wind that had been so chilly all day had vanished, yet the cold remained, feeling like knives against my skin.

Officer Rowe had found the North Star as well. "The *Californian* is to the north of us," he mumbled. "If only they'd answered our call. We might've saved everyone." Then more loudly, he said, "The *Carpathia* will come from the southeast. Let us turn the lifeboat in that direction, to be sure they will find us."

"How long must we wait?" someone asked.

"Another hour. Maybe two."

Which should've been some comfort, but I couldn't make myself care. I was shivering with cold, or maybe with fear as well. I could last another hour or two.

Those who had descended into the water could not.

I looked around at the other lifeboats. No one was going back for people in the water, even those with more than half their seats still empty. Even those in the boats with stiff wooden sides that could tolerate someone climbing in. They didn't go back either.

"Will no one help them?" I cried. "How can we sit here and not help them?"

"They would make the same decision if our situation was reversed," Mr. Ismay said. "We will do them no good if we find ourselves in the water too. Now sit down, please!"

I obeyed, but I could not stop myself from hearing the calls for help. Then I heard one familiar call. "We're here!"

Charlie?

I turned, and there in the distance, I saw a small number of men standing on what appeared to be an overturned lifeboat—the collapsible lifeboat Charlie had been trying to assemble earlier.

"There! He's there!" I cried. "We can rescue those people. They'll cause us no harm."

"Our ship is too full as it is," Mr. Ismay said. "Now let us row."

I sat again, straining my eyes to see Charlie on the overturned lifeboat. As other survivors swam close, the men there leaned down to pull others up with them. They were risking themselves to help others. Why couldn't we do the same? Why couldn't any of the lifeboats here help?

Once we were farther away, Officer Rowe pulled out a light and lit it. "The other lifeboats will see this and stay near us," he said. "We are saving them too."

They could all speak as proudly as they wanted, congratulating themselves on their rescue efforts, but I was furious. I stared back at the night as the cries for help continued.

"At least you saved your bag," Miss Hellström said. "I left everything of mine on the ship. Don't even have my shoes with me."

I looked down and saw her feet in evening slippers, soaked through. Her feet were probably nearly frozen by this point, yet she wasn't complaining.

"What was in that bag worth saving?" she asked.

"Nothing at all." I began pulling on the strap to free the

bag from inside my life belt. Once it was in my hands, I looked inside. Some of the money from my mother was still there, but it was so wet, I doubted it could be saved. Then I reached for the metal case that Mrs. Abelman had given me. I explained to Miss Hellström, "This is only a notebook full of questions for a story that I will never write. Not now."

I pulled the notebook out. The edges were wet with water that had seeped in, but for the most part, the pages were dry. I folded the notebook shut once again and went to put it back in the box, then saw the papers that had been left in the metal box before Mrs. Abelman gave it to me.

I had assumed the papers had belonged to Mr. Waddington, but when I opened the first, I saw a letter, hastily written to me. Using Officer Rowe's light, I read:

Dearest Hazel,

In only the short time of our acquaintance, you have become dear to me.

Almost from the first moments on board, you reminded me of my daughter. She was as adventurous and brave and strong as you are. I never wanted her to work in that garment factory, but she insisted that she must build her own life.

So must you, Hazel. But your future is not in a factory. You will write your own future with a pen in your hand and notebooks to fill. You have so many questions. Now go and find all of your answers.

The questions are the best part of you, for they will guide you into a future better than you can possibly imagine right now.

I have one last gift for you. Use it wisely and it will allow you to live as you choose.

With all my love,

Mrs. Ruth Abelman

I pulled out the second note from the box. At the top, it read, *The Last Will and Testament of Ruth Hannah Abelman.* I scanned only a few lines, enough to see the words, *my full inheritance to Miss Hazel Rothbury.* Behind that paper were several other papers, all of them titled as Stock Certificates.

I folded the note again, then stuffed it back into the metal box, closed it tight, and returned it to my bag.

Then I cried.

I vaguely felt Miss Hellström pat my back a few times, offering me words of comfort I barely heard and certainly could not care about.

And that's where I remained, where time did not pass at all. I wondered if I would be in this very position forever. Adrift. Lost. Sad beyond repair.

I did not look up again for a very long time, and only when

someone reported seeing a spark of light in the distance.

"Signal flares," Miss Hellström whispered.

Officer Rowe gave an audible breath of relief. "That will be the *Carpathia*," he said. "We are saved."

Not all of us were.

FORTY-FOUR

When Dawn Came

The *Carpathia*'s mast light became visible soon after the flares were launched. Yet the ship cut its engines and for several minutes, there seemed to be no movement from anyone on board.

"They can't see us," Mr. Ismay said. "Rowe, raise your light again."

I hadn't even realized it had gone out, but Officer Rowe shook his head. "It's burned through its kerosene. We'll have to hope some of the other boats are luckier than ours."

"And if they're not?" Miss Hellström asked. "Will they assume we've all gone down and pass us by?"

Her answer came in the distance, from a green lantern raised on one lifeboat, then from a light going on in another. The *Carpathia* immediately powered on its engines, and the entire side of the ship lit up. Some people in the lifeboats closer to the ship shouted that they saw rescue boats coming toward us.

Ours was not the first lifeboat to be rescued, but I hoped they'd come soon. Some of the third-class passengers had gotten into the lifeboat already soaking wet. Their complaints of being cold had turned to numbness, and I worried that some of their lives were still in danger.

I believed that I was cold too. I knew I was, but that was nothing compared to the ache I felt inside. I only wanted to get on board the *Carpathia* and fall into a deep sleep. Or better yet, to wake up and realize that all of this had been a horrible nightmare.

We waited for some time until one of the rescue boats reached us. The feeling of being seen by a rescue boat was greater than I could possibly describe, and it was the first time I knew that I would survive. They towed us to the edge of the ship, where ladders were extended to us from one of the upper decks. The weakest among us had to be lifted by the ship's crewmen, but I was proud to be able to climb for myself.

When I reached the deck, I was greeted with a warm blanket pulled over my shoulders. "There's hot drinks available ahead," a crewman said. "You're safe now, miss."

I stumbled forward, still numb, when I heard a cry of joy and there was Sylvia, hugging me. "You're alive! Hazel, I hardly dared to hope for you, but Miss Gruber kept telling me that you would make it."

"I never doubted it," Miss Gruber said, more solemnly adding, "I should never have doubted *you*."

I looked around the deck, where other survivors were sitting on deck chairs or on the deck itself, some too weak to take another step farther. They all seemed to share the same expression of sadness and horror and exhaustion. And for the first time since I had left Southampton, perhaps for the first time ever in my life, nobody seemed to care which class we had come from. We were all mourners, and all survivors. And all of us trying to take our next breath through shattered hearts and exhausted minds.

I looked around one more time, hoping my eyes had missed someone before. But I hadn't.

Charlie wasn't here.

"Did Mr. Waddington make it to a boat?" I asked Sylvia.

Sylvia shook her head. "I don't think so."

"What about Officer Kent?"

Again, she shook her head, then she lowered her eyes as Mrs. Mollison neared us. She stopped directly in front of us and said, "I have no right to ask forgiveness from either of you, and I can offer no proof of my sincerity. But I want you to know that I have been punished for my crimes. Everything I thought I cared about went down with that ship."

I stepped forward. "Mr. Mollison saved my life. I thought you should know that."

Tears spilled from her eyes and she choked on her final words. "Then he died a good man."

I exchanged a glance with Sylvia, then we both walked forward and wrapped our arms around Mrs. Mollison, letting her cry for her husband, as I cried for those I had lost.

"Thank you," she said after a moment. "I hope that when we meet again one day, we will meet as friends."

She nodded at each of us, then walked on, refusing the offered blanket and drink, and sitting on her own at the far end of the promenade.

"This is the last boat," an officer called. "But be careful unloading it. This one is overfull."

I stepped back, making room for the survivors. The women came first, and a child or two, followed by some men, all of them soaked through. These weren't the well-dressed men from first class, though. These seemed to be dressed as crewmen.

The same crewmen as those I'd seen on the overturned lifeboat!

I rushed forward just as Charlie climbed onto the deck. With a cry of joy, I closed him into a hug, with Sylvia behind me to wrap her arms around us both.

We held each other for several minutes, all in silence, until finally we separated.

Each of us was handed a mug full of warm tea. I stared at my cup for only a moment before I raised it and solemnly said, "To those who we lost, especially those who gave their lives so that we might live now. A toast in their honor."

We clinked cups, then drank our tea, once again in silence.

FORTY-FIVE

For the First Time

The total number of survivors was seven hundred and five. Just over seven hundred survivors from twenty-two hundred passengers and crew on board.

Even after three days on board the *Carpathia*, I still couldn't begin to comprehend that.

But it might have been worse. One crewman told me that when the distress call came from the *Titanic*, the *Carpathia*'s Captain Rostron ordered all heating and hot water to be cut off so that the full power of his ship could be put into the fastest possible race through a field of ice, all in hopes of saving as many people as possible.

The rest of our journey to New York was slowed by rain and fog, but none of us seemed to care. Maybe we needed the time to accept our losses before we'd be greeted by the crowds at the dock.

We arrived Thursday evening, on April 16, one day after

the *Titanic* had intended to enter New York's harbor. The night was cold and rainy, but I tried to ignore that as I stepped down the gangway. Other passengers on board had donated clothing and supplies, which meant I left the *Carpathia* dressed better than I was when I boarded the *Titanic* back in Southampton.

The crowd that greeted us was immense, with locals and government officials, with family and friends, and with journalists from what must have been every newspaper along the Eastern Seaboard. By now, I had written my story of the *Titanic*, but I preferred to keep it to myself. I would become a journalist eventually, but I was still young and in no hurry to grow up too fast. For now, it was enough simply to be alive.

Sylvia pointed out her father in the crowd, a tall, distinguished-looking man. "You may stay with us for as long as you wish," she said. "Father has already sent a telegram to your mother, telling her not to worry, that you are safe with us. But if you wish to return home, we will pay for your ticket."

I smiled over at her. "I am in no hurry to be on the ocean again. Thank you for letting me stay."

"Stay as our guest, if that is all you wish," Sylvia said. "Or as my companion, if you want that. Or as my friend, always."

I no longer needed the money. In my satchel was Mrs. Abelman's signed will, completed in some of the last minutes of her life. Never once had I expected such a gift from her, but I would be forever grateful to her for it. With this inheritance, my family's worries about money would be over.

"I still want to be a journalist," I said.

Sylvia took Miss Gruber's hand. "Miss Gruber has offered to teach you everything you want to know."

"It's my way of repaying the debt I owe the Thorngoods," Miss Gruber said. "Within a few years, the finest newspapers in the country will eagerly put anything written by Hazel Rothbury on their front pages."

Sylvia continued, "My father will be so grateful to you. You only need to ask the favor and I know he will grant it."

"Can he find work for Charlie?" I asked. "He's a hard worker and loyal, and—"

"Consider it done," Sylvia said. "He can work for us, but Father will see that he is educated as well. He always wanted a son, and I think he will enjoy having Charlie around."

So would I.

I had boarded the *Titanic* alone and worried that my life would end once I was forced into the factories.

Instead, I had come ashore in New York with friends and newly discovered family. And now, my life was about to truly begin.

FORTY-SIX

I Began to Live

"*The Story of the* Titanic"
By Hazel Rothbury

O f the 2,224 people on the *Titanic*, who should tell its story?

When I first boarded the *Titanic*, I thought it should be me. After all, I was curious, I asked questions, and I wanted answers. How arrogant that seems now.

I met a boy who worked on that ship. He was brave and honorable, and tried to always do the right thing. Maybe he should tell its story.

But how could the *Titanic*'s story be told without those in first class, those who saw the ship in all its glory? Maybe some walked with their heads held too high to see the others on board, but in those final hours, nearly every man in first class stood aside, with his head bowed low enough to help even the smallest passenger into a lifeboat first.

And there were many in all classes who never failed to be kind and generous. I saw the wealthiest among us tend to the needs of the least important on the ship, just as I saw those in the humblest of positions show pride and nobility worth the crown itself.

The *Titanic* foundered with fifteen hundred souls on board, good people who deserved better than what fate gave them. They would have stories too, of lost dreams and promises. Of the greatness that might have been theirs.

The ship's story could be told by its crew, though in the end, who will we measure as being the most valiant? Certainly those who stayed below, working until their final breath to keep the lights on, allowing time for as many passengers as possible to get into the lifeboats. It could be the service staff, who offered food and comfort to those who were waiting and kept everyone calm. Perhaps the musicians, who continued to play, even as the water rose below their feet. The ship's officers were valiant to the very end, each man to his duty, each man placing all others before himself.

I believe now that the *Titanic* has 2,224 stories to be told. It also has one single story, to be told 2,224 times. That is the story of courage, of compassion, and of heroism. That is the story of life.

And so, for today and every day ahead, that will be my story. I intend to live.

AUTHOR'S NOTE
TITANIC FACTS VS. FICTION

Although I try to keep the world as accurate as possible when writing any historical novel, there will occasionally be departures from a few facts. Can you guess the answers to each of the questions below? Find out if you were right on the next page.

1. Did anyone actually stow away on the *Titanic*?
2. Was there really a fire on board and could it have affected the sinking?
3. Was there an Officer Kent among the crew?
4. Was it possible to sneak from third class into first?
5. Were there any card sharps or swindlers on the *Titanic*?
6. Could Hazel have heard the tapping of Morse code from outside the Marconi Room?
7. Did the passengers really play with the ice that was sheared off the iceberg?
8. Did wireless operator Jack Phillips really tell the operator on the *Californian* to shut up when the operator tried to warn the *Titanic* of ice?

9. Were there really explosions as the *Titanic* was sinking?

10. Did J. Bruce Ismay really refuse to watch his ship sink into the water?

1. **UNKNOWN:** It is possible. Stowaways were always a problem with any passenger ship. However, there are no surviving records of anyone having been caught, so if there were stowaways, they likely went down with the *Titanic*.

2. **FACT:** There was a coal fire on the *Titanic* that could have been burning for two to three weeks prior to the ship leaving Southampton, and it did continue to burn until the night before the ship struck the iceberg. Coal fires were not unusual on ships, though, so this would not have been considered an emergency. There is some debate among *Titanic* experts over the impact of the fire. Some believe it had no serious effect on the sinking, while others believe it created a weakness in the bulkhead that caused it to fail, instantly filling two areas with water.

3. **FICTION:** Officer Kent was fictionalized to avoid altering the personality of an actual ship's officer. However, Captain Smith, J. Bruce Ismay, Officers Lightoller and Murdoch, wireless operator Jack Phillips, and Quartermaster Rowe were all real,

and their actions in the story are consistent with what happened on board the *Titanic*.

4. **LIKELY FACT:** Most of the gates separating the classes were only waist-high, with a sign noting that third-class passengers were forbidden to enter. Those with third-class tickets would have nearly always obeyed the signs. After all, they were provided with better food and accommodations than on nearly any other ship on the seas, and they often experienced better living conditions than what they had at home. There was also a respect for the different classes and for the ship's rules—so much, in fact, that even when the ship was sinking, many people were reluctant to cross those signs. Finally, for most third-class passengers, if they did try to sneak into first class, their clothing, language, and manners would have instantly given them away and they would be sent back anyway, so it wasn't worth the risk.

5. **FACT:** The *Titanic* had at least three professional gamblers on board who attempted to draw passengers into their games of chance. They were enough of a concern to White Star Line that a warning was sent to all passengers discouraging them from any gambling. All three of the gamblers survived.

6. **FICTION:** Not likely. The door would have been closed to keep out noise, so unless it was very

quiet outside and she had excellent hearing, Hazel would not have heard any messages.

7. **FACT:** Yes, several did. Those who came out onto the deck considered it a novelty rather than any sign of danger to the ship.

8. **FACT:** He did. The Marconi operators had a large stack of messages to send while they were within range of land, and wanted to send them because that was how they earned their salary. So when the warning came in from the *Californian*, the two ships were so close that the message would have been loud enough to hurt wireless operator Phillips's ears. In his hurry and irritation, he shot back a reply to the *Californian* to "shut up." Twenty minutes later, the *Californian*'s operator went to bed, where he was when the *Titanic* hit ice, meaning there was nobody in place to receive the message when the *Titanic* messaged the *Californian* for help.

9. **LIKELY FACT:** At least three survivors described hearing explosions as the ship was sinking. It is possible that these could be explained by other causes, such as the smokestacks breaking off and tumbling into the water. However, there is also an interesting theory about the explosions and their effect on the sinking ship.

   After the *Titanic* struck the iceberg, the decision was made below to keep the boilers working so that the ship's lights could remain on. This was incredibly brave of the crewmen below, but it also may have made a big problem even worse.

As the ship sank lower into the water, the electrical wiring became exposed to the salty ocean water. This created hydrogen gas, which is highly explosive. The copper wiring in the ship mixed with the seawater and created chlorine gas, which is highly poisonous. With the boilers running, a single spark could have ignited the explosion, sending the ship down much faster.

If this theory is true, then it means hundreds of lives might have been saved, if only they had turned off the lights.

10. **FACT:** Yes, he rowed away from the *Titanic* without ever turning his head to see it. For getting into a lifeboat rather than going down with the ship, as Captain Smith had done, whether he deserved it or not, Mr. Ismay was branded a coward by many in the media and in his personal relationships, a charge that would follow him throughout his life.

ACKNOWLEDGMENTS

Ultimately, any story about the *Titanic* will be a survival story. It will speak of courage, heroism, honor, and trust. Perhaps what appeals most to us about the *Titanic* is that life itself is a survival story. At some point, we must each face our icebergs. Some are more difficult than others, but the solution is always the same: Get on the lifeboat.

That lifeboat is a friend or family member, or anyone you trust to keep you afloat. So if at any point you feel like you are sinking, don't stop; don't freeze. Just get on the lifeboat.

For this book, I am most grateful for the efforts of two amazing women: my agent, Ammi-Joan Paquette, and my editor, Lisa Sandell. Both professionally and personally, they are lifeboats to me. More importantly, they are friends.

As always, dearest to my heart is my husband, Jeff, along with our children and their spouses. To Chase, Ale, Logan, Sierra, and Bridger, I love you all.

ABOUT THE AUTHOR

Jennifer A. Nielsen is the acclaimed author of the *New York Times* and *USA Today* bestselling Ascendance Series: *The False Prince*, *The Runaway King*, *The Shadow Throne*, *The Captive Kingdom*, and *The Shattered Castle*. She also wrote the *New York Times* bestseller *The Traitor's Game* and its sequels, *The Deceiver's Heart* and *The Warrior's Curse*; the *New York Times* bestselling Mark of the Thief trilogy: *Mark of the Thief*, *Rise of the Wolf*, and *Wrath of the Storm*; the standalone fantasy *The Scourge*; and the critically acclaimed historical thrillers *A Night Divided*, *Resistance*, *Words on Fire*, *Rescue*, and the *New York Times* bestseller *Lines of Courage*. Jennifer collects old books, loves good theater, and thinks that a quiet afternoon in the mountains makes for a nearly perfect moment. She lives in northern Utah with her family and is probably sneaking in a bite of dark chocolate right now. You can visit her online at jennielsen.com or follow her on Twitter and Instagram at @nielsenwriter.